QUICK-KILL
& THE GALACTIC SECRET SERVICE

K.J. HERITAGE

SYGASM

For all the tek-heads

CONTENTS

PART ONE
QUICK-KILL

I SQUEEZE THE LASER AND, with a crackle and hiss, a beam of fiery light slams into the shoulder of the escaping mark.

I let him run just for the fun of it, tracking him as he criss-crosses the dusty alleyway between the old buildings of the abandoned spaceport, followed by pools of harsh white light courtesy of my few remaining drones.

With the power outages this far out of town, the area is as dark as a tomb—an excellent location for villains of all types to hang out.

The mark is Rollo Barla, a low-life high-tek data-cracker. A rotund ball of quivering fat in his late fifties. By the look of him, he'd drop dead from a heart attack if I let him run any further—red-faced and sweating with the effort of trying to stay alive. But killing is my profession… and I love my job. The beam spins Rollo around, slamming him face down into the dust. He struggles onto his back, screaming in pain. But we both know it's over for him.

I take off my hat and let my long auburn hair spill. Classy, but nothing more than a wig. Quick-Kill Jane ain't the type to leave her DNA lying around. A swift touch up of crimson lipstick and I'm ready for Rollo's big moment.

Things need to go quick this evening. Later on, I'm all set to go meet my latest squeeze, a cute little cityblok-chick called Angie. We've been going at it for a few weeks. A business agreement. After tonight, she says, I don't need to pay no more. She wants us to be legit—when I settle her rent and her bills, she's all mine. No other johns.

Nice.

Rollo kicks at the drones, pushing his immense bulk up onto his feet with his one useful arm. A quick glance over his shoulder and I wave the laser at him, smiling. Other killers become bored, but I always get a thrill from seeing desperation shining in doomed eyes. The realisation that *time has been called.*

He runs again, holding his injured shoulder, his other arm useless—flapping around like a wet stocking on a windy tenement washing line. The fat of his belly also flaps, and I can't help a sneer of disgust. But Rollo is typical of the losers trapped on this backwater planet. The low-grav allows them to carry a lot more weight. And there ain't much else to do here other than eat, screw and defecate. And, by the look of him, Rollo had no interest in sticking his dick where it wasn't wanted, unless it was in someone else's pie.

I'm not so much an inventor as an *enhancer.* The laser was originally a mining tool, industrial, and too heavy for me to handle—even in this low grav. I'm petite, standing just over five foot—not that I'm any less dangerous than a man twice my size—*or any man.* A few modifications here and there, shrinking the laser's size and augmenting the different functions and—using a sturdy but discreet exoskeleton worn under my clothing—I'm a walking one-woman laser turret.

A quick flick on the control butt to alter the beam and I fire again. The widened heat-ray setting of my own design hits Rollo in the legs. His stretch-corduroy trousers catch alight and he screams but carries on running.

I walk forward, watching him stumble, flames licking towards his face. He finally falls to the dusty alley floor, desperately rolling around, extinguishing the fire only to lie motionless and smouldering in defeat.

The drones converge on him, their machine guns cocked and ready, focusing lights onto his face.

"Rollo Barla," I say all business-like, standing over him, toying with my red hair and pursing my ruby-red lips.

It's always nice to let the mark know it's a woman who is gonna do them in. A bit of icing on the cake.

"Why'd you run off like a frightened cat?" I ask. "You know Quick-Kill Jane ain't never failed to deliver. You somehow think you can beat my hundred percent record?"

"Don't do it," Rollo splutters from a red and sweaty face. "I got kids and family. I was only looking out for them. I can pay you double."

Angie is waiting for me and I don't wanna be late. I already wasted time letting this mark think he had a chance of getting away. "You've been a naughty boy," I say, the words rolling easily off my tongue. "Judging by the amount of money on your head, you must've pissed off some very bad people."

"I ain't done nothing," he blurts. "I've kept my head down, kept schtum like always. This ain't fair."

"I can tell you all about unfairness," I reply. "Don't pretend you don't beat your wife in front of your kids every night. You're a bully, Rollo. A nasty piece of scum. If anything, I'm doing your family a favour." I alter the setting of my gun and stand back.

"Bitch!" he spits from a screwed-up face. A sudden, sharp pain behind my eyes makes me blink for a second.

I raise the laser and let him have it.

Rollo explodes in a conflagration of blue flame. The laser's beam intensifies and engulfs him. Fat and skin boils, catches fire and is turned to quick ash. The ash glows white and becomes a molten slurry into which his bones crumble and disappear, leaving only a charred stain in the red dust of the alley. No body, no DNA… just ash fused into glass. When you hire Quick-Kill Jane, you get the full service.

I replace the laser in its holder—the heat-sink warm against my thigh. The sensation of a job well done.

I'm a professional and take pride in my work. Sure, being a dame used to put some clients off, but they soon learned that gender ain't no bar to the art of murder. More than anything, I've a rep for know-how and getting the job done. That matters in this town. As for Rollo? He's gone to wherever people go to when I off them.

Just another day and another mark.

I straighten my hat and command the drones to return to the Loft using my enhanced cerebral wafer—a top of the range illicit job with all the latest tek. Brain augmentation ain't new. I was dubious about the procedure—and the thing cost me plenty of hard-earned bucks—but the result? Hey, I'm now a walking library with a perfect memory. I can also patch into my augmented phone or access the net. Cool. Sure, the wafer's illegal but Quick-Kill Jane ain't the most law-abiding of gals.

I flick open my phone and patch through to my contact. A guy called Tewis, who set up tonight's little date with Rollo, although I doubt Tewis is his real name—but who am I to quibble about using a pseudonym? "Hello Tewis."

"Is it done?"

"Yeah, no problems. I'm expecting your transfer asap."

"Did Rollo say anything… before he died?"

I snort. "Just the same old regular bleating of a john who realises his time is finally up."

"Tell me exactly what he said."

I shrug. "Everything is recorded by drone. Minus my little part in the show, of course. I ain't stupid. I'll patch the vids over to you now."

"Yes you will, just as it states in the contract. But I also want you to tell me."

This ain't the normal procedure for a post-kill chat, yet I ain't too bothered. So what if Tewis is a little uptight?

"Sure," I reply, "I'll even mimic his damn whine for you. He said, *Don't kill me. I got kids and family. I can pay you double.* That was it. Apart from calling me a bitch."

"Rollo didn't attempt any other deal? Offer you anything?"

"Like I said—take a look at the vids. And if you want, I'll send you a copy from my own personal wafer. But that'll cost you more."

"A wafer?"

"Yeah. Top of the range and highly illegal. Is that a problem?"

Tewis is quiet for a few seconds. I've wasted enough time on this conversation already. "You gonna make the payment, yes or no?" I smile at the edge of threat in my voice. Everyone understands you pay assassins their dues, anything else would be stupid.

A few clicks and whirs. "Payment made." The connection ends.

The conversation was odd, but in my profession, you get to deal with odd every other day.

I make my way to my transport—to all intents

and purposes a '69 Dodge Charger …*custom*. A five-hundred-year old design but she still makes heads turn. She's electric, not that pollution is a problem on the backwater planet of Plenty—the most unfortunately-named world there ever was. The oil reserves didn't pan out as they were expected to, otherwise this baby would roar like a monster. Petrol is a luxury even I can't afford. I slip inside, start the engine and head for town.

THE SPACEPORT LIES A GOOD thirty miles from the city. Back in the day, the port was a bustling town of arrivals and take-offs, of trade and barter.

Now? Ships are few and far between.

Since planetary living has become unfashionable, it's mostly empty apart from the low-lives who hang out there. Rollo Barla for one.

I did my homework on the mark. Rollo was a safe-cracker. One of the best. He possessed an advanced cerebral augmentation similar to my own wafer patched into some impressive hack-based software of his own design. An artist, by all accounts. But despite all that extra cerebral power, he was too dumb to take his profits and get off this rock. And, to be fair, the chump was so overweight he would've never survived take-off.

But escaping is my plan. If you wanna do anything in life you gotta think big. Rollo Barla was a small-time criminal and he died a small-time death. That won't happen to me. Not to Quick-Kill Jane. As for my real name—*you know what?* I've never even had one. Yet growing up on the streets alone, with no family and no one looking out for me, that name just started to follow me around. I was quite the ace with the catapult and then with a gun, although the name Quick-Kill Jane didn't come from my skill with all weapons but from how effectively I used them. In the end, I took the name as my own. Why not? It instilled fear and respect. And despite Angie, or any of the other girls, I'm a one-woman operation. And once my pot of bucks hits a certain size, I'm taking the first available rocket out of here. It'll be goodbye Plenty and hello Good Times.

I push my foot down hard on the pedal and the Dodge picks up speed. No auto-drive for me. I like to be in charge of my own destiny. Besides, auto-drive puts you on the system. The cops may turn a blind eye but you never know when that might change. When I drive anywhere, I drive anonymously.

Amsterdam City is ahead, silhouetted against the dark night sky and lit up like an electric red thistle. The lower gravity means that it boasts some of the tallest high-rises and skyscrapers in this forgotten solar system. But the money has long-gone, leaving decades ago to invest itself in the 'next big thing'—which happened to be space habitats.

Amsterdam is Plenty's first and only city, its buildings mimicking the red of the surrounding landscape. The conurbation was once considered a marvel. But now? It's nothing more than a crumbling prison, home to thirty or so million people wishing they were someplace else. No towns, no resorts… *nothing*. Just a few outlying industrial farms and the spaceport. The locals—who I do not count myself a member of—call it the *Forgotten City*. And I can't wait to put it out of my memory.

I enter via the ring road, taking the turnoff that brings me close to Angie's apartment. At this time of night there's little traffic.

I park outside, amongst the other transports. I open the boot, take out the tarp and drape it over the Charger. It serves a double purpose—keeping out the red dust and hiding my ride from prying eyes.

Sure, a Dodge is gonna generate attention, which,

considering my occupation, is counter-productive. But hey, what's life if you can't indulge yourself once in a while?

Talking of indulgences, I cast my eyes up to Angie's windows. Her lights are unexpectedly off, and my inner alarm bells start ringing. She should be waiting for me, all dolled up and a meal prepared. A celebration. Tonight, of all nights, she'd be there with the lights on. And she ain't the type to throw a surprise party. Besides, she's like me when it comes to friends... she can't see the point. That's why we get on so well. That, and our disinclination towards men.

The foyer is an oasis of light on the dark street. Just inside, I spot Joe, the robo-doorman. He's seen better days. His once colourful costume is faded, as is his absurd top hat. I push open the doors and head for the elevator.

The metallic face inclines towards me. The eyes sunken and slightly sad. "Are you here to see Miss Angie?" he asks in servile bass tones.

I see the gun in his hand long before he can raise it against me.

I snap out my laser and play the beam over his face which collapses in on itself. The cooked bio-circuitry smells like a pie in the oven. Which reminds me... I'm hungry. Whoever's upstairs waiting for me hoped Joe would do their work for them.

Mistake.

I flick the laser beam over the rest of Joe's twitching artificial body. He collapses into nothing more than a few whirring, metal cogs and smoking servitor modules. I never did like the condescending creep. Good riddance. If I had my way, I'd melt all these robotic half-breeds to glass and laugh while I did it.

My next action is easy. I get in the elevator and arrive

on Angie's floor a few seconds later. I step out, make my way to her apartment and knock. I shout, "Honey, I'm home!" and sidestep a hail of bullets that turn the door into plastic shreds.

I power up the laser again and play it at head-height across the wall. It punches through the extruded pseudo-cement like, well, like a high-powered industrial laser through a cheaply-manufactured living module. I know Angie is in there, I'm just hoping she's got her head down.

I flash the laser across the wall a second time and the whole thing collapses. I stare into the smoking ruins of the room. Angie is tied up in a chair, her hair singed from where the laser caught it. Good girl, she'll survive. Shame about her apartment. I guess I won't be eating anytime soon.

For my attacker, it's another story. He lies on the floor, his head a burnt mess.

Nice.

I make eye-contact with Angie. *Anymore goons?*

She shakes her head and, as I push through the rubble, Angie's binds suddenly fall away and she fires a pistol at me.

I take the shots in my midriff, twisting away from the bullets, swinging the barrel of the laser at her head. Metal meets flesh with a clunk and she falls forward, her neck broken. The exo is a useful tool but a little heavy-handed.

Damn, and I thought me and Angie were a match made in heaven.

I grab the pistol from Angie's still twitching fingers and fling it aside.

Under my clothing, is pretty much the most expensive and lightest armour a gal can buy, incorporating a one-molecule thick nano-mesh. At the close-range I was shot,

I'm still gonna bruise. But I'm alive and, in my game, that's all that counts.

I go over to the dead guy and rifle through his pockets. A hired goon. And there's the first mistake. The whole thing with Robo Joe and this now dead wannabe wiseguy is one fatal misstep. If you want rid of an assassin, you employ another assassin, not someone like this joker. There may be honour amongst thieves but assassins will take anyone out for the right amount of cash.

Tewis is behind this. He must be. Something to do with Rollo Barla. This whole ambush stinks of last-minute thinking, which means my kill didn't go to plan. I don't get it—I took out Rollo with no fuss. A straightforward job. Something must've gone wrong… but what? I'm gonna go find Tewis and ask him, before I make him eat his own giblets that is.

I take one final look at Angie. She was a real honey. My guess is that she was offered more money than she was able to say no to. Angie took her chance to get out of this hole, but the dice didn't roll her way. Shame. Yet she tried—and I respect that. A real stand up gal. I'll miss her… and her cooking.

I walk back onto the landing to be met by worried faces poking out from the other rooms on this floor. Losers, the lot of them. Trapped in a decaying tenement on a dead-end planet with no exit plan.

"Nothing to see here," I say. "And remember that, because if anyone of you blabs, I'll be coming back. You understand?"

The doors close with a chorus of bangs and clicking locks and bolts. Like I said… *losers*.

I exit via the stairs, jumping over the bannister and dropping down the twelve or so floors to the ground. The exo absorbs the shock. The artificial outer-skeleton is not just a powered cage giving me the strength of many, it's also a means of transportation and escape. I'll never match a man for bulk or weight but why should I need to when my brain is by far the bigger muscle? And besides, wearing my exo, I could pull apart the biggest man and dance on the pieces.

A few seconds later, I'm running through the back door and into the side-streets.

I can't return to the Loft—my rooms on the top floor of the Heinrich Hotel—a modest apartment where I eat, sleep and tinker with stuff. If Tewis knew about Angie, it's a good bet he knows where I live.

As to how? I'm gonna have to pump Tewis for that information. But first… I'll need back-up.

I patch a signal from my wafer into the phone and silently call my drones. I increase the power to my exo and jump up onto a low roofed building, and then hop to the next, making my exit via rooftop, putting quick distance between myself and Angie's destroyed apartment.

This is no blind run. I may be Quick-Kill Jane, I may drive a Dodge Charger and spend a little bit too much on the show of it all but that doesn't mean I don't plan for contingencies. Sure, I love my Dodge and all my gadgets, but should I ever need to, I can disappear in a puff of smoke—or so it would seem to anyone who came looking.

I keep to the shadows, using alleyways and shaded rooftops, heading for a bolt-hole. I have various hideouts around town and tonight is all about 'Just in case'.

I need to lie low and think this through… before I go after Tewis. He must know that if he doesn't get me, I'll get him. That's gonna make him desperate, and desperate guys make mistakes.

The almost silent whir of rotors—a sound that only I would recognise—and my flying helpers arrive. All three of them. But something is wrong. The drones are lit up like Christmas trees and, as they close in on me, I hear the click and snap of their machine guns, readying themselves for firing.

I dive behind a roof dumpster, almost deafened by the cacophony of bullets slamming into its metal sides.

I can't afford to be angry but I'm certainly irked. These are my machines.

No one touches my stuff and gets away with it!

To be honest, since I created the laser, I've used the drones as threat only. A way to round up a mark who wouldn't give in to the inevitable. Luckily, they work on the principle of point and shoot. There's nothing intuitive about their programming. Whoever is controlling them, has not keyed in a stop command.

I wait till the barrage comes to an end, the magazines clicking and whirring as they reload, and jump out of my hiding place.

The laser makes a quick job of their props and they come crashing down.

I have no time to waste. I grab their data-links and throw the remains in the dumpster.

Below me I hear the sound of approaching vehicles. But I refuse to be trapped. I drop down the opposite side of the rooftop into a darkened alley, run to a nearby drain cover, and disappear into the sewers. A click of my exo's beams and I'm soon racing down the circular tunnel, scaring rats and splashing through shit and piss.

TWENTY MINUTES LATER, I'M IN one of my bolt-holes and I ain't happy. Far from it. It's one of many lock-ups in the industrial end of town nestling beneath the arches of a long-abandoned railway.

To any intruder or perp, it's a room full of junk. The kind of stuff cheap motels throw away every day. Beds, mattresses, tables, chairs, wardrobes, bits of service-roboes and other worthless rubbish. All stacked up and covered in crap.

At the back, there's a hidden door to one of my hideouts, leading to a room that has everything I need in an emergency, and I slip inside.

First things first, I heat up a food pack. This is a lot more than a simple set of cardboard-like plastimeat and nutrients. I had time to set up these places and made sure I stocked them with the best money could buy. Pretty soon, I'm sitting back eating a plate of sliced beef, potatoes and vegetables covered in thick gravy and sipping from a hot mug of milky tea.

I don't do booze. In my job, I need to keep my wits about me.

By now I should've been cuddled up with Angie. Something else I can blame Tewis for. It's time to find out what all this fuss is about. Tewis was worried about what Rollo said before he died. *Why?* I power up the digiscreens, that fill one wall, and patch-in one of the data-sinks scavenged from my damaged drones.

White noise and flickering replaced by the scene from the spaceport alleyway.

I observe myself holding up the laser. I sure am a fine figure of a woman. My exo is invisible, following the curves of my body seamlessly.

Angie made a bad choice. Loyalty goes a long way with Quick-Kill Jane. Hell, I might've even taken her off planet with me when the time came. But the offer of serious money can turn a gal's head.

I turn my attention back to the screen. A flash of the laser, and Rollo goes down. A second flash, and he's on fire. The drones now close in on him.

I turn up the volume.

He says his last words just as I remember, except for one glitch. I replay the vid. But there can be no mistake. After Rollo calls me a *bitch,* the vid feed crackles and drops out for the briefest of moments.

The data-sink captured all three drones' cameras. I replay the other two angles and get the same result. Rollo died. I don't doubt that. The laser turning him into a quick stain of blackened glass, but he did something to me…

I remember the brief stab of pain from behind my eyes. Shit! A flash-dump to my wafer.

My interface is back at the Loft. I can't perform a diagnostic, but I can still bring up the directory files. The screen blinks, and there it is. An extra folder, tetraquads in size.

But how?

My wafer was supposed to be hack-proof. Having said that, Rollo was just about the best file-smasher on the planet—a very small insignificant planet with one city, but impressive all the same.

What did that bastard do to me?

I try to open the file, but it's security locked. Copying and deleting gets the same result. For now, the file is stuck in my head—the last place I need it to be.

For Rollo to flash me that file before his fiery end means it's damn important. Tewis wanted Rollo dead, and these files destroyed with him. That's why the contract was to leave no trace behind. Yet the mark did something unexpected.

Still, Tewis can't be sure I have the file, he can only suspect. But I went and told him I have a wafer didn't I? Showing off again. I damn well knew that one day my swagger would get me into trouble. Tewis won't rest until I'm dead and also disintegrated.

I take another long drink of tea and shuffle my options.

One. I stay here and lie low. I've enough rations to last me many weeks. But I'm not the sitting around type.

Two. I go find someone who can get this file out of my head, or maybe get me access to it. Knowing what I'm dealing with may give me a bargaining option.

Three. I further investigate Rollo Barla, his associates and his family. See what they know. But Rollo was a career criminal who always worked alone, it's unlikely that avenue would throw up any information.

Four. Go find that bastard Tewis, and ask him direct.

I finish the tea and stand up, resting my weight on the exo.

I'm going to make Tewis pay, there is no doubt about that, but a bargaining chip—such as downloading the file and saving it elsewhere—will get me close to the bastard without him shooting on sight.

One and three are no-goers. Four, although my favourite, is too dangerous. I decide on option two—

find someone who can get this file out of my head.

Like Rollo Barla, I work alone, but I have associates. People who I go to for expertise. People who can be trusted. Like the guy who boosted my wafer…

I replace my clothes with a disguise I've worn many times. A quick augmentation of the exo, widens my shoulders and thickens my arms and legs.

I look at my reflection in a full-length mirror and, if not for my hair and make-up, I'd be easily mistaken for a man.

A hasty wash of my face, a new short-haired wig, my cheeks padded out with an injection of gel, and I complete the look.

The exo even gives me a few more inches. I ain't ashamed of my height. If anything, it makes me a damn sight cuter than other chicks… and more dangerous.

I pick up a hat and a raincoat and fasten the belt. I finish the tea and slam the mug down on the table. It shatters, but I'm not concerned. Adrenaline is still pumping through me, and the exo is an extension of that. But it gives me an idea.

I locate a rack of stims and place them in my pockets. Like I said, I prefer to remain in control but stimming myself to the eyeballs may be an option I will need later on.

I pull the hat down over my face and exit into the night.

I close the graffiti-covered metal shutter, fasten the lock and make my way to the steps leading into the local station and catch a tube-train to Amsterdam Central. Here, I dummy out to the West-End and take an autocab south-westward to the mainly run-down area of Heim.

I find a suitable bar—an old dive of mine called *Mama's*. Not that the place has the motherly touch. Quite the opposite in fact. It has a roof area and three other exits in case I need to escape in a hurry. I find a booth that gives me an eye on all three exits and the stairs, sit down, order a tea, and wait. Watching for anything out of the ordinary. Anything off-key. *Anything odd*.

My phone ain't your bog-standard model. Yeah, I enhanced it a little. Put my mark on it and made it my own. For a start, it possesses stealth tek. I checked it back in the hideout and got the same result—there's a constant sweep looking for my phone's ident. *Looking for me*. But the signal is too broad and bouncing off too many towers, for me to track it backwards.

The handheld has another special feature—a short-range weapons detector. I got it from a police contact. One of the few chicks who's allowed to wear a badge, and she's cute with it. A piece of hush-hush software that only law-enforcement is supposed to know about. It can't identify a gun, but it can sure detect their presence up to two-hundred feet. A series of red dots on an electronic map. Something to do with the ambient signals from gun-specific circuitry present in all modern weapons. Damn effective, and the reason why I switched to my trusty laser.

Guns are commonplace in New Amsterdam, used for 'home-protection' as the saying goes. But carrying a gun outside the home without a license is against the law.

My phone will alert me if any weapons are close by. So far, it's showing nada.

I access the net to check out the news and, via an ear-piece, to eavesdrop on the supposedly secure police channel. Both bring up nothing of interest.

I wait another ten minutes. I order my second cup of tea and speak a single word into my phone: *Dynamo*. It's a stupid name, sure, but who am I to judge?

"Jane?" says a surprised voice at the other end.

"I'm data-patching you my location. Come see me. And make sure you're not followed." I hang-up and sit back. If anyone can help me, Dynamo can.

He arrives in the bar twenty minutes later.

Dynamo is a tall, skinny, stretched rubber-band of a kid, his almost white hair sticking up in the style of any regular twenty-something tek-boy. I wave him over.

Sure, I've taken the piss out of his name. Lots of times. Dynamo comes from the Greek word 'dynamis' meaning 'power'. The kid is the antithesis of command—all nervous, twitching limbs and mumbled half-words. But I get it. Wafers have been around a long time now. His expertise is in boosting their capacity whilst keeping power demands low. Anything that is charged by the electrical-chemical balance of the brain ain't gonna receive much in the way of current, not unless Dynamo is on the case.

He stares around, confused.

I hold up my cup of tea and, smiling in realisation, he comes over and squeezes into the booth. A long-legged spider sliding into its hole.

"Why the public place and the neat guise?" he says, staring into my eyes.

I glance at my phone. No red dots. "I needed to make sure you weren't followed. Assassin one-oh-one—don't walk into an ambush."

"An ambush?" Dynamo's manic blue eyes dart around the bar like a cat following a blob of light. "What the hell is this, Jane?"

"Mention my name again, and I'll kill you where you sit. Understand?"

Dynamo's head nods on a long neck, his Adam's apple bobbing up and down. "Yeah, sure. Sorry," he replies—a scolded puppy.

I give him a precis of recent events. "Things are shit-serious right now, okay?"

"Sure. I get it. Serious shit." The head nods again, eyebrows furrowing in exaggerated apology. "So you got me here. What do you need?"

"You heard of a creep called Tewis?"

The name has no effect on the kid and he ain't no actor.

"Who is he?" he asks. "One of your marks?"

A quick shake of my head. "A client of mine. An ex-client as it happens. Soon to be ex of this life if I can find him. I just wanted to judge your reaction. He might've gotten to you first, and I need to be careful. I think you're clean."

"This Tewis sounds dangerous."

"He is… I want you to do a job for me."

"Sure. Anything. *For a price.*"

I smile. "There's a file wedged in my wafer. Stuck fast. Encrypted. I need it out of my head, asap."

Dynamo's blue eyes search my face, as if trying to peer inside my skull. "I can give it a go. But I'd need to see it for myself, to get the measure of what we're dealing with. Tewis is after this file?"

I nod. "Seems like he'll move heaven and earth to destroy it. The only problem—I'm in his way."

"We'll need to return to my lab."

"No way."

"But all my equipment is there."

"No."

"You gotta understand. I want to help you, but without my tek, I'm useless."

I take a sip of tea. "I've my own place nearby," I say, "a hideout. You can bring what you need there."

A quick shake of his head. "It isn't that easy. I can't… even if I…There's just no way to do that."

I've trapped Dynamo and he's frightened. But he hasn't the guile to try and trick me. And he's genuinely afraid of getting on my bad side, so I make the decision. "Okay. We'll do it your way. Return home now and I'll follow you."

"Will I be in any danger?"

I lean forward and fix him with my meanest stare. "You try and pull any nonsense, and I'll burn your face off. Understand?"

He swallows. "Sure."

"Good. Now get your shit outta here."

NO RED DOTS WHILE I follow Dynamo home.

It's possible Tewis knows about my associates, that he's having them watched. He could even be waiting back at Dynamo's den, hoping the tek-boy would bring me back to an ambush. It's unlikely, granted, yet he somehow knew about Angie.

Damn! I'd been sloppy with her… but a chick like Angie can do that to a gal.

I'm reminded of the goon at her apartment and his half-assed attempt to off me. From what I've seen of Tewis's methods, he ain't subtle. If he'd had Dynamo followed, his attack would've come in the bar—he wouldn't miss a chance like that and I don't think he's the type to play the long game, which gives me the advantage.

Dynamo enters the crumbling tenement he calls home while I hang around outside in the shadows for the required amount of time. Satisfied all is okay, I call the single elevator and ascend the thirty or so floors up to his room. The only way in and out… unless you possess an augmented exo that is.

I crouch, sliding the door open, laser on standby. Dynamo's den is empty, apart from a nervous looking Dynamo and his extensive tek stacks.

"You're sure putting the sweats on me, you know that?" he says.

His den is an open-plan apartment. The only other

room is a small bathroom, the door open—empty. I stand up and holster the laser. "A gal can never be too careful."

Dynamo relaxes. "I have my own security system should anyone try to creep up on me." He nods his head to a screen from which a camera angle shows the building's foyer, the fire escape, elevator, the alleyway below, roof, and various other shots. He sits on a battered office chair and powers up his screens. "I take it you want this to be quick?"

"As quick as it can be. Encryption ain't one of my skills."

"That's why tek-boys like me exist."

Dynamo gestures to a couch and I dutifully lie down. He places a monitor on my forehead and goes back to his screens.

I've been here before and had a similar procedure. From my position, I've a great view. Dynamo is suddenly all action. Gone is the nervous twenty-something, in his place is an artist totally in control. His hands wave through the air as if conducting a vast and complicated orchestra, his fingers occasionally typing on an archaic keypad.

My wafer appears on the main screen and, below it, a list of folders. I don't even have to tell him which is the offender, nor remind him all the other folders are private. I'm the top of the tree in my profession and Dynamo is no different in his. There are few boundaries on this world but people like me and Dynamo recognise and respect them.

"What the hell is that?" he says, eyeing the offending file with an excited raise of his eyebrows.

"That's what I want you to find out."

A few more hand gestures, and the interloper glows

red. "Was this flash-dumped?" he asks, not taking his eyes off the screens.

"Yeah."

"You were lucky it didn't fry your brain."

"I don't believe in luck."

"You're right. This wafer is top-of-the-range. The best ripped tek money can buy. You know some of these components come from the Key Systems, huh? All held in perfect balance by a Slash-Stak bio-controller, and a host of other bits and bobs. I installed and designed this baby myself and, when it comes to wafers, I know my job."

I laugh inside at Dynamo's unconscious arrogance. "You think the flash-dump was an attempt to kill me?"

"Could be. But why encrypt the file? No. Whoever sent this, wanted you alive."

"You can open it? Get inside?"

"There ain't no file Dynamo can't get into… Shit!"

"What is it?"

Dynamo leans into his screens, squinting. "The wafer has fused with the bone-tissue of your skull. It's the heatsink I designed."

"What about it?"

"It's supposed to 'float' on top of your frontal lobe. This has become a part of your brain and skull."

"Bad?"

"Brain damage is minimal, so no. But you won't be able to remove it. Not without some serious surgery from someone who knows their shit inside and out. And guess what? There ain't no one like that on this backwater planet."

I shrug. "That's not important now. I just need to know what's in the folder. How long will this take?"

"Shh!"

Being shushed by a kid like Dynamo irks me but I forgive him. He's in the zone. Doing his thing. I sit back, close my eyes, and let him get on with it…

"Jane!"

My eyelids part to reveal Dynamo's face next to mine. "Did I nod off?"

"Yeah, it was kinda cute actually."

"Back off, Bud!" I push him aside. Behind him, all the screens are flashing red. "What the fuck?"

"I managed to open the folder," Dynamo replies. "And whatever was inside took over my system… or tried to," he added, sounding more impressed than upset. "My tek stacks are protected. Walls within walls and then some. Whatever was inside the folder was trying to get out."

"It didn't make it?"

He shook his head. "I'd stake my rep on my security cols, but I think it's still a good idea we get out of here."

"Tell me what you found," I say, stumbling to my feet.

"An invasive program of some kind," Dynamo replies, flinging a selection of wafers and other tek into a satchel. "I'm guessing military or something else. Programmed to attack."

"Did you get it out of me? Or make a copy?"

A shake of his head. "The contents are hard-wired into your wafer, happened in the flash-dump. And like I said, you can't get rid of it without serious medical intervention." Dynamo runs over to the window and pushes it open. "Come on. Down the fire escape."

I rip off the monitor and follow him out. The kid clatters down the stairway. But other than his urgent, metallic footsteps, the area is quiet. No approaching vehicles, and a quick glance at my phone tracker shows no active guns in the vicinity.

A thought crosses my mind. Is Dynamo double-crossing me? Did he put me to sleep and arrange this little scenario? It's possible but the way Dynamo is rattling down the steps tells me otherwise. He's genuinely freaked.

Instead of dropping down, I use the exo to jump across the street, landing on a rooftop of a smaller block below.

Dynamo is still a good ten floors above me.

I check my wafer. The folder still won't open.

Damn!

Things are going from confusing to downright infuriating. I want to run, to get away from here. But I've put Dynamo in danger, he at least needs my protection and could still be useful. I'm about to jump up to him when… the world explodes in a ball of blinding white.

I WAKE UP COUGHING, COVERED in dust and rubble. A quick once-over tells me I'm not injured.

I stand, brushing more dust from my coat and stare in disbelief at the scene in front of me. Dynamo's tenement has gone. Disintegrated. Cut cables spark and water gushes from many broken and exposed pipes. There's no explanation other than the building was hit from orbit.

What the hell is in my head?

In the distance, I hear the approach of emergency vehicles. But they can do nothing. Dynamo, the block and all its inhabitants have gone. Broken apart at the molecular level is my guess.

I can't hang about. Whoever blasted the building from orbit may have the capability to see me standing here. And I'm the target. Or whatever's in my head.

Plan two didn't work out for me.

Only one option is left—*go find Tewis.*

Ten minutes later, I'm a long way from the destroyed building. I access the news channel via my wafer, but the streams are quiet. It means only one thing. Whatever is going on here—is government sanctioned.

I enter the second of my hideouts—a cellar under a row of shops and slip inside the fusty smelling room.

After what happened to Dynamo and his building, I can't stay in any one place too long. My visit is a quick one. I grab a stash of credits, recharge packs for my laser and exo, a range of grenades, flash-bombs and gas pellets, and a few extra guns with ammunition. What I can't wear, I place in a holdall.

As for my appearance, I decide to stay as a man—swapping my dust-covered clothing for something less conspicuous. I even change my hat. Then I'm back out on the streets again.

The back alleys somehow feel more dangerous. Instead, I head towards the centre of town, down one of the many high streets. They aren't exactly crowded but there's safety in numbers.

A chirrup from my phone. A quick glance tells me it's Tewis. I answer the call.

"Hi there," I say with forced calm. "You getting all sweaty that I'm still alive? Cos I hope so." The guy has been able to call in some pretty big guns. He's connected and, despite my plans for revenge, getting to Tewis ain't going to be as easy as I'd hoped but he doesn't have to know that. "And guess what? I'm coming for you, understand?"

"I'm afraid Mister Tewis won't be making any more phone calls," replies an officious sounding woman. "In fact, Mister Tewis won't be doing much of anything anymore."

"I can't say that news makes me sad," I reply, my mind racing. Of course! Tewis was too small to be behind all this. Especially after the strike from orbit. Bigger players are involved, that much is for sure. "Who the hell are you? And what's all this about?"

"I can tell you in five simple words. Alpha. Renegade. Purple. Angst. Drumroll."

"Huh? What the hell is that?"

"Just a little something for you to ponder on. I take it you're the girl causing everyone so much trouble?"

"Trouble is my middle name, as is 'get to the bloody

point.'"

"Quite. You've heard of the Galactic Secret Service?"

The question takes me aback. The Galactic Secret Service is a ghost organisation. A name bandied around the backrooms of gangster hangouts, seedy barrooms, millionaire clubs and political headquarters, as the main reason behind any number of imagined gripes. These gripes ranged from shipment seizures and disappearances to assassinations and regime changes.

"Yes, we do exist," the woman continues. "And we are here on this shit-end planet of yours, which must highlight the seriousness of your situation. Now, before we talk further, I've got a little question for you… You've been on this line for over thirty seconds. How come we can't track you? That's impressive."

I decide to bluff this out. "I'm an impressive sort of gal. Now what's the damn lowdown?"

"Before we move onto that, I've another question for you. Do you want to live?"

"You're threatening me?"

"No. Not a threat. More of a choice. You've done a good job of surviving so far. You've shown yourself to be resilient, resourceful and your augmented tek is borderline genius, but believe me, without the protection of the Service, you won't survive the evening."

"I can do without your protection," I say, wondering why I haven't hung up, but I'm intrigued. "I saw what you did to that building."

"You think that was us? The service isn't beyond blowing up civilians when deemed necessary but it's those who want to destroy the information inside your head that are responsible."

"So you're not the bad guys, huh?"

"Let's just say some other bad guys are out to kill

you. Today, it's us bad guys from the Service wanting to keep you alive."

"For the wafer inside my head?"

"For what's on the wafer, yes."

"This is all fine and dandy, but I'm running low on trust tonight. So forgive me when I tell you to *go to hell!*"

"I thought you might be like this, so here's a little bit of encouragement."

A sudden, high-pitched whine from the ear-piece makes me wince and the phone becomes hot in my hand, sparking like a firework, and dying. I throw it into the gutter and stalk quickly away. I have no idea where I'm going but standing still seems like inviting trouble.

The bloody Galactic Secret bloody Service! They actually exist?

Going to any one of my hideouts is now a mistake. Staying in one place also seems like a dumb idea. Sooner or later, they will catch up with me. And besides, I have everything I need on me.

There's nothing for it, I need to improvise. I pull up my own schematic of the sewer system, what I've christened the Rat-Run, and superimpose it over the street. Most of the shops are closed for the evening. I duck down a side alley and find my way to a set of tradesman's entrances.

There's no lock in this city that I can't tek-crack. Within moments, I've let myself into the back of a shop. I find the alarm system and disable it before it can trigger. I take out my laser and punch a hole through the floor, quickly dropping into the sewers.

I don't want to admit it, but I sometimes feel more at home here in these pipes than I do elsewhere. They should call me the Sewer Rat, not Quick-Kill Jane. But I digress, all my considerable brainpower is telling me one thing, and one thing only…

I'm done for.

The Service or the friends of Tewis will find me. It's just a matter of time. The only thing I've got to bargain with is fused into my head. And to try and bargain would literally be serving my head up to them on a plate.

Maybe this is how the marks feel after I've caught them? The terrible sense of no way out. And worst of all. I'm missing Angie and her wonderful pies.

I take a left, a right and, pushing full power to my exo, run as fast and as far as I can, heading for the city outskirts in as roundabout a manner as possible.

You may try and corner Quick-Kill Jane, but she ain't too proud to run away. As to where I'm heading, I'll work that out when I get there. But I'll find something. Come up with a plan. I've never yet failed to come out on top.

I access my wafer and play the last conversation over again. I'm sure I missed something in the heat of the moment.

What did the woman say?

Alpha. Renegade. Purple. Angst. Drumroll…

What the hell does that mean? But it's too late. Before I can curse my own stupidity, the folder locked inside my head unzips, and all hell and damnation breaks loose. proud to run away. As to where I'm heading, I'll work that out when I get there. But I'll find something. Come up with a plan. I've never yet failed to come out on top.

I access my wafer and play the last conversation over again. I'm sure I missed something in the heat of the moment.

What did the woman say?

Alpha. Renegade. Purple. Angst. Drum-roll…

What the hell does—! But it's too late. Before I can

curse my own stupidity, the folder locked inside my head unzips and all hell and damnation breaks loose.

THE OVERPOWERING SMELL OF AMMONIA under my nose and I'm jolted back into consciousness.

I'm tied to a chair in a white room with soft edges and even softer lighting. A deep hum from behind the walls irritates my hearing.

A quick glance down shows I've been stripped and placed in a black skinsuit of some kind.

Without my exo and nanomesh armour, I might as well be naked.

Twin wires are attached to my temples, connected to a large tek stack.

I remember the folder opening in my head and the wave of horror emanating from it. I unconsciously access my wafer again. The folder hasn't been removed. For now, it's inert but threatening.

What the hell was inside there, and how the hell did I get here? Wherever here is.

A worn-looking woman in her forties, wearing a similar black skinsuit revealing a honed physique, stares at me intently while leaning against a white table seemingly extruded from the floor. She possesses beady eyes sitting under a wrinkled brow, above which perches long black hair twisted into a rough bun. A sense of controlled power emanates from her and, although she's no looker, there is something about her.

"Hello," she says.

I know that voice. The woman from the phone call…

I'm in the clutches of the goddamn Galactic Secret Service!

I wriggle, trying to get a sense of my bonds, aware that the gravity has increased. I'm either on a different planet or this room has artificial grav.

"They call me 'Mother'," the woman continues.

"I never had a mother," I say, although she ain't the type to be changing diapers, that's for sure. "I grew up on the streets and found my own way in the world without a damn family. But it's no sob story—all the hard knocks were dished out to any and everybody who got in my way."

Mother ain't listening. Her eyes narrow. "You sure are one difficult girl to catch," she says. "But credit where credit is due. You led us on a merry chase alright. Luckily, we were mostly one step ahead. Mostly. We thought we'd lost you when that cityblok was fragged from space. But no, you turned up again."

"And here I am, wherever here is," I reply, searching the room for anything that might aid my escape. "And if you think I'm gonna let this pass," I continue, "you've another think coming, you get me?" The place is more of an office than a holding cell. I'm relieved to find my equipment laid out on a shelf to my left. Nanomesh, exo and the rest. I just need to get untied and dressed, and I'll be back to being a one-girl army.

Mother shrugs. "You might want to stop the threats and start giving out some thanks for saving your stubborn ass. You were in a hell of a mess down on that planet of yours."

I snort but the information jolts me—I'm on a spaceship. I've finally got away from Plenty. Just not the way I envisioned. From a practical perspective, I'm trapped—even if I do manage to get free of these bonds and out of this room. "So where are we, still in orbit?"

Mother sits back on the desk and hits me with a quizzical look. "I'm asking the questions. And you have me flummoxed. Just who are you? I'm pretty sure you weren't christened with that ridiculous name you go by… *Quick-Kill Jane?* How very quaint."

She picks up a sheaf of plastic sheets. "You've no DNA profile. Well, nothing that can be left behind or traced, which is quite some trick, don't you think?"

"I have no idea what you're talking about," I snarl at her. "The cops have never scanned my DNA cos I ain't never been stupid enough to get caught. Even so, I ain't the type to leave such obvious evidence lying around. And if there's a prize for the most ridiculous name, you'd win that hands down."

Mother's quizzical look remains stuck to her face, as if my words have no impact on her. "I might expect to see something like this in the Key Systems," she continues, planting a hand on the curve of her thigh while her eyebrows furrow. "Or on the mediscan of some antigov rich-kid from one of the Gaiaspheres but not from some cheap assassin in the back end of nowhere. How'd you afford it? The procedure costs more than the GDP of your whole goddamn trashcan of a planet."

I've always prided myself on my ability to read people face-to-face. Mother doesn't appear to be lying. If anything, she's surprised by what's she's found. I'm also shocked by the information—mainly because it's not true. "There ain't anything augmented about Quick-Kill Jane," I announce. "I'm perfect and untouched. Just as nature intended."

"You're telling me you don't remember the procedure?"

"What possible reason would I have to lie?"

She takes in my words with a rise of her eyebrows.

"If that's the case, there is only one conclusion—shortly after you were born, someone hid your identity. As to who or why, I have no idea, but they sure went to a lot of trouble over you."

"What do I care?" I reply. "You think I'm like every other orphan who dreams they're some lost princess? Give me a damn break. And besides, why should the Galactic Secret Service care one jot about—how did you put it?—*some cheap assassin in the back end of nowhere?*"

"How old do you think I am, Jane? Forty? Fifty maybe?" she asks. "Well think again. The Service doesn't pay well but they have a great medi-plan. I'm over a hundred years old and seventy of those years have been with the Service. I've survived all this time because of my gut. My instinct. Some might call it clairvoyance or telepathic insight. And all my insight is telling me there's more to you than…" she stares intently into my face. "…than meets the eye."

"I know who I am and that's enough for me," I reply. If I only had my laser, I'd burn that quizzical look off her face. First, I need to get untied and to get out of this place. "Now, tell me… what the hell am I doing here? After what happened when I activated that damn file, I pretty much thought I'd wake up dead."

Mother puts down the sheaf and grimaces. "You nearly did. But you are the resilient type. What we in the Service call a 'survivor'. You also show a disdain for authority and an almost paranoid lack of trust—which I personally find admirable. But trust is what I need from you."

"You ain't getting anything from me."

"Sure, trusting the Service is not always the best option. But in this instance, you need us—or, more importantly, you need me. I'm in your corner, although you don't realise that yet. There are some quite nasty people desperate to retrieve what you've got stuck in that stubborn head of yours. So let me be honest, the Service doesn't care one single jot about you. To them, you are just a container, and very much expendable. My orders were to retrieve the missing data and get it out of the system and back to headquarters. And believe me, it would be a lot simpler to cut your head open to do that. But after such a long time in the Service, I get a certain amount of leeway. I'm putting myself in the firing line by keeping you alive. So cut me some slack."

Mother is telling me pretty much what Dynamo said earlier. There's no way to access the file without removing the wafer from my head. I don't trust Mother, her intentions are all too foggy, but I must admit that what she says is plausible—and most of all, I don't wanna die. "Okay," I say. "I get it. You're keeping me alive. So why keep me tied up?"

"Once we intercepted Tewis, we found out everything we could about you. And you know what we came up with?"

"Not very much."

"Exactly. That's impressive right there. After we brought you aboard, I had time to check out your tek. You designed all that by yourself?"

"Sure. There ain't no walk-in armoury on Plenty. I had to improvise with what I could find. And I like to tinker."

"You sure do. Which means you're dangerous. You will be kept in restraints until we can get to headquarters. We're en-route via voidwarp and I've scheduled surgery to get your wafer removed. If you survive the operation, we'll talk again. I think we may be of use to one another." She pushes herself up to her full height, looking to leave.

"You ain't gonna tell me what's stuck in my head? Even if I say 'pretty please'?"

"You want to know what's in that folder?"

I nod impatiently.

Mother stares intently into my eyes. "Quite simply… we went fishing."

A LOUD REVERBERATING BANG ROCKS the ship. The room jolts sideways, and Mother is thrown to the floor.

My chair is bolted down, my restraints preventing me joining her. The white light of the room suddenly flashes red and sirens blare.

"Status update!" Mother bellows.

A voice over booming speakers: *"Three cruisers, a fourth closing in. Took us by surprise."*

Mother straps herself to her desk chair. "How'd they find us so quickly, Captain?"

"The Cabal must've tracked the shuttle bringing the package from the surface and followed our wake into voidwarp. Inertial dampeners are offline and we—BRACE FOR EMERGENCY MANOEUVRES!"

The Cabal? The name rings a series of bells inside my head. They are as mythical as the damn Galactic Secret Service. A sort of super-mafia.

Another jolt, and the background hum increases in volume. I'm slammed into my chair, my spine crushed by a sudden upsurge in gee, knocking the breath out of my lungs. More gee, flinging my head in every direction. Like some kind of rag doll.

"Two more cruisers ahead. We're not going to be able to hold them off, Mother," the Captain blurts over the com.

Mother is all controlled calm. "How long do we have?" she asks, her hands sweeping over what I guess is a desk readout.

"Two minutes, maybe three…"

"I'm afraid you're going to have to keep those ships occupied for as long as you can, Captain. You know the contingency."

"…Yes, Mother," the Captain replies after a short pause. *"Inertial dampeners are now back online."*

Mother unstraps herself and comes over to me. Without any preamble, she cuts me free. For a second, I consider kicking her aside—an automatic reaction—but I sense she has a plan to get us out of this. I damn hope so.

"Follow me!"

I don't need telling twice.

Mother opens the door and we race down a corridor, rocking side to side from multiple impacts, red lights flashing.

We arrive in a hub-room hung with similar skinsuits to the one I'm wearing.

Mother punches at a control panel. A door opens. We dive inside an escape vessel of sorts. Long, thin, and barely large enough for the two of us. The door slams shut and the dash flashes into life.

"Strap yourself in." Mother punches at more buttons and the craft begins to hum. "We're ready, Captain," she says into the com.

A sudden jolt of gee and we're ejected out of the ship, followed by a booming explosion seconds later.

"This is gonna be rough," Mother barks. "Brace!"

Everything goes black. My mind is wrenched from my skull to be scattered across the cosmos like so many broken shards. I want to scream but I remain trapped, inert, until… *I'm back.* "What the—!"

"Quiet!" Mother orders, wrestling with the controls. The ship bucks but comes under control.

I peer over her shoulder. Star maps and navi-readouts. "Where are the other ships? What the hell happened?"

"A contingency measure," Mother answers. "In case of emergencies. We took an escape raft and were jettisoned just before the captain blew the ship. A loss of a few brave men and women. But they knew the risk and their duty. Their families will be well looked after. Hopefully we weren't tracked. We dropped out of voidwarp at the same time as the explosion… I did say it was gonna be rough." She punches at the navicom with quick fingers. "This ship is one big voidwarp engine with room for one or two passengers. But we aren't clear of danger quite yet—we need to evade those pursuing Cabal ships. It's only a matter of minutes before they work out what happened."

"Then let's get outta here," I reply, trying to control my voice, but recent events have jolted me somewhat.

The Cabal—a loose collection of illegal gangs, mafia families and violent, secretive underhand groups of organisations of all types—want me dead. It's one thing to piss off a few hoods and local kingpins but the mythical Cabal? That's a lot to take in.

Mother saved my life—I know that she's protecting what's stuck inside my head, but I can't ignore the fact she kept me alive against her orders. I'm not sure if I would've done the same if I was in her shoes.

Do I trust her?

No. Not for one moment.

Right now, she's calling the shots and seems to be actively trying to keep me alive. And Quick-Kill Jane ain't too stupid to realise sometimes she's gotta go with the flow.

"We don't possess the power for an immediate jump," Mother replies calmly. "We have to wait for the engines to recharge. A few minutes but if we can get out of here before those cruisers arrive, there'll be no way to track us."

"A waiting game?"

Mother nods. Outwardly, she is cool personified, but I can plainly see beads of sweat on her brow.

"Headquarters is out of the question," she says. "I've plotted a course for the Outland Systems. Sometimes the best place to hide is amongst the unwashed… but we have to get there first."

I drum my fingers against my thigh, missing the sure presence of my laser, yet I'm still capable of putting a tight arm around Mother's throat, forcing her to tell me what all this is about. Even so, my sixth sense is telling me that would be a bad move. I get the feeling Mother may be as dangerous as I am. I try a different tack… "Are you gonna explain to me about what is in my head? And what exactly did you mean by *fishing?*"

A small laugh escapes Mother's tight lips. "We put our line in the water, dangled our bait and waited to see what sharks would bite. That file you have stuck in your head… was the bait. Although it's less of a file and more a piece of highly volatile but effective code. A half-aware information gatherer. Or to put it another way—an intelligent spy working on behalf of the Service."

"Intelligent?"

Mother nods, her eyes still fixed firmly on the voidwarp readout. "You've heard of Encephalic tek?"

"Sure," I reply. I might not have had an education back on Plenty, but everyone knew about that. "Artificial intelligence was banned hundreds of years ago. They're supposed to be illegal."

"Remarkably illegal but we in the Service have a certain leeway with what's lawful and what's not. The code welded into your wafer isn't a full Encephalic intelligence—not even close—although it has objectives and self-preservation skills." Mother shrugged. "We call it a *Ceph*. And for a Ceph to function properly, it needs a certain amount of suitable hardware... A few years ago, we created our own little illegitimate operation. Designing, manufacturing and supplying illegal tek to anyone and everyone willing to buy it. We flooded the illegal market with high-quality wafer components of our own particular design, making it easier for this operation to work."

A name flits into my mind, complete with a rotating logo. "You mean the Secret Service is behind Slash-Stak? The part of my wafer Dynamo was bragging about? I have damn secret service tek welded into my head?"

Mother nods. "Yep. One and the same. The problem... Slash-Stak was far too successful. And, as supplying top-class tek to a growing bunch of dangerous illegals was starting to raise a few eyebrows, we were forced into entering the second part of the operation without being fully prepared. Under the guise of Slash-Stak, we arranged a robbery. An 'audacious strike against the Secret Service', or so the Cabal was led to believe—the theft of a supposed list of our operatives and operations. The file was indeed 'stolen'. Or what they thought was a file. It was our burrowing worm. Our information gatherer. The Ceph. Like I said... we went fishing."

I digest her words. "Okay, the Ceph is part of your operation, of your plan. I can see that. It makes sense. Sure it does. But what was the Ceph doing on Plenty, a planet in the ass-end of nowhere? Inside some low-life scum?"

Mother turns away from the readouts, contemplates me for a few seconds and shrugs. "As your friend Dynamo discovered, the Ceph can't be copied or cracked. It was passed around from one underground organisation to another, exactly as we anticipated, while collecting as much Intel as it could. But as I said, Slash-Stak was an unprecedented success—too damn successful. Soon after the Ceph was 'stolen', our plan was leaked. All hellfire was let loose as those compromised organisations used their considerable resources to find the Ceph and destroy it. The Ceph has a certain amount of guile. It tried to hide. Flitting from one illegal wafer to another. Seeking an opportunity to call for help. Until it became wedged inside you."

"Okay," I say, taking in the information. "But that doesn't answer why I was contracted to kill Rollo Barla. Why employ me when they had all that firepower circling in orbit?"

"Like I said, the Ceph has a certain amount of guile. We'd lost it for a few weeks. It did what it was programmed to do—the Ceph went underground. That's why it ended up in the back-end of nowhere. But the bad guys weren't idle. The Cabal panicked and began eliminating anyone and everyone who may be carrying the Ceph in their augmented Slash-Stak wafers. There's been a plague of assassinations, hundreds over the last two weeks. That's how you became involved. Tewis wasn't sure what he was looking for, but he was ordered to eliminate anyone with an illegal wafer and to data-beam anything unusual to his superiors."

Mother pulls her lips into a tight smile. "Six cruisers—a mishmash of mafia families, clanships and illegals—voidwarped to your planet in the last hour. We followed them, arriving shortly after, masking ourselves as a family merchant vessel. But we were just as blind as the bad guys who were looking for you—until the

Ceph sent us a message, that is. Courtesy of your friend Dynamo. But in contacting us, the Ceph revealed its position to the Cabal ships and they destroyed the building you were in. Then it was just a matter of who could get to you first. We had one advantage though, the Ceph broadcast an encrypted message, allowing us to get to Tewis first. You were tough to catch, granted… but here you are."

A beep from the com and Mother's head darts back to the readouts. "Multiple incursions! The Cabal will be here in moments but that's all the time we need." The navicom flashes green and Mother punches the voidwarp activation code.

This time the lurch into voidwarp is not as jolting. All my sensations slip backwards and forwards and loop around themselves then return to relative normal. Sure, the experience isn't particularly nice, but neither is it so injurious.

The stars of voidspace flow past us on the screens. I've seen them many times before, on the public streams but not for real. They are nothing like what you see on a cold, clear night from Plenty. The spectrum of human eyes is too narrow. But in voidspace, the stars are revealed as vast, luminescent, jellyfish-like structures, floating past us as if we're underwater, not in a wormhole. "It's beautiful," I hear myself saying.

"It's your first time in the void?" Mother asks. "Everyone reacts the same."

I never thought I'd miss Plenty but now, in this moment, all this is a little overwhelming. I shake my head, deciding that to survive, I'll have to adapt. Having nostalgic thoughts, about a place I spent a lifetime trying to escape from, doesn't sound like Quick-Kill Jane. "Tell me, where are we heading?"

"I mentioned the Cabal… we're now entering their heartlands. I've set a course for the Barrens."

Clever. *Always do what the enemy doesn't expect.*

Back when my escape plan had been simple, the Barrens was going to be my first destination once I left Plenty. A place to meet the right people and to enhance my skills and my fortune. And Mother is taking me right there. If it wasn't for this damn Ceph stuck in my head, I'd be elated. For now, I'll need to hold off until Mother can sort out my wafer. Having to rely on somebody irks me but, unfortunately, Mother holds all the cards. "You got friends there, huh?" I ask.

"The Barrens is a hive, full of paranoid off-gridders, pirates and clans. You should fit right in. But I also know my way around. It's where I grew up."

"You came from there?" My voice sounds more incredulous than I intended.

Mother laughs. "Where do you think service operatives are made? At some elite training compound where only the best of the very best end up?"

"I suppose so, yeah."

"Well think again. My childhood was… problematic. But I'm like you, a survivor. I was a master-thief and an assassin. Until the Service caught up with me."

"Well more fool you."

"Fool?" Mother says, turning to face me. "It's not *me* getting shot." She pulls out a blaster and fires point-blank into my chest.

I AWAKE, GROGGY AND UNCOMFORTABLE. I'm lying down—or at least I think I am—my body feels heavy and I'm unable to move even fingers or toes. I must be somewhere in high-gee or held by some powerful restraint field.

And then my memories come flooding back in the bright flash of a blaster discharge. I was shot!

"How is the patient?"

I recognise the voice immediately. It's Mother. I try to curl my fists but, again, I'm powerless.

"Under stasis," replies another voice, male and ancient-sounding—nothing more than a reedy whine. "All readouts are well within acceptable parameters. The procedure was a resounding success."

"Thanks Abe, I knew we could rely on you," Mother says. "Time to revive the patient."

"He's already listening to us," the man replies.

I'm confused. I thought they were talking about me. Who is this 'he'? Some other sap? Sudden panic floods my mind. Am I dead? A disembodied consciousness trapped in some mad scientist's lair? Mother shot me at point-blank range with a blaster. Even my nanomesh wouldn't have protected me from such a gun.

She killed me… *Didn't she?*

"Release him, let's see how good you did." Mother again, a pleased tone to her normally efficient words.

A weight is lifted from my body and I gasp for air,

my chest heaving. I try to lift an arm but it's too heavy. I'm also aware of my heartbeat—a loud, slow thud, reverberating from inside my chest. I try to speak but my mouth is dry. I cough—the sound is different—it's not my cough. What the hell is happening to me?

I struggle to part my eyelids and they finally peel apart. Harsh, bright light slams into my brain.

I try to speak again but the only sounds I make are low and guttural—like some brain-damaged ape.

Slowly, my eyes adjust. I become aware of an aged man staring at me. His face a mess of vertical wrinkles cutting deep into his skin. His eyes watery, and surrounded by thin red veins.

Again, I try to lift my arms. I want to strangle him and then Mother, but the effort is just too much.

"It will take you some days to regain any semblance of strength," he says. "But you are breathing on your own and your bodily functions are very much in the green. In the meantime, you need to rest and re-orientate."

I feel pressure against my neck and I slip into unconsciousness.

The next few days are spent flitting in and out of drug-induced sleep. My waking periods are characterised by what feels like physio, my limbs massaged by some machine whilst electrical impulses make me jerk and twitch.

After I don't know how many more days, I wake again. It takes me long minutes to make sense of where I am—the drugs slowly being leached from my system, I guess. But finally, the blurs resolve themselves and I find myself in a small room, sitting up in bed. Mother and Abe are here, both looking at me.

"Welcome back to the land of the living," Mother says.

"You shot me!" I blurt, but something is wrong. My words are not my own. They sound harsh and loud. I raise my hand and baulk at what I see. It's not my hand. It's too large, the fingers fat like sausages.

"What the hell have you done to me?" I growl.

"Saved your life," Mother replies. "With the help of our chief *meat technician,* Abe, here. But you don't have to thank us just yet."

"It will take you a short while to adjust to your new body," Abe says, "but in a week or two, you will be up and about and able to leave us."

I stare down at the bed. A hideous ape is lurking under the bedsheets.

"I know it's an imposition," Mother says matter-of-factly, "but with the Cabal looking for you, there was no way I could enter the Barrens with you in tow. I'm afraid I had to dump what remained of your body in voidspace. But I kept your head and… *here we are.* As for the gender reassignment, that's standard procedure for a new agent."

"You've turned me into a goddamn man!" I croak, finding this difficult to process.

"Can it!" Mother replies harshly. "You're not on that backwater planet no more. Your issues with gender are old-fashioned and out-moded. But don't worry, your proclivities remain unchanged. You will still have the same sexual urges, but they are now confined within a male container."

"You bastards," I spit, staring down at my spatula-sized hands. I curl them into twin fists.

"That may be," says Mother, coming closer—close enough for me to put my hands around her throat and squeeze the life out of her, but, more than anything, I need to hear what she's got to say.

"I know how much we become attached to our physical selves," Mother continues. "You are still intrinsically you, but this…" she puts one thin hand onto my arm—it looks tiny in comparison to my vast biceps. "…is the male version of Quick-Kill Jane. If you're going to work for the Galactic Secret Service, you need a completely new identity."

"You really think I'm gonna work for you after this?"

"I'm sure of it. First off, we recovered the wafer from your head and replaced it with something far superior. Secondly, we reassigned your gender ID. A complicated procedure for those not diagnosed with gender dysfunction before puberty—but as you might have seen in the streams, it's also become a fashionable procedure that the rich and sexually promiscuous are happy to endure for the thrill of the different. Here in the Service, it performs another function. All new agents are gender-reassigned and their DNA homogenised. They become entirely original individuals, retaining everything other than the body they had before."

"But I didn't ask to become an agent," I snarl back at her, aware of an edge of animal violence I've not felt before—those active male genes, I guess. But I'm sure the old me would still want to rip Mother's head off, even if I needed my exo to do it.

"No one is asked," Mother continues. "We are all *recruited*. And before you start flexing all that new muscle, you'd better realise that if not for the Service, you'd be dead. I saved you and gave you a chance at a brand-new life. And I must admit, the male version of yourself is impressive. I told Abe to give you a body to match that iron-will of yours and he's certainly come up trumps."

I'm flooded with an intoxicating mixture of emotion.

Betrayal, loss and—most of all—*anger*. But at heart I'm a logical pragmatist. The only way I survived on Plenty was to roll with the knocks and not let anything or anyone defeat me. To turn every setback in to an advantage and to take every chance at revenge without looking back. Above all, Quick-Kill Jane is a survivor.

"There's one more thing," Mother says. "Abe managed to find a strand of your original DNA in that brain of yours. When we get the time, we'll chuck it through our tek stacks. You never know, you might be a princess after all."

"Don't bother," I reply. "I know who I am. I don't need no goddamn back story."

Mother shrugs. "As you wish, but we'll keep it on file for you."

I review the facts and can't ignore them. Without the intervention of Mother, I'd be dead meat. I'm still alive—not in the way I wanted to be—but I can play the waiting game, even if it's a different heart beating in my chest. And, the less I know about what they've put between my legs, the better.

"Can I ever get Jane back?" I ask, guessing Mother's answer.

"The old you?" She shakes her head. "I incinerated the body and dumped it into voidspace. "But if you live to retirement, the Service has a great medi-plan, or didn't I mention that? When you retire, you can start again, live any life as you wish, as anybody you want to be—within reason—with a few mega-bucks in the bank courtesy of the Galactic Secret Service. And with that DNA we found, we can even grow your old body back… if you still want it."

I take in the information with a nod of my head. A body is just a body to Mother and Abe. I get that. But

I've been violated and I ain't never gonna let that wash. I have to admit it, they've got me but Quick-Kill Jane ain't nothing if she's not resourceful. I'll find my way through all this and come back for revenge. First, I must play their dumb game with a goddamn smile on my face. "You're holding me as a hostage while I go and do your dirty work for you, is that it?"

Mother nods. "That's exactly it. Although for someone with your talents, it won't exactly be work. More like a helluva lot of fun. You'll need some training—how to use that new body of yours for starters—but once you're done with that, you'll pretty much work on your own. You'll become an independent special agent operative. And, let me tell you, you're quite the looker, despite the dumb expression plastered all over your face. We'll send jobs and missions your way and, if you do well, I may even let you take me on a date." She laughs.

I try to pull a smile on what I guess is my new face, but my lips feel as clumsy and over-sized as the rest of me.

"The name 'Quick-Kill Jane' might've suited you on that dead-end planet we rescued you from, but it won't do for the Service. We will need a codename."

I shake my head as vigorously as I can manage. "You've taken everything else from me but you ain't taking my name!" I blurt. "I'm Quick-Kill, that's all I've ever had that's been mine and mine alone."

Mother contemplates my words for a moment and shrugs. "Okay, your codename from now on is *Quick-Kill*. Keep it secret. It's for Secret Service use only. A way for you and other operatives to identify one another. The Service will issue you with any number of false IDs, but your codename will always remain the same. You understand?"

I lean back and laugh loudly. I'm still angry, and this body is going to take time getting used to, but another emotion has joined all the others vying for my attention—*elation*.

I didn't expect that. But I know why... I finally did it. I got my ass off Plenty, got myself a new life and... got myself a new body. It's not how I envisaged escaping, and living life as a man is gonna take some getting used to, but I'm up for it. Although, there's no way Quick-Kill is gonna bend the knee for the Galactic Secret Service for long. "Okay," I say. "I'll do it. How long before I can get my old look back?"

Mother shrugs. "Seventy or so years, give or take a decade."

"Then I'd better get started."

"I knew you'd adapt quickly to the situation. You are a survivor after all—a one-in-a-million that the Service is always looking for."

I openly scoff.

"Maybe the odds are not that high, but we service men, women and all shades in between, come from the same stock. So believe me when I tell you that all your thoughts of payback, punishment and whatever else you are feverishly planning in terms of revenge, are a waste of time. Every agent has lain in a bed similar to your own and, in coming to terms with what's been done to them, has planned what you're planning. I won't tell you to forget that, it's who you are. It's why you've been recruited. But you will find the Secret Service hard to shake off. You've spent most of your life working on your own selfish goals. Today that has changed—you now work for the greater good. You've been recruited."

"What next?" I ask, my new voice a guttural growl.

"First off, I suggest a shave."

I rub a hand across my jaw. My chin feels enormous, jutting out of my face like a slab of granite, bristles rasping against my skin. "This is gonna take a lot of getting used to."

"After that," Mother continues, "we have a little job for you. Nothing too strenuous but you will need to be at the peak of your strength. You'll have four weeks to learn how to talk and walk—without falling over that brand new dick of yours." She salutes. "Welcome to the Galactic Secret Service, mister."

I sit back and groan. Seventy years before I can get my old body back? No way in hell! Mother has underestimated me. I ain't like her or any of the other saps the Service has 'recruited'. I'm not one-in-a-million, I'm one of a kind… I'm Quick-Kill!

PART TWO

THE DO OR DIE

PLANET-FALL IS NO FUN. No fun at all. Or at least that's what I'm discovering. I'm crammed into a goddamn flying coffin, heading feet first into a planet's atmosphere, like some shooting star with a death wish.

You'll become an independent special agent operative, pretty much working on your own, is how Mother explained my new life.

Was that only four weeks ago?

So far, the opposite has been true. I've been surrounded by doctors, trainers, and psych-specialists—all eager to get their mittens on me. Until the Galactic Secret Service stuffed me into this bloody cigar tube that is. My first solo mission—I was told—yet I'm to meet another agent on the surface.

I guess Mother doesn't trust me to work on my own after all.

I'd emerged from Abe's medical section—Abe being the ancient son-of-a-bitch who performed this gender-swap on me—as a new man. Literally. And things haven't gotten any better. Although I've accepted what I am… *A male. A he. A goddamn guy.*

Sure, I went through the exhaustive body-reorientation crap, took the self-defence modules—which I thought I didn't need, until I fell flat on my face on day one. This lumbering body of mine is a helluva lot different than what I'm used to. But the thing is strong, I'll give it that. Not as robust as my exo, but powerful and controlled.

I used to love to dress up… you know what I mean? When you've got the curves, you show them off, right? But now, *what's the point?* My clothes have become functional and boring. And don't even get me started on shaving. Legs are one thing, but this stupid face? It's like trying to shave a chimp. No wonder some men prefer beards.

The benefits?

As far as I can tell, apart from the increased upper body strength and height (I'm a good foot and a half taller—which all the bumps on my head can attest to), there ain't any. Not one.

And as for everything *down below*… You don't want to know. Hell, even I don't want to know, and I have to live with the annoying things. I've been avoiding that area as much as physically possible. But its uncomfortable. Moving around, getting trapped, changing size when I least expect it. And in the mornings? *Yeugh!* The sooner I'm a woman again, the better. This six-foot-ten lump of hyped-up muscle is a step down the evolutionary ladder.

Sudden buffeting and I'm forced to stab my sausage-sized fingers at the navicom to compensate. A couple of mashes at the console and I'm careening over the terminator into the morning of a brand-new day on this green and blue planet. I'll tell you one thing… it sure is pretty. Vast glinting oceans surrounding a single, impressive continent. Nothing like my home planet of Plenty—a forgotten, ugly ball of red dust.

I glare at my chump hands. It took a lot of getting used to, but I learned to use these fingers. The Galactic Secret Service may have taken my body, but my intellect—my superior brain—remains intact. More fool them.

The Service gave me gas pellets, darts, and grenades,

but I enhanced them. Adding my own little tweaks, you know what I mean? The uniform I'm wearing as cover for the planet below is stuffed with surprises. They also let me have a laser. I worked on my design some more. Now it's compact and light enough for me to carry around like a regular blaster. Sure, the previous me, *Jane,* would've struggled with its weight without her exo. But not the new me with all these macho muscles.

More buffeting and the navicom tells me I'm through the worst of re-entry.

I find the beacon—a weak signal some twenty klicks away—level out and head straight for it.

A minute or two later, I'm bringing the flying coffin in to land. My first ever solo flight. *Textbook.*

The thing ain't a patch on my Dodge Charger—the transport lacks any style—but hey, I'm loving every minute of it. The freedom, the control. The more the Service teaches me stuff—like how to fly ships like this—the sooner I'm gonna use those skills to escape. First, I'll need to steal back my original DNA profile. I don't plan on playing at *Mr. Man* for the rest of my life, that's for sure. But the Service keep that stuff well and truly hidden. It's gonna be quite some hill to climb… *but never underestimate Quick-Kill.*

I pop the lid and pull myself out. I'm in a small wooded copse of some kind. And I admit it, I'm impressed. So much greenery. Back on Plenty, you didn't see many plants, unless you visited the out-of-town greenhouses. Which, I can tell you, ain't no fun day out.

The sky here is blue and empty of clouds, not the dull purple I'm used to. I take a deep breath of air. It's full of exotic smells and an early morning freshness. And then it hits me… *I'm on a completely new planet.*

Fuck, *yeah.*

The transport casing is still hot from re-entry, so I'm extra careful when I grab my equipment. A satchel containing laser, grenades, darts, stims and a stylised kit-bag—all part of my disguise. I'm already dressed in the local garb for this mission. Although I have no idea what the mission is…

A snap of wood behind me.

I whirl around, laser in hand, my finger ready to punch heat.

I see a woman clad in a tight, green leather stylised uniform similar to what I'm wearing, standing with one hand on her hip. She's mid-thirties, with sandy blonde hair framed around a boyish-looking face.

"What the hell was that entry?" she says, her voice full of scorn. "You want to bring every goddamn twat with a tracking device to this location? I know Mother said you was still wet behind the ears, but that show of yours will have alerted the whole goddamn planet."

I don't get it. Even with my stupid ham-hands, I nailed the landing. Like I said. *Textbook*.

"Don't just stand there, idiot!" She tosses something past me and into the transport. "That's a multiphase stealth grenade. You don't want to be in the field when it deploys, or you'll be cut in half."

She takes off, and I angrily jog behind her.

A few moments later, I hear a dull pop and turn around to see the transport disappear. "I thought the plan was to destroy it?"

"Don't worry yourself, Sweetheart. If anyone gets too close without a code, the thing will explode." She shakes her head at me. "You're Quick-Kill, huh? You're sure gonna be quick-dead if you don't buck up soon, you get me?"

I grab her arm with one powerful hand. "Shut up,

just for one jazzing minute."

She spins out of my grip, twists my hand, and I land face down in the dirt.

"Don't you ever touch me, okay? Or I'll break your face. You're under my command now. You mess up again and the report says you died on impact. You get me, Mister?"

I nod, and she lets me go.

Just who is this lunatic woman?

I stand up, brushing myself off and realise I'm a good foot taller than her. How did she manage to push me into the goddamn dirt? That wouldn't have happened when I was Jane. No way. I need to hone my reflexes and my fighting technique if I'm going to make any headway in this damn body.

"I'm Pistol-Whip," the woman says. "And if you mess me around one more time, you'll come to learn why that's my code name first hand, understand?"

She offers me her hand and I take it.

A foot to my thigh, a twist of my hand and I'm face down in the dirt again. "And don't ever forget who's in charge…"

AFTER HER CHARMING INTRODUCTION, PISTOL-WHIP says nothing. She motions me to follow her and soon we're jogging through a dense, bushy wood. The trees are overwhelming. I've never been this close to so much vegetation. The smell is cloying, the air full of strange noises.

I focus on my breathing, chasing Pistol-Whip, who's damn nimble-footed in this terrain. I lumber behind her, my footfalls loud in comparison to hers.

A crashing bull chasing a darting deer.

I've had dark moments since the gender swap was forced upon me, but as I watch her elegant thighs, tight upper body, and compact arms, I'm swamped by envy.

Ten minutes later, we reach a rocky outcrop. She flits upwards, bouncing from rock to rock and suddenly disappears. I follow a few paces behind and realise she's entered a cave of some sort. Pistol-Whip waits for me inside.

I open my mouth to speak, but a quick finger darts to her lips.

If there's anyone close enough to hear, I'm not aware of them. This place is quiet, apart from the occasional breeze rustling the trees and vegetation. She pads towards what looks like a tent made from similar material to her uniform, and slides inside, beckoning for me to follow.

Once inside, she closes the flap and relaxes. "We're

safe in here. Undetectable."

"It's very nice," I reply.

"Weren't you told that this was a covert mission? You were supposed to land unnoticed."

I shrug. "I thought I did."

She sits back. "Really? You put my life in danger, Mister. And I don't like that."

"I did what Mother told me, what I was trained to do. To come in fast and hard and to head for the beacon."

"You came in fast and hard, alright. Half the bloody continent knows you're here."

"Okay," I say, sitting back, wondering why she's giving me such a hard time. "Tell me what I did wrong. If anything, the flight was easier and more straightforward than the sims they put me through beforehand."

She closes her eyes and shakes her head. This close to her, I see that, despite the boyish demeanour, she's attractive. Damn dangerous, but quite the looker.

"Your first sonic boom woke everyone up and the second told them where you were heading."

"Give me a break! That was my first flight outside the sim."

"Your first goddamn flight?" She opens her eyes to give me a disapproving look—an adult chastising a disobedient child. "Next thing you'll tell me this is your first mission."

I shrug.

"Goddamn Mother! If this mission wasn't difficult enough, she's saddled me with one of her *trial runs*. Dammit!"

"What do you mean by that?" I spit back.

"Your first mission is a way for the Service to see if you've got the balls and the brains to survive as a Service agent."

"I've got the ba…" I begin, before deciding to rephrase my answer. "I've got the brains."

"The survival rate of new agents is less than one in ten, which means I'd be better off killing you here and now. You've already compromised the mission."

"Well, do it then!" I reply, tensing. Pistol-Whip may be cute, but she sure is starting to piss me off.

She digests my words for a few seconds. "I should."

"Which means you're gonna let me live." I slump back and give her another shrug. "So ditch the attitude and explain the mission to me."

"You weren't briefed?"

"Sure I was. Follow the beacon, land on the planet, meet up with a field agent and get delivery of mission details."

"And that's it?" She shakes her head again. "Welcome to the Galactic Secret Service," she says with a mock salute.

"You gonna fill me in on what we're supposed to be doing here?"

Her green eyes focus on mine. "Do you even know the name of the planet?"

"Mother said you'd be giving me everything I need to know."

"Let me get this straight, you were told you were on a mission and you didn't ask where it was or what it was about?"

Pistol-Whip is right, dammit. "I had other things on my mind," I say, pointing to my new body in explanation. She must know I've been gender swapped. The same thing probably happened to her, though she got the better deal.

"This is the planet Palladia, in the Prometheus System," she says. "The smallest of the Triumvirate, but where all the power of this jumped-up little system is centred, you get me?"

"Got it."

"I can tell by your dumb expression that you've never heard of it."

"Cut the insults and get to the damn point."

"The problem with the Triumvirate is that it's run by some quite nasty people."

"I thought that was the problem everywhere."

"It is, but the Service don't like the present nasty people in charge and want to replace them, with other nasty people. Nasty people the Service approve of. Is this getting too complicated for you to follow?"

I pull my lips back in a sarcastic smile. "Like I said, just give me the deets."

"The Triumvirate is a dictatorship. They work the same the galaxy over. You know the deal—some small-dick sits in charge with a group of other small-dick generals handing out the punishments and the rewards."

I feel a strange urge to tell this woman that I ain't no small-dick. That, despite my negative feelings about my new anatomy, I'm reasonably well-endowed. And then it hits me. That's a stupid man-thought. *Space!* Mother and her Secret Service friends have turned me into an idiot obsessed with the least interesting and most uncomfortable part of his new body.

"You listening?"

"Yeah, sure," I reply, feeling myself flush. "I get it, this place is run by small-dicks."

Pistol-Whip gives me a sideways look. She's not impressed.

I take a deep breath. The next time, assuming there is a next time, I'm gonna insist on working alone.

"The other two planets in this system are Pluton and

Protactin," Pistol-Whip continues.

I recognise the names as based on some of the three-hundred elements on the ever-growing Periodic Table, but planet-naming hasn't been one of humanity's strong suits—as those unfortunate enough to be born on the planet *Blessed* found out. Space knows why anyone would choose to live on that dangerous rock. Surviving to adulthood there was quite an achievement, due to a wide range of environmental challenges from extreme changeable climate to flora and fauna that would kill you rather than look at you. Old age? An impossibility.

I jerk my attention away from my inner dialogue and back on to Pistol-Whip's words.

"Those planets are both significantly larger than where we are," she continues. "Here, grav is zero-point-eight. Lighter than Earth-normal. The other two planets are heavier, both at grav one-point-five. All three planets of the system were colonised in the early part of the Expansion, but over time Palladia gained a natural authority. They were taller than their squat compatriots—or 'dirty nuggets' as they call them—from the other two worlds. All the best universities and schools, the military and the government became based here. Richer, more influential families either moved here or sent their children to grow up here. And, inevitably, a division occurred. The nuggets and their masters. A two-tier system. And, also inevitably, so did a civil war. The upshot of this potted history is that the Palladians won. They instigated a dictatorship that controls this system with a clichéd rod of iron."

"Our job is what, exactly? To support a coup. To bring down the Palladians?"

Pistol-Whip's face splits into a grin. "Slow down soldier. We're doing nothing of the kind. The Service works gradually—using its illegal ceph-tek to keep the galaxy in balance, while pulling at many intertwining threads. I'm not even sure if they understand what they're doing half the time. My job here was, and still is, to infiltrate the Palladian high-command. And, just so you know, this system has been officially designated 'backward'."

"Backward?" I repeat. "Huh?"

"The Prometheus system has been formally struck off the Galaxy Charter of Planets and Systems. Which means it's embargoed, hit with a whole raft of sanctions. They're not allowed access to the tek that they want, to the trade to support that tek, or to any personnel who can develop that tek. Get it?"

I shrug. "Yeah, I get it. But why? What did they do?"

"Let's just say they're not very much into human-rights. Or any goddamn rights for that matter."

"But I guess there's now a fantastic opportunity for black market dealings, huh? Nice of the Galaxy Charter to make that work available to all the bootleggers and dark-runners."

Pistol-Whip snorts. "That may be, but these guys don't care. They are very happy being in power and reaping the benefits of being in power. To be honest, until a few years ago, they were isolationists, but that changed. It's one of the reasons the Service are suddenly interested in them. So far, the Palladians, and their jumped-up little Triumvirate, have no idea we're here and we want to keep it that way. Your job is to break out a prisoner. Some nugget kid. The Service says he can't die. That he's vital for this, that or the other."

I can't help but laugh. "A moment ago, you were threatening to kill me, and saying I've a one in ten chance of survival. I don't see how I could help rescue this kid if

I was dead or died trying."

Pistol-Whip purses her lips and tilts her head to one side. "Like I said, there are lots of threads. If the Service don't manage to pull this one, there'll be others. The way I hear it, everything is a *vital mission*. Failures just lead to adjustments. The Service will get their way, somehow. You fail today and maybe things will take that little bit longer to put in place. Maybe there'll be another nugget kid, from another nugget family. Who knows?"

"Do I have a cover name? Mother said you had an ID set up for me."

Pistol-Whip nods, producing a device like a cigar-stub, carbon-coloured with a glowing end. She grabs my chin and brings the device up to my right eye.

"What the hell?" I say, pulling free.

"You've not seen one of these things before? You're greener than an Eridanus Emerald Fish! It's a retinal transmuter—a nifty piece of kit. A Galactic Secret Service special, designed for missions on backwater worlds like this one. You are now… *Warrior-Colonel Sub-Lieutenant Danton*. Which, on this dump of a planet, means your retina will be regularly scanned. If that happens, this'll ensure you don't ID as anything other than who you should be. Get it?"

I nod begrudgingly. "I'm taking on the identity of someone else."

"Don't worry, you won't be bumping into him anytime soon."

Her expression tells me Warrior-Colonel Sub-Lieutenant Danton ain't around to complain about someone stealing his identity.

"Sit still." Pistol-Whip grabs my jaw again. Her hands are soft and warm, her body close to mine. Intimate. If she wasn't holding my face so tightly, I'd shake my head with frustration at what I've become—*this man-thing.*

I long to be myself again…

A blast of white light and an intense sting then she moves to the next eye. "All done," she says.

"What about my face?"

"You're very pretty? What of it?"

"You know what I mean. My eyes may pass their scanner, but I ain't the real McCoy."

Pistol-Whip shrugs. "The Palladians rely on their scanner tek alone. It's fool-proof, or so they think."

"I'm a Warrior-Colonel? Is that a high rank?"

She scoffs. "You wish. No, I'm the one with rank here. Warrior-General Third Class Vabre. And from now on, even if it's not necessary, you address me with this rank at all times. And never mention my code name, okay?"

"Sure," I reply with a smirk.

"You think you're the only one with a monopoly on dumb-sounding names?"

I take a breath to reply, but she silences me with an irritated wave. "Your job is to get in and out with as little trouble as possible. I'm flashing over everything you need to know about how to survive on this messed-up rock, and the info to pull off this gig."

I sense a spike in my cerebral wafer and suddenly, her knowledge is my knowledge. I review the info. It's more than just ranks, but names and faces, coupled with a full history of this system and its present oligarchy.

And my own back-story as Danton.

There's also a large file on Pistol-Whip herself, or as she is known on this planet, *Warrior-General Third Class Vabre.* Her career, up to eight months ago, is flagged as facsimile. Her back-story, I guess. The rest details her work in the Ministry of Alteration—a shady organisation that, as far as I can tell, is part of the regime's torture and control section. An apt name as many of the people it deals with appear to be altered from being alive to being dead. "Just how deep does your cover go?" I ask. "You torture and kill people?"

"We all do what we have to do. If not, it's our necks on the chopping block."

"Okay… so what happens next?"

"We discuss the mission."

Another spike in my wafer and a mission folder appears.

"Let's go over the details," Pistol-Whip says with no preamble. "First off, when we get back to the city, we'll split up and that's the last you will see of me. You'll make your way to the visiting officer's barracks. You get settled in, spend a quiet evening and tomorrow you'll be doing the normal things that out-of-town hicks do—which is sleep and take drugs to kill their jet-lag before heading out for a typical night on the town. Your cover is that of an out-of-towner unused to the ways of the city… you get me?"

"Yeah, got it."

"You'll drink, make merry and get yourself into trouble. Nothing out of the ordinary. It happens all the time. The MPs will take you to a holding cell. Come the right time, the security cameras will be disabled, and you will escape, making your way via a short, predetermined route to the Ministry of Alteration."

"Escape?"

She gives the barest of nods. "Don't fuck it up."

"I won't… Warrior-General, sir!"

"We're gonna lie low until night-time."

"Night? But it's only morning!"

"Take the time to review tomorrow's mission. And

if you're clever, you'll do what I'm gonna do. See you in seven hours." She lies down, closes her eyes and is immediately unconscious.

PISTOL-WHIP AIN'T SLEEPING, THAT'S for sure. My guess is she's using a trance inducer, a cerebral enhancement allowing her to pass time in the blink of an eye. Mother promised me a top-grade Service wafer, but I have to earn my enhancements. She explained that it was all to do with survival. *"Wafer augmentation may enhance your wits,"* she told me before I left. *"But they can also certainly dull them. You earn your enhancements as you go along. Mission by mission."*

Nevertheless, what now sits in my cerebral cortex is a more complex and advanced wafer than poor Dynamo, my recently deceased tek guy, could even dream of. It has its own stealth tek, appearing like any bog-standard wafer on a typical scanner—or not appearing at all, if that's what I command it to do. Also, I can now literally split my thought streams, allowing me to work on one problem while dealing with another. It has invasive patch software—so I can hack and commandeer tek—and an autonomic systems interface, giving me conscious control over every part of my body—from blood flow, tone of voice and accent, to stemming my urge to pee. My guess is that it's this autonomic part of Pistol-Whip's wafer that is enhanced.

Sighing, I slump back against the tent. Sitting around ain't much fun, especially after being so pumped by getting on an actual mission at last.

I've got some chill-tabs that would knock me out, but, when it comes down to it, I suppose I prefer to be awake. I've slept for too long in the last few months. Instead, I find myself staring at Pistol-Whip again. At her slight form. At the curve of her hips and her compact shoulders. Her wide lips. Her small, but rounded breasts. At her chest moving slowly in and out. Yet despite her size she's powerful, resilient, and strong.

I look down at myself. At this thing I've become.

I've lost so much of myself…

I shake my head and throw those negative thoughts aside. I have more important concerns. I need to get out of the Service and this body they've trapped me inside as soon as possible. But first things first… surviving this goddamn mission.

Leaning back, I close my eyes and flip through the assignment file on my wafer. I'm impressed. It's extensive and informative. I'm keen to play the 'hick out-of-towner' on secondment from one of the less exciting settlements on the West side of the continent. We are presently in the East. A hedonistic place. Seeing as I don't drink—and I'm not exactly best equipped at the moment to deal with dames—a night of carousing is gonna be tough. I've tried to push that one part of becoming a man as far away from my mind as I can. Yet it won't budge. Sooner or later, I'm gonna have to bite the bullet.

I shake my head again.

The mission seems straightforward. A get in, grab the kid, and get out kinda job. Pistol-Whip has set everything up, but it's up to me to pull it off. And it is a solo mission after all, just as Mother promised. I shouldn't have been too quick to judge.

My target is a Pluton kid named Siruv Melan.

Kidnapped as a child from his influential, but

vertically-challenged dirty nugget family. Now nineteen in adjusted years, he's been held here for most of his life, although from his perspective, he's been pampered and well-educated.

I know the score—it's a ploy used as far back as the Romans on ancient Earth. Abduct the children of your enemies, educate them in the ways of Rome, and then send them back home to rule in their name.

But I can't see how that would work here.

If Siruv ever returned to his gravity-bound planet, his height would not be well-received, regardless of his birth right. Politics was never my strong point, though. I'm just the one who points the gun and shoots, the why is for others to decide. The Service obviously has plans for Siruv. He must be in trouble—why else is he being shipped to the Ministry of Alteration?

Ah. I chuckle as I reach that part of the file. Seems he's been mouthing off about the Resistance. A typical rebellious teen. That's the problem with pampered youth, they don't realise the consequences of speaking their mind. When I was his age—not that long ago—I let my laser do all my talking.

Siruv's image pops up in spinning 3D via the wafer and I'm surprised. They've kept the kid in higher-grav. He's as squat and squashed as the rest of his nugget-kind. A neat little trick if the Palladians' plan was to send him back home. He may be nineteen, but he looks older. Sturdy legs and arms, although his big brown eyes and spotty skin betray his obvious youth. Siruv doesn't know anything about the rescue. His IQ has been augmented, though, so he should be able to grasp the situation.

The Service has an ID set up for the kid, which, if we escape the cell where's he's being kept, should allow us to exit without too much fuss. Sure, he's gonna grab attention with his squashed, off-world nugget-looks, but the plan takes that into account.

Hopefully, before it's noticed he's gone, we'll be back in orbit with Mother.

I go over the mission details many times. And somewhere along the way, I fall asleep.

I'm awoken what I guess is seven hours later, Pistol-Whip shaking me. "This capsule tent we're sitting in makes us invisible on all spectrums, unless you walk into it. The only downside—we can't see out," she says as if carrying on the conversation where she left it all that time ago.

For her, no time has passed at all.

Pistol-Whip slings a satchel over her shoulder. "C'mon!" She peels open the flap and crawls outside. I follow.

A scanner of some sort appears in Pistol-Whip's hand. "Good," she says. "We're alone. But it's a long way back to the city. And these twats love their checkpoints." A quick tap on the tent's flap and it shrinks down to the size of a small pouch that she pops into her satchel.

"Checkpoints?"

She points at a golden chain hung around my neck. Part of the absurd military garb I'm wearing. The end is hung with a large, ruby-like gem. "That's your other ID—used for payment and stuffed with credits. I'm the one who risked her neck to get it for you. Don't lose it."

"I know what it is," I reply. "Your mission docs were… excellent."

If she's flattered by my compliment, she doesn't show it. "One more thing, while you're on this world you need to get used to the fact that these guys don't have wafers. They've no cerebral-tek or any implants. Not all of them, you understand? As you guessed, the black market has been flourishing, but that kind of tek is reserved for those in power. Us grunts are not even supposed to know wafers exist. So I suggest you turn on stealth-mode. The scanner-tek down here ain't that advanced, but it's not worth taking the risk."

"And I thought where I grew up was a backwater. This place is practically prehistoric." I send the command to my wafer and if anyone was scanning me right now, they'd see the thing disappear. Cool.

We exit the cave into the dark of the forest.

At night, the perfumed air is heavy, and even more creatures are moving around. I access my wafer and get a rundown on local fauna and flora. There's nothing large or carnivorous out there, just a few poisonous insects and pseudo-snakes. Still, I'm out of my comfort zone. "Where are we?"

"Zenda Province," Pistol-Whip answers. "One of the recreation areas for use by the elite. Which would've been our cover if you hadn't messed up your landing."

I access the planetary map. Zenda province is a small green area—one of a few—that surround Zenda City, where I guess we're heading.

"How are we getting there?"

"There's a walkway about three klicks from here."

"A walkway? You mean a road?"

"You'll see. First, we need to create a little distraction."

She jogs away and, again, I'm forced to follow. I orientate my wafer and realise that we're heading away from the road, towards what looks like a small collection of outbuildings. I decide not to ask any more questions. Pistol-Whip knows the lay of the land, knows what she's doing. I won't get in her way.

Twenty or so minutes later, we come to a perimeter fence. Pistol-Whip produces a blaster from her satchel and wastes no time in blowing a hole into the compound. We run through, sudden alarms blaring around us.

So far, this doesn't seem like such a great plan. We arrive at the back of the buildings I saw on my wafer map.

"Time to take some pot-shots," she says matter-of-factly. "You got a gun?"

I nod, producing my laser.

"Shoot everything." She tweaks her blaster's settings and blows a hole in one of the buildings that collapses in on itself. Inside occupants run around on fire or lie dead or unconscious. She looks at me. "What you waiting for?"

I fire my new compact laser, it incinerates the vegetation like a flamethrower. I stab at the controls and tighten the beam.

Soldiers emerge like wasps from a smoking nest, but don't seem to notice us. Pistol-Whip picks them off with her blaster, while I decapitate the others with a sweep of my laser's beam.

"That's a cute weapon," she says. "For a man. But I think we've done enough for our needs. C'mon." She holsters her weapon and casually heads towards the main gates of the compound we just attacked. More soldiers emerge, running around like headless chickens. But no one challenges us. "It should be here any second…"

A transport of some sort flies towards us from the direction of the road, making a beeline for the compound, engines whining. I check my wafer. It's a ZB07D patrol vehicle. Two occupants, fitted with fourteen cannons. A slight overkill for what I realise is an outer city patrol vehicle.

"Just as expected," says Pistol-Whip. Her blaster re-emerges, and she fires, disabling the vehicle's com array and then the engines, before targeting the cockpit. She must be perfectly capable of taking over the ship's systems using her wafer, yet she blasts it out of the sky. The patrol ship erupts into a series of explosions and careens into the ground, taking out more compound buildings.

I get what she's doing. Drawing attention to the attack, so we can return to the city without being stopped.

Impressive.

"We're done here, let's go."

Moments later, we're under cover of the forest and jogging along. "I don't get it," I say. "Why did no-one shoot at us?"

Pistol-Whip keeps running, her back to me. "It's simple," she says. "Everyone is so brainwashed on this goddamn planet—from the grunts upward—that they just don't expect an attack from one of their own kind."

"Huh?"

"This is Palladia, remember? They are geared up for attacks from nugget rebels from the two other planets, and they are mostly squat, short, thick-necked and piggy-eyed. Like that nugget-brat you're here to rescue. After all these hundreds of years, they're a breed apart. It also helps that we're wearing the right uniforms. We needed a distraction, and we needed that patrol ship out of the picture. After that show of yours earlier, I want their focus elsewhere. Not on where I've been and who I'm returning with, you get me?"

Pistol-Whip is saying all the right things, but she seems distant, unfocused. Like her mind is elsewhere. But who am I to talk? I was also famous for my professional detachment. Dealing out death was, and still is, my goddamn day job.

A short while later, we arrive at the walkway—a moving road. My home planet of Plenty had a few similar automations. Pistol-Whip jumps aboard with me behind her. And soon we're quickly zipping towards a brightly lit city squatting on the horizon.

We exit the walkway before we hit the outer-limits.

"This is where we part," she says. "You will be staying in one of the city's military barracks. It's important for the mission that you make a big noise tomorrow night. Stay low until then, drink and dame hard—or whatever takes your fancy. Just remember to play your part. Give me your satchel."

I pause. I've read the plan for tomorrow, but giving up my stuff…

Pistol-Whip's eyes narrow.

I pass it over. "Be careful with that," I say. "A lot of it's my own design."

"Hey," she snaps back. "I know better than to mess with another agents' kit." Pistol-Whip salutes and I salute back. "Good. You salute anyone and everyone of rank. Don't forget that." She jumps onto the walkway and disappears.

I follow her ten minutes later, hitting an intersection, swapping walkways multiple times. As I approach the inner city, I notice other people. They hurl along, non-military personnel keeping their heads down, whilst officers and other officially-garbed men and women salute me.

I find the military barracks, a depressing-looking building, and I'm taken to a single, bleak room by a spotty young intern.

"You on a two-day layover, sir?" he asks politely, a glint in his eye.

"Yeah, I sure am," I reply, using the West slang, my voice augmented by my wafer. "I'm gonna be sleeping off all those klicks I put in today. Tomorrow night will be my last night here. You have some places in mind where a guy can find a drink and… dames?"

He nods. "I know just the place."

THE RATHER UNIMAGINATIVELY NAMED 'CAFÉ Fun' is like the sleazy dives I frequented many a time on my home planet of Plenty. Sure, Plenty's hard-working criminals, creeps, and low-level politicos have been replaced with military officers and soldiers, but I understand places like this. The décor is more upmarket—flock wallpaper, pseudo-antiques, and art-deco lighting. But the café has the same old, laconic, balding barman, dark booths, and the requisite number of working women. Palladia is one of those 'moralistic' places that frowns on vice, while its highest dignitaries partake of it daily. Gotta love a good old double-standard.

My home planet of Plenty was one of those worlds that suffered from 'gender issues'—and that's putting it mildly. Gal-on-gal action was officially outlawed, along with other 'non-conventional' sexual relations. Being very much a committed gal-on-gal girl, I always had to be careful. Cops could have thrown me in jail just for looking at a woman. Not that anyone would dare cross me. But if my enemies or rivals wanted to bring me down, that was one of the ways they could've attempted it. And I'm not about to give anybody an opportunity to get one over on me. No matter how small.

Palladia ain't no different. Just another backward, puerile little world. And yet, sitting down on my own at the bar, taking a few tentative sips at a double rye and soda, I'm struggling with how different things are now that I'm outwardly a man.

Women openly stare at me. Giving me the come on. Flirting. Sure, they're working girls, but I'm not used to such directness. I plied my trade in a secretive, closed-off world where the barest glance, the momentary lingering touch of a finger or a single suggestive word meant so much.

This is a unique experience. And not one I'm enjoying. It's crass, tawdry and the opposite of anything remotely erotic.

It wouldn't be so bad if it wasn't for my stupid man-face. I'm still not used to it, but it sure does grab attention. A chance thing, Mother said. *"Agents need to blend into the background. You, on the other hand, stick out like an attractive but very sore thumb. Maybe we'll give you another face, to help you blend in more."*

I look at myself in the mirror behind the bar. Square-jawed, with powerful cheekbones. Thick, black hair trimmed short for this mission. Blue eyes complete the brooding package.

Mother's threat may have been empty, but despite my reservation, I'd prefer to keep the face staring back at me. Another change would be one change too many.

Yesterday was dull. I ain't the type who likes sitting around waiting. I'm a doer. Still, I'm now out and on-mission. If all goes to plan, I'll be off this rock tonight and kicking back in orbit with Mother, discussing a job well done.

I glance at my timepiece.

I've got half an hour, maybe forty minutes before things need to kick off. Causing trouble in a place like this shouldn't be too hard. A group of young, drunken officers, loudly carousing at the other end of the bar, is a likely starting point. Instead of bouncers, this place uses

MPs—Military Policemen. If anything spoke of official sanction, it's their presence. This brothel is run by the military, which means no police problems.

But I've still got time to kill. *Time for…*

I down the rye and order another and down that too, finding the courage to nod at the tall blonde who's been giving me the eye since I arrived. She's like all the women in this bar, long-limbed and lithe. I prefer a few more curves. But she sure is easy on the eye.

She traipses over. "You on leave, officer-sir?" she asks with false coquettishness.

I'm on a mission, I tell myself, wondering if this part of the show I'm supposed to be putting on tonight is necessary for my cover. "Have a drink with me."

"Oh, you're from the west," she says, nodding knowingly to the barman. "I do love a western accent. Sends me all a-quiver."

She's coming on way too strong for my liking. But hey, a gal has to do what a gal has to do… even when she's in a man's body. Been avoiding this for too long. Time to get this over and done with. "You have a room?"

"Of course, officer-sir," she replies with an exaggerated curtsy that draws a few shouts and jeers from the officers at the bar.

"Give me a bottle of rye," I tell the barman. Tonight, I won't be getting drunk, just giving the impression of it. And I am a teetotaller. My wafer allows me to control the absorption of alcohol into my blood, a mixed blessing right now. Despite my present situation requiring of a stiff drink, I need to make sure I have a clear head.

"Sure, son," says the barman, waving a payment device over my ID crystal, and hitting me for what I guess is an obscene number of creds.

"I'm Honey-Rose," says the blonde.

"Yes, you are," I reply.

She leads me upstairs, and instead of the usual excitement I would feel in this position, about to spend some special one-on-one time with another dame, I'm nervous and uneasy.

"You okay?" Honey-Rose asks.

"It's been a while," I reply.

"With those looks?"

I shrug.

"Don't worry, you'll soon remember…"

We enter a smart, clean room also decked out with pseudo-antiques. Dresser, gold-fittings, red-wallpaper, and closed velvet curtains. A screen hangs on one wall— no doubt for us to watch ourselves, or others, should that be desired. Honey-Rose closes the door, turning the latch. I go over to the bed and sit down, deciding to allow some of that rye into my system.

Honey-Rose quickly removes her outer dress to reveal a sexy number underneath. "You like?"

She is indeed a sexy gal. I was too hasty in dismissing her curves, they were there the whole time. I lean back on the bed. "You're every gal's dream," I reply.

Shit. Too much rye.

A quick frown crosses her face, but the smile remains stuck. Honey-Rose is a pro.

"Before we start…" she says, nodding towards my ID.

I get the meaning. "How much?"

She grabs a payment scanner from her nightstand, ambles over to me, waving it playfully. It beeps, and she shows me the pay-screen. "This should do for starters, unless you want anything special…" Honey-Rose puts the scanner on her dresser and sits beside me on the bed, her hand resting on my thigh. "You sure are a handsome one."

I gaze into her eyes, which are blue like my own. For a moment, I'm transported away from my mission, from this military-sanctioned humping den and my gender reassignment. It's just me staring eye to eye with a sexy gal. I move in to kiss her, but she pulls away.

"Hey," she says, raising a warning finger. "You didn't pay for anything special. You want mouth to mouth, that's gonna cost you, okay?"

The moment is broken. But I get it, there's no way she wants to kiss some random John, even if he is good-looking. If this was two women in the same situation, I know lip-on-lip action wouldn't have been a problem. But I ain't a woman no more, not in body, at any rate. Damn. I should've never come upstairs. The mission didn't require indulging in all the facilities of Café Fun before the main event. No, I've been trying to run before I learned to walk. I stand up, deciding to leave.

"Where you going?"

"This was a mistake."

She looks up at me from the bed. "Sure, go if you want, but remember, there's no refund at the Café Fun." She rubs a suggestive hand over her naked shoulders. "But why not stay? If you want kissing, you pay for kissing." Her eyes widen suggestively. "I'll do anything you want… for a price."

A wave of anger passes through me. "You shouldn't be working in a place like this," I spit.

Honey-Rose smiles. "Sure, you western boys are a little backwards at coming forwards. I know places like this go against your strict upbringing, but deep down, you men are all the same, whether you realise it or not. You want the same things. And you certainly pay for it with the same money."

"Don't you want to get out of this?" I ask, remembering saying pretty much the same thing to my last squeeze, Angie. "This is no place for a woman with your style. You could do so much better."

She stares at me as if I'm the sappiest of saps. "You think I don't run my own life? Well think again. I'm no Palladian." Her accent drops away and I realise she's come here from off-world. "I'm what you call a freelancer. Working my way across the systems—where the best work takes me. The goddamn skinny women on this planet are all too stuck up to work in a place like this, and the gentlemen like their women tall and leggy. Working here in this officer's bar is quite some gig. So don't you worry about me, sugar. I'm making a fine living. Doing what I'm doing. Enjoying it… *mostly*. As for my looks, I didn't start out like this. I paid for this body and now people pay me for it too. This is my choice, mister. But there's one thing I don't like about this job, and it's johns like you, telling me what a woman should do with her body. If anything, it's you who needs to buck up your ideas… you should leave this system, check out the other worlds, meet some real women and lose your backward-thinking ways."

"You don't know me, you don't know me at all," I splutter, but Honey-Rose's words ring true. I'm still thinking like Jane, a girl trapped upon another backward planet. If I was a woman saying these things to Honey-Rose, would I get a different reaction? But I'm not a woman—at least not to her. Which is something I'm just gonna have to get my head around. The last thing I should be doing is lecturing Honey-Rose on her career choices. Especially since mine landed me in an unwanted body on a backward planet working for people who don't care if I live or die. I ain't on some ill-advised moral crusade, I'm on a damn mission.

Honey-Rose pulls on her clothes. "I thought there was something different about you. Guess I was wrong. Now get out."

I grab my bottle of rye and stomp onto the landing amidst a loud argument. A drunken guy being dragged out of a room by a typical-looking MP—all muscles and no neck. I push past them and head downstairs. What just happened gave me some much-needed perspective—now I've become a john, sleeping with prostitutes is downright ugly. That's not my style anymore. I've hated Johns all my life. No way am I becoming one.

A glance at my timepiece tells me I'm now within the window for tonight's main performance. I return to the bar, grab a glass, fill it with rye and down it, aware that the carousers at the bar are watching me. I give them my best sneer. "What you staring at?"

This gets their attention and one of them—their leader, I guess—comes over. A red-faced kid in his early twenties. Ginger hair trimmed short, a freckled, pointy, slightly reddened face sitting underneath. "That didn't take long," he mocks in a rather posh version of the clipped eastern accent, flicking his head upstairs. "Did your gun go off unexpectedly?"

His friends jeer and laugh.

I say nothing.

"Where you from anyway?" he continues, looking me up and down like I'm some kinda joke.

"Outta town," I reply, casually picking up my glass.

"I can tell that by your accent," he says to more jeers. "Come on, what happened up there?"

"I decided that I was too much of a gentleman, what of it?" The irony of telling the truth isn't lost on me.

He laughs again. "You don't look like a loser, but you

sure sound like one."

I glance at him. The officer system on this damn world is over-complicated, but I can see I'm out-ranked by the kid, and probably his mates as well. That's why he's so cocky, and it's all I really need to know about the guy.

He claps me on the shoulder. "I think the bar you need is down the way. You know the one… with the blanked-out windows and the *pretty* boys."

His mates guffaw.

Male aggression is all about who can talk the loudest, who can punch you down, who can win. I understand winning—I usually enjoy it. Real winners don't need to crow about their superiority. Yet I feel something stirring within me.

Something animal.

"I think you better get your hand off me," I growl, surprised at the controlled malice in my voice.

"I'd be careful how you talk to a superior officer, off-duty or not." He turns to his mates. "What d'ya think, lads?" he says, purposely clapping me on the shoulder again. "Should I order this low-ranker to give me his rye and get the hell out?"

His mates jeer in the positive. I smile inside.

"Calm it, boys," says the barman. "He ain't bothering no one."

The kid points to the complicated mix of chevrons on his cuffs. "Don't talk back to me. I'm Under-Major Gemn Tavk. A name you're gonna hear a lot of. I'm on my way to the very top. That's why I'm out. Celebrating another promotion."

"I'm sorry, sir," the barman replies dutifully. I guess he knows how to deal with dickheads like this.

Gemn pauses, before once again turning his attention

back to me. "Now gimme your bottle, soldier!"

I shrug and slide the bottle of rye over to the kid.

"Good. You know how to follow orders. With that in mind… get out."

I sit unmoving at the bar.

"Probably best you get along," the barman whispers to me.

"Another bottle of rye," I reply, and the bar suddenly hushes.

The barman frowns at me, and all the chatter from the kid and his mates stops. My heart thumps in my chest so loud I wonder if anyone else can hear it. I let it thud away, consciously increasing my oxygen uptake and sending more blood to my muscles.

"You've had your fill. It's time you went," the barman says, nodding over my shoulder to what I guess are the MPs I spotted earlier.

"Give me a bottle," I say, consciously slurring my words. "I'll take it with me."

The barman shrugs and grabs a bottle from under the counter. He places it in front of me, lifting the payment scanner.

"Thanks."

Here we go. One distraction, as ordered.

I grab the bottle, jump off the barstool and bring it crashing down on the kid's ginger head. The bottle explodes in a crescendo of powdered safety-glass and escaping whiskey.

Gemn goes down hard.

I let loose the full power of my adrenal glands and an overwhelming desire to fight rushes through my veins. It's more than a physical response—I'm angry. Angry about Honey-Rose. Angry about what Mother did to me. Angry about what I've lost.

I grit my teeth as the next guy comes for me. A young spotty kid with a flat, gormless face.

I kick my stool up into my hands and roundhouse it into his midriff. He crumples satisfyingly to the floor, his mouth open like he's diving for apples.

The rest pull back in alarm. I drop the chair and raise my fists. "Come on then!" I shout. "Or are you easterners all mouth and no action like we're told back home?"

A thickset guy steps forward, followed by a few cheers. He's packing a lot of muscle, most of it in his face. He's not too tall, giving him a low centre of gravity. He'll be tough to knock down, but I'm filled with red mist. I let off a right hook, surprising him—and myself—with my reach. My fist makes a satisfying *thwack* as it connects with his nose. I jump backwards, ready for him to come back at me. But instead, a confused expression crosses his overblown features before he collapses face down on the carpet.

Emboldened, I launch forward, throwing my fists at anything that moves, punching, elbowing, and kicking—glorifying in the strength of this body—until I'm hit on the back of the head. I crumple to my knees, blows raining down upon me.

"Enough!" Two burly MPs grab me from behind, pulling me away.

I struggle against them, realising I have the strength to break free but… this is what I came here for, *isn't it?* To get arrested. Logic is one thing, but I still have a terrific desire to fight. A visceral feeling deep inside of me. I take a deep breath and relax, shutting down my adrenal glands and slowing my heart. The red mist disappears and, in its place, a feeling of euphoria…

I've seen men fight before. Laughed at them as they've strutted around—metaphorically beating at their chests like the long-dead apes of Earth. I never realised that there could be enjoyment in it. Sure, a gal also needs to let it all hang out. To allow her physical side to take over. To give in to those basic urges and needs. I'd be a fool not to. Yet what I've just experienced is something different to just letting go—it was more primal. Deeper. *Almost animal*. One thing is for sure… men are quite disgusting.

A smile comes to my lips and I laugh out loud for the first time since this gender-swap was forced upon me.

"What the hell are you so pleased about?" the MP says, slapping cuffs onto my wrists. "You're in deep shit, mister."

A hand grabs at my jaw, lifting my face up—Gemn, his uniform covered in whiskey and blood.

"You're gonna pay for this!" he growls. "You just attacked a superior officer."

I try to stop laughing, but this bloodied, ginger runt is just too funny.

"He'll be up in front of the local beak," says the MP. "And he sure don't like out-of-towners." He turns to face me. "Expect to lose one or two of those stripes, mister."

"Good," says Gemn, before sucker-punching me in the gut.

I crumple, the wind and my laughing knocked out of me. But hey, I've done exactly what I came here to do. My first proper brawl and…

…*it felt good*.

I'M TAKEN OUTSIDE AND THROWN into the back of a waiting transport, already full of other worse-for-wear soldiers of varying ranks and states of inebriation. My feet and hands are manacled. The transport takes off—a high-gee vertical ascent—and the guy lolling next to me vomits over himself. Luckily, I can now control my autonomic reflexes.

I shut down my nose and give rigid instructions to my gut.

We make a few more pick-ups and the transport finally arrives on the rooftop of what must be the local lock-up. The back doors open and a mean-looking Sergeant-at-Arms is waiting for us. His nose curls at the smell of vomit. A few moments later, the back of the transport is doused in disinfectant.

We're dragged out one by one and taken to an elevator that opens into a depressing prison block. After a few twists and turns, I'm thrust into a cell shared by twenty other prisoners. The guy who vomited on himself and a few others are thrown in after me. A holding tank until morning. The door slides shut with a bang and a red light flicks on—signifying we're locked in. Even with my nose shut down it's a grim place—reeking of shit, piss, and vomit. A single toilet squats next to the far wall, accompanied by a basin.

No way am I gonna use that. A gal has got to have

standards.

Everything goes quiet apart from the odd moan and groan. There's no bunks here. Bodies crash on the floor. The lights go out, replaced only by the eerie red glow of the security light and a green dot from a surveillance camera. I find an empty bit of floor, lie down, and allow myself to doze.

A signal from my wafer slams me back into the conscious world. The green dot on the camera is no longer illuminated.

It's time…

My heart thumps heavily again. I don't think I'll ever get used to it reverberating loudly in the barrel of my chest. I slow its beat, slip off my boots—part of my basic Service kit—and remove the laces. My socks are nano-pads, an advanced, soundless slipper that confuses pressure sensors. I wrap one of the laces around the cell bars and, with a simple command from my wafer, the highly advanced laser-lace glows green and easily slices through the primitive metal alloys. I catch the freed bars, placing them gently on the floor. The red light above the door doesn't even flicker.

I slip out into the corridor and find my way back to the elevator. This is no high-security prison, just a holding centre for drunks. The elevator arrives, and I step inside. If this was a simple escape, I'd take the elevator to the roof, overpower the guards, grab a transport, and fly away. But that ain't my plan.

I press the button for the basement.

The doors open to reveal a wide, pipe-filled service-way. I navigate using my wafer, following a prescribed route until I find a grate. I pull it aside to access a ladder, descend, and pull the grate back in place above me. After I reach the bottom of the ladder—a good fifty feet below—I bring up the schematics and make my way westward, towards the Ministry of Alteration.

Quick-Kill is back in the sewers again. And I must admit, for the first time in a long time, I feel right at home. The sewer system on Plenty saved my bacon more times than I could count. It's a place the authorities always overlook. The smell offends them. They can't imagine others braving such foul air to gain an advantage. And there are advantages to be had—sewerage systems, no matter how well-designed, have evolved from older tunnels—from covered streams and forgotten piping. Maps don't show everything. There are places to gain entry or hide.

Pistol-Whip must be a sewer-rat like myself. She'd personally mapped the under-city warren using its access and exit points to build her plan.

I must admit, I was impressed when I read her mission details.

This is gonna be easy.

I slide through a disused pipe and, a few minutes later, emerge into what appears to be a storage room. My military uniform features eight buttons on each cuff, lapel insignia and twelve buttons on my shirt—all small, explosive-packed grenades with enough punch to take out a wall or two—and a few extras added by myself. I slip free a grenade, arm it and throw it on the floor—ready to be detonated at my command. An explosion in such a small place is sure gonna get everyone's attention—when I need them to be looking the wrong way, that is.

I exit into a corridor, pausing only to place more of my little surprises.

The whole basement is unguarded. Typical of an arrogant dictatorship more concerned with prisoners getting out than anyone breaking in. I find another storage room, filled with what looks like cleaning fluid. I toss in a grenade and close the door. More grist to the mill. I clip my remaining grenades back on my cuffs and head upwards.

I wish I had my laser with me, but that's where I'm heading—to the prearranged place where Pistol-Whip left my kit.

The next floor is a warehouse lit by faint light. Hundreds of plastic barrels stacked from floor to ceiling. I know what's inside and shudder. It's where the bodies of those who have been 'altered' are stored before being shipped away to some landfill or other. Sure, they don't have to pile the bodies so high, but I guess it makes them feel good to come down here every now and then to survey the results of their handiwork.

I may be Quick-Kill, I may have worked as an assassin and I may have killed my fair number of marks, but there's something about officially-sanctioned murder that turns my gut.

Blowing this place is gonna be sweet.

The barrels are unmarked and somehow this makes the entire process even more sinister. These people have not only been tortured and murdered, they've become anonymous. The containers are hardly large enough to fit an entire body. Then again, there's probably not much left of the victims.

Only one barrel is different.

It's dented. Almost unnoticeable, but it's the barrel I'm looking for.

While I was busy getting myself into trouble, Pistol-Whip was doing her bit—leaving my kit here for me in a place no one would think to look. I can't wait to get my hands on my laser. If things go tits-up, I can burn my way out of trouble. I don't care what Pistol-Whip thinks about her blaster, my laser could cut a hole in the side of this building and I could walk straight out if I wanted to.

If only that was the goddamn plan!

I pad over to the barrel and take a deep breath. The lid is nothing more than nano-sealed plastic. A quick tug and it peels away.

I jump back. *What the shit?*

Instead of my kit, I'm staring at the corpse of a naked woman, her face hidden under a flock of sandy-blonde hair. She's been thrust inside, limbs bent at odd angles. Another victim of this goddamn planet's dictatorship. Her skin is mottled and bruised. I shudder. Death may be my job, but sometimes it ain't pretty.

I check around… but this is the right barrel. No mistake. Pistol-Whip's plan was meticulous. I pull the girl's head free and push blood-matted hair away from her face…

It's Pistol-Whip.

BEFORE I CAN REACT, I'M blinded by harsh lights, my ears full of the sound of boots thumping against steel. My vision returns to reveal thirty or so soldiers surrounding me, their primitive, but no doubt still effective blasters, pointing at my head.

Something hits me between the shoulder blades and I go down, followed by what feels like the weight of two or three bodies pushing me into the floor. But there's no fight in me—what's the point against so many?

Shit!

This mission has been smooth as glass up to this point. But if Pistol-Whip got herself killed then it sure looks like the same could happen to me. What the hell did she do wrong? This should've been a simple 'sneak-in-and-sneak-out'.

"Take him to the Chamber," says a thin, tight eastern voice.

I don't like the mention of this 'chamber'. But all I can do now is play along and see if I can find a way out of this mess.

I'm dragged along a metal floor to another elevator, taken up a few floors and pushed into a dank, circular room. I'm hit by the stench of shit, blood, and bleach. They strap me into some kind of tek-chair, connected by many wires and industrial-looking cables to banks of ugly, humming tek. The floor is one large stain that's been bloodied and cleaned many times. A stain I'm sitting in the centre of—which isn't filling me with confidence.

But then, it's not supposed to.

A helmet of sorts, also festooned with wires, lowers over my head while my hands and ankles are manacled by copper bands that snap into place using what I guess is a tek-controlled locking mechanism.

A scanner blasts my eyes—an ID check. The officers then exit the room, the lights go off, and I'm left on my own.

At least they didn't strip me. I've still got a few surprises up my sleeves—my whole uniform is a goddamn arsenal. And once I find out what these guys know, the mistake that Pistol-Whip made, and any other information I can squeeze out of them, I ain't gonna be sitting around here for much longer, that's for sure.

I test my restraints, nothing I can't handle. I've dislocated thumbs, wrists, feet, shoulders and more to escape in the past. 'Double-jointed' they call me, though the medics have a different name for it. Sure, that ability belonged to my other body, but I ain't been idle since my rebirth. Part of the integration into my new body was pushing the boundaries of what it could do. I was pleased to discover that the Galactic Secret Service gives the double-jointed ability to all their reborn agents.

Wriggling free of these restraints is a real possibility. But I can do better than that. I'm gonna commandeer those humming tek-banks sitting behind me and free myself using my wafer. The only problem? The tek is so damn primitive that I'm finding it almost impossible to hack the antiquated system. I'm working on it in the background, using my wafer's split consciousness function. If I can't break the chair, things will be a lot harder, that's for sure.

But, as I said, escape ain't my plan… *not yet*. I'm

staying put until I find out what happened to Pistol-Whip. By the state of her body—her head was still intact—they were not aware that she possessed a wafer, which means they probably don't know who she was or what she represented. But somehow, they learned how I would enter the building. And…

I'm disappointed and a little annoyed that she gave me up so easily—unless Pistol-Whip ventured that information willingly, which is unlikely. And if so, why kill her? Maybe she was protecting someone else? Another agent, perhaps? Someone more important than me? And I can't forget Pistol-Whip, a supposedly competent agent, didn't manage to escape with her life.

Whatever the reason, I can't underestimate these guys.

These thoughts swim around my head while the other half of my mind is working furiously on hacking the tek-chair. I'm having to write a specific program just to penetrate the outer-core alone. Once that's done, I can then try and attempt a crack. But it's taking time. Time, it seems, they are willing to give me. But I know what they're doing… leaving me alone to contemplate my fate. A classic technique that would work on most people. But not Quick-Kill.

My wafer allows me to shut off any or all bodily sensation, should I need to, so I'm not worried about any torture. I'd prefer to be kicking back in the Fun Bar, that's for sure. Damn. I should've gone with Honey-Rose when I had the chance. At least I'd have my 'first time' to think about.

A breath next to my right ear startles me and I jump.

I try to turn my head, but I'm trapped by the helmet. Another breath and, from somewhere behind me, I hear a growl. And then I suss it. This torture-machine of theirs incorporates some kind of hallucination inducer. *Good news!*

I interrogate the signal back to source. Giving me a way into the chair's core program. And there's one more thing, these guys must not be aware that I'm fitted with a wafer, which in turn, confirms that they don't know who I work for. I bite down a smile, just in case they are watching me, and decide to play along with their little show. "Who's there?" I ask, adding an extra nervous twang to my voice.

A vague shape takes form in the shadows to my right. Some kind of arachnid, lurching forward on horrible, twitchy legs.

I yell before I realise what I'm doing.

It's just an hallucination, but one based on my own phobias. The planet of Plenty had its version of such a creature. A kind of dust spider. Totally harmless, but likely to jump on you for no discernible reason other than to freak you out. I quickly tell my wafer to countermand the effects of the device they have me wired into, but I'm forced to spend the next twenty minutes wailing and shouting. You can guess the kind of thing. A display put on to impress these grunts. But inside, I'm still working on hacking into this damn prehistoric chair. Splitting my efforts.

A door finally opens, and the lights flicker on. A pompous-looking man in his late fifties enters. His hair is badly dyed black—grey showing at the roots. He's followed by two grunts, big guys, carrying primitive-looking devices, designed I guess, to put the fear of space into me. Bolt-cutters, hammers and knives. All rusted and covered in dried blood.

The dye-job comes over and stares at me through piggy glasses, his dead eyes magnified into twin grey saucers.

"Pleasure to meet you, Warrior-Colonel Sub-Lieutenant Danton," he says pulling up a chair and purposely invading my personal space. "But that isn't your real name, is it? As for myself, I do not need a pseudonym. I'm Glick. Walthus Glick. I'm sure you've heard all about me."

The way he says his name makes me think it's supposed to either impress or terrify me.

A quick search through my background files and I find him. *Warrior-General First Class Walthus Glick.* The system's most ruthless interrogator.

Glick produces a single, brown, cardboard file from a leather suitcase and flicks it open. "We seem to have a problem," he says deliberately. "You see this person here?" He shows me a photo of a rather sad specimen with sticky-out ears and acne. "This is the real Warrior-Colonel Sub-Lieutenant Danton. Unfortunately, his body was found a few hours ago, washed up by the city tide. He didn't drown. No. It appears he had an unfortunate accident with a blaster." He shows me another picture of the same guy lying on a beach with an impressive hole in his chest. "What we have here," Glick continues, "is an inconsistency. A very disturbing anomaly. Our retinal scanners tell us you are Danton, and yet, quite clearly, you are not. Do you have anything to say about that?"

I'm disconcerted about the appearance of Danton's body. That was sloppy work by Pistol-Whip. Not what I'd come to expect from her. But the woman got herself killed. Maybe she wasn't the top-class agent she pretended to be? I toy with the idea of bluffing the guy by acting all dumb but that won't get me anywhere.

"Of course, I'm not Danton," I say. "I murdered him

and stole his identity."

"You may have stolen his ID, yet you have a valid retinal scan. That quite simply cannot be. An anomaly that must be investigated. I attempted to extract this information from the woman masquerading as Warrior-General Third Class Vabre. But she… resisted."

Of course she did, you malicious twat.

"Why did you kill her?" I ask, finding myself suddenly angry at this stupid world and its violently idiotic people.

"That was unfortunate. She died under routine questioning before I had finished my evaluation. Sometimes the heart will stop under duress. But not yours. You are a stronger, more superior specimen." He smiles at me, a vile upturning of thin lips. And I decide, in this moment, to kill him first chance I get. Offing Glick wasn't part of my mission-plan, but neither was getting captured. If he should get his head accidentally blown off when I escape? All the better. However, there is one small problem with my thoughts of revenge—I have to get out of this chair and find myself a weapon. But I'm not being idle. I've broken through into the chair's core program and I'm now attempting a direct rewrite of its primitive operating system.

"The imposter pretending to be Warrior-General Third Class Vabre told me of your mission," Glick continues in his deliberate fashion. "That you would be making an appearance tonight—and where you would pick up your kit."

My kit! Damn! I'd forgotten about that. "You know why I'm here?"

"To assassinate Consul Siruv Melan, of course."

I smile inside. Pistol-Whip must've strung Glick a line before she died. I decide to play along. "Sure," I say. "That's why I broke in. To go show him what the resistance does to collaborators."

Glick shakes his head, as if talking to an ill-informed child. "Consul Siruv Melan is no collaborator, but one of our most promising operatives. And a vital asset to our subjugation of Pluton, of keeping that rabble in line. But you know that because it's the Plutons who've sent you here to kill him." He turns towards the room's entrance. "You can come in now," he says.

I hear a door opening and approaching footsteps. A squat figure waddles into view. A kid in his late teens, dressed in the military garb of this planet. I recognise him as Siruv Melan. But he ain't anything like my mission description.

Physically, yes, but he's no moralistic rebel, I see that in the curl of his lip. In the way he carries himself and the twitchy hand resting on the butt of his holstered blaster. I'm surprised to notice Siruv is carrying my satchel. Why hasn't Glick mentioned what was inside? He must have been intrigued by the laser and my other gadgets? But I cast those thoughts aside. My kit is right there for the taking. All I need to do is get free from this damn chair.

"Will he be receiving full punishment?" Siruv asks hopefully.

"That will be for him to decide." Glick turns his attention back to me. "Mercenaries are not uncommon in the Triumvirate, but if so, they are usually in our employ. It's rare to find anyone willing to work for those dirty nuggets on Pluton. And yet here you are. A gun-for-hire. A professional paid to take risks others are afraid to. Which means you know there's always a chance you'll get caught and executed. With that in mind, what I'm going to say to you will not come as too much of a surprise. You will die. We both know that. The manner of your death, however, is up to you. You can expire slowly and painfully in that chair, tormented by your mental demons as we remove your extremities bit by bit—my preferred technique—or you can tell me what you know now, and your end shall be far less agonising. We understand each other?"

"Sure," I reply. "You're a sadistic nutter, working for a sadistic nutter regime by practising advanced sadistic nuttism on hundreds of innocent people—does that about cover it?"

Glick's dead eyes close for a moment behind the thick lenses of his glasses, as if he's struggling to keep his composure. "I will now repeat my previous question. I will ask it only one more time and I seriously advise you to be very careful with your reply."

"Go on," I say, nodding my head with false-enthusiasm. "I'm ready."

Glick's brows furrow in consternation. "Tell me, how did you fool the retinal-scan? I need places, I need names and I need them now. Otherwise…" He indicates towards the two grunts with a delicate hand. I notice well-trimmed fingernails and a roughness to his fingers. The hands of a surgeon… of sorts.

I shrug within the confines of my chair. "Okay," I say. "It was Vabre. She had a device. Small and cylindrical. Like a cigar stub. I'd search her stuff if I was you."

Glick sits back and sighs, a look of disappointed benevolence plastered across his nasty pinched face. I bet he practises this look in the mirror, but it doesn't fool me. The man is seething. "A convenient answer," he says. "Of course, we examined every part of Vabre's life in minute detail and found nothing. No illegal tek of any kind… This is just for starters." He nods to one of his lumbering assistants, who brings down a hammer onto my right hand.

Two of my fingers snap and I scream in pain.

"Now, I'll ask you again," Glick says through gritted teeth whilst, behind him, Siruv Melan smiles. "Places and names. I want that tek and I want it now."

The grunt raises his blunt hammer over my hand again.

I stem the pain coming from my shattered fingers and prevent the tissues swelling. A stab of panic hits me square in the gut. I wonder if, like Pistol-Whip, I'm gonna die in this goddamn chair—

A green light flares in my wafer and I relax. At goddamn last! I've finally rewritten the chair's prehistoric code.

"You know what?" I say to Glick, who seems confused by what I guess is the look of elation on my face. "I'm sick and tired of you and this vicious little planet of yours. It's about time someone kicked your elongated butts."

I broadcast two signals, one to my grenades in the basement and the other to the chair's wrist and ankle cuffs. They flick open while a series of large booms rock the building from below.

I jump to my feet and elbow Glick in the head, unclipping a couple of stun-pellets from my shirt and throwing them at the two grunts who drop like electrocuted cows. I grab a shocked-looking Siruv with my injured hand, wincing at the pain, and remove his blaster with the other. I turn to Warrior-General First Class Walthus Glick, who is trying to scramble away.

"This is for Pistol-Whip," I say, and blow his head clean off.

GLICK JOINS THE GRUNTS ON the floor. His death was too quick for me, but sometimes a gender-reoriented gal has to live up to her goddamn code name.

Alarms ring throughout the building, accompanied by the sounds of people running and the frenzied shouting of orders. I grab my satchel, eager to retrieve my laser and other equipment. But it ain't there. It's my satchel alright, but these are not my weapons or tools.

"What the hell?" I dump the contents on the floor. There's some advanced tek, but nothing special.

"Where's my stuff?" I shout at Siruv, but the half-shocked, half-confused expression on his face tells me he knows nothing.

I order Siruv to remove his jacket, revealing a white tee-shirt underneath, while I straighten out my broken fingers. I punch him hard in the face, once, twice, three times, until his blood leaks from his nose and onto the pristine white. I rip his jacket and make a gag, tying it in place, while the kid attempts to struggle free. A punch to the kidneys soon quiets him. I manacle Siruv's hands behind his back and march him out of the door into the corridor. I remember the way I was brought in and head for the elevator.

My cover ain't great, but I'm hoping what Pistol-Whip told me would hold true here in the Ministry—that no one will question an officer frog-marching a goddamn dirty Pluton nugget.

I hold my breath as officers and soldiers rush past, but they don't give us a second glance. I blast the elevator doors a few moments later and toss in more grenades. I want the thing out of action if my plan of escape is going to work. But my actions haven't gone unnoticed. Two officers run towards us, unsure what's going on. I rip free one of my tunic's buttons and throw it towards them. The tiny grenade sparks into life, zipping down the corridor, bouncing from wall to wall, leaving a trail of thick smoke before exploding and bringing down the corridor roof.

I find the stairwell and I push my prisoner upward, throwing more grenades behind me, preventing pursuit from the floors below. Siruv resists, digging his heels. I turn him around, thrust him against a nearby wall and remove the gag. Before he can say a word, I remove another button from my tunic and shove it in his mouth, replacing the gag.

"You want your head blown away like your friend Glick? Then I suggest you continue resisting, because I can do this with or without you."

The look in his eyes is all the confirmation I need.

We race up the stairs and arrive, a few flights later, on the roof. I drop my remaining grenades ready to be remotely detonated and push Siruv out into the chilly night. An important-looking transport is parked opposite a command post—five or six men raise their weapons simultaneously. I drop my blaster to my side and nod towards the transport. Pushing Siruv in front of me.

The men are unsure what to do but I was right in assuming that they wouldn't shoot. They come over to me. "What the hell?" says their leader, an older guy who outranks me.

"Help me get this prisoner on the transport, sir," I say in my best posh eastern accent, pushing Siruv forward. The leader may be above my rank, but my accent tells him my social rank is higher than his. I'm hoping this will sway him.

"I'm not doing anything until you explain yourself," he replies guardedly.

"The Ministry is under attack, sir," I say. "Someone is after this prisoner. Warrior-General First Class Walthus Glick himself ordered me to get this dirty nugget out of here using any and all means. I'm sorry, sir, but you must defend the roof. They're coming after us."

I command the stairwell grenades to go off and they explode, creating an impressive plume of smoke that pours from the stairwell into the night sky. That's all the group leader needs to make up his mind. He orders his men to take up positions to repel the 'attackers' and I head for the transport. I push Siruv inside and he falls face down. I hit him on the back of the head with the blaster's butt and he goes limp. *Good*. The last thing I want is for him to get in my way.

I scramble into the pilot's seat and power up the machine, patching directly into its systems, focusing on its navicom. Other vehicles are heading this way. Command procedure and pilot protocols flash into my mind. I punch the dash and I'm hit with a blast of gee as we take off vertically, thrusting up into the dark sky. I command the ship to turn off all lights and any com signals—and manually cut the engines.

This is no glider, but from what I can tell of the ship's schematics, she should be at least temporarily manoeuvrable before she crashes—a controlled dive of sorts. Like all the vehicles on this paranoid planet, the ship is over-compensated in the cannon department. And fully loaded.

Good.

We sweep down just as the other vehicles land on top of the Ministry of Alteration.

I turn the power back on, spin the ship and let the Ministry have it with everything the ship has got. The building rocks with cannon-fire. Plumes of flame and exploding masonry. I keep on firing until the whole building is burning and collapsing.

I punch the dash again and head out of the city at full speed towards the pick-up point.

This is *not* how the mission is supposed to go down. Nowhere on the spec did it say for me to kill Walthus Glick or destroy the Ministry of Alteration. But then again, it also didn't say what to do if the mission was compromised. Happily, improvisation is one of my skills. As is shooting guns. If Mother gets upset by that, then she should've sent someone else on the mission.

And besides, Quick-Kill will do anything to get the job done.

I bring the craft in to land at what's supposed to be an abandoned refinery. Lots of rounded, reflective surfaces confusing the limited scanner-tek of possible pursuers. But I'm hoping what happened to the Ministry building will keep everyone busy for at least a few hours.

Killing Glick went some way towards making myself feel better about Pistol-Whip. And, even though I know blowing up the Ministry won't stop the torture on this planet, I feel I gave those that died a bit of closure. Sure, there must've been other prisoners in the building. And I'm probably responsible for their deaths. But after seeing all those goddamn barrels stacked up in the warehouse, I certainly did them a favour.

Siruv is still out like a light. I put him over my shoulder and make my way through tree country towards the rendezvous point located a few klicks to the south.

The sun is just making an appearance over the horizon when I approach the pick-up, accompanied by two bright and beautiful-looking early morning stars. Pluton and Protactin—the other two habitable planets of this messed up system.

I'm glad to be leaving it all behind.

Hopefully, my other missions will take me to the Key Systems. I want to see more of the galaxy than backwater hellholes. But I have to escape this particular backwater first. Pistol-Whip's mission document says there should be a small air-to-space vehicle waiting for me, auto-programmed to take me back to Mother's cruiser in hidden orbit above.

I sense a change in the air as I approach the co-ords—warmer, accompanied by the smell of engine fuel and burnt vegetation—and head towards it.

I find the still-glowing ship in a small glade. A diminutive female figure standing at its edge, petite arms crossed over her chest. I do a double-take, but there can be no doubt about it.

The figure is Pistol-Whip.

"WHAT THE HELL?"

Pistol-Whip shrugs. "Welcome back, Agent Quick-Kill. I, for one, didn't give you a cat in hell's chance of completing your mission. But here you are, and you've even brought the mission objective with you. Nice."

"You what?" I throw Siruv unceremoniously to the ground.

"Hey, don't get all up in my face. Every agent must complete a *Do-or-Die*. This was your assessment. And hell, you passed with flying colours."

"This was a set-up from the goddamn start?"

Pistol-Whip shrugs. "Yes and no. The Service decided to pull out of this system a few weeks ago. Which meant my stint as General Vabre was ending. I hung on just long enough to come up with that mission of yours. It forced you to improvise. Gave you scope to do your own thing and to get yourself out of that mess I put you in. And here you are. You made it."

I'm not sure what to think. Part of me is elated at my success, whilst another part of me is damn angry that I've been set-up. My good hand tenses on the grip of my blaster. I'm Quick-Kill and no one double-crosses me and gets away with it.

Or they didn't.

I grit my teeth and shake my head. I'm now playing a whole different ball-game. I'm fuming, pissed off, and…

I start laughing. A loud, reverberating chuckle. I

throw the blaster to the ground and shake my head. "You sure made a sap out of me," I say. "Good job."

Pistol-Whip relaxes, and behind her, one of the ship's mag-rail guns powers down. "That was the last part of the Do or Die," she explains. "Not everyone can take being double-crossed. Hence my back-up. And be assured, you won't be lied to ever again." She stands to attention and salutes. "Welcome to the Service, Agent Quick-Kill."

"I'm not quite ready for salutes," I say. "And I don't think I ever will be."

"I was cheering for you all the way, you know that?" Pistol-Whip says. "And I don't always get personally involved. It sure was fun beating up on your dumb ass."

"Thanks… I think."

"We don't have time for idle chit-chat. Let's get off this dump of a planet." She steps back towards the ship and I go to pick up Siruv.

"What're you doing?" she says. "Didn't you hear what I just said? We're finished here."

I untie the kid, who's still unconscious, remove the gag and rescue my whizz-bang from his mouth.

"You might as well off the bastard," Pistol-Whip says. "From what I know about the nugget, he's a nasty little scumbag."

I shrug. "Nah. I think I'll leave him to face Palladium justice. I'm sure they'll be looking for a suitable fall guy after what went down at the ministry."

She laughs. "And there I was, thinking you'd gone all soft on me."

We enter the ship and, within seconds, we're soaring through the atmosphere and into space.

"So, you gonna tell me why you call yourself Pistol-Whip?" I ask.

The girl winks at me. "Well, it sure wasn't to do with

my gun skills."

I'm confused. "Huh?"

"I used to be a man," she says in explanation.

I decide to change the subject. "The body in the barrel… I was convinced that was you. And Glick told me you died under torture. How did you pull that off?"

"Easy. You brought my clone with you. Packed into your entry vehicle—I made a big noise about you drawing attention to yourself, but your landing was indeed textbook. I made that stuff up just to piss you off. No one was after us. But wrong-footing you from the start was part of the test. I made the body-swap back in the tent. You remember when you suddenly fell asleep?"

"That was you?"

"Yeah. And while you were conveniently unconscious, I replaced myself with the surrogate. A clone of sorts. But with a wafer instead of a brain. Remote controlled by me up in orbit—so I could give you even more of a tough time. I took the transport back up to Mother and we waited. We weren't sure you'd make it, but then all hell broke loose at the Ministry and we figured you'd made your move."

"My escape was a little crude, but very effective," I say. "And it sure was fun blasting that goddamn building to bits."

Pistol-Whip turns and smiles at me. "To be honest, before your mission became part of my exit plan, I was going to kill Glick and destroy the building. So I'm grateful for what you did."

"Which means you owe me one."

Pistol-Whip turns her gaze back to the ship's controls. Mother's cruiser looms up in front of us and she guides us in. "No, I don't," she says. And I believe her.

"What's next?"

"Next," she says, a cheeky smile on her lips. "Next is a goddamn party! Afterwards… who knows? But it's gonna be fun and damn dangerous."

"More fun than Palladia?"

"You telling me you didn't enjoy yourself?"

I contemplate her question for a few moments. "I sure did. Even with all that crap you gave me. It's the most fun I've had in a long time."

"Looks like you're made for the Service," Pistol-Whip replies.

I grin back at her. I still resent Mother, Abe and what they've done to me but… "Shit," I reply, shaking my head. "This might be the best job I've ever had."

PART THREE
BLUETONGUE

I TIGHTEN THE WIDE, EMERALD sash around my fat belly, straighten my thawb—the name of the local knee-length tunic—and perform a few last-minute checks on weapons and grenades. Everything flashes green as expected. My wafer offers me reams of diagnostic information, but I don't take any of it in.

This is habit. Rote.

A way to calm my nerves—one better than instructing my wafer to mess with my autonomic system.

Robbing banks is certainly different from my previous line of employment. An assassin plans to the same degree, but they cut down all the variables. Not so much with thieving. For a start, there are more people than I'm used to, crammed into this sprawling structure that mimics a desert tent popular in this hot, dry system. To call this building 'a bank' doesn't do it credit. It houses various financial services, from pawn-brokers and lending sharks to investment advice and financial services—all under the auspices of the Gilligan Corporation. The Hejaz system—a tightly-knit sector of planets, moons and asteroids—is controlled by this single, dominant ginger-haired clan.

At least two hundred locals mill around the space, arguing with one another in the many queues. And that doesn't include the roboes. In short, the entire situation is messy and unpredictable. But the tension is necessary. Without it, I may get sloppy and getting sloppy is a sure way to get dead.

The queue I'm in lurches forward. I act annoyed at the slow progress and curse in the local language, pretending to play the Hejaz system's popular game of Seega on my battered handheld device. The game is akin to checkers, but with various levels and… *you get the gist.* It's just part of my cover as an overweight, middle-aged down-at-heel merchant going by the name of Finley Shaddeed—one of the many disguises I've been using over the last few months as part of my so-called 'crime spree'.

The line moves, and I float forward on my hoverchair. An accessory that the low gravity—a quarter of one gee—allows for. But it ain't no regular chair. I've spent the last few weeks in my workshop perfecting it.

The tall robo waiting in front of me doesn't move. I give the thing a hefty kick on its mechanical arse. The domed head swivels and an array of optical interfaces check me out. The mechanical has a snooty look, like it thinks it's better than me. Good luck if it's trying a scan—all it will see is what I want it to see. A harmless old merchant wearing a pair of battered sunglasses under a headscarf, sitting on a hover-chair and clutching a bag on his lap. Exactly like every other overweight, middle-aged loser on this moon—although my bag contains enough weaponry to demolish the building in a couple of seconds.

That's not the plan—but close enough.

I offer the robo a fake smile of apology and turn my attention back to my game.

The head swivels back in place and it glides forward on long legs—a gawky desk lamp with attitude. The Hejaz system uses roboes for everything. Even the poor own a robo or two, although only richer, well-connected clan-families can afford well-maintained bio-mechanicals like this one. I've always hated the 'mechanical men', as I called them as a kid. Never liked them, never will. Even with my interest in tek and tinkering, the closest I've ever wanted to get to one of these machines is blaster distance.

Time to go to work.

I kick the robo again and swear loudly in the local language, causing a few heads to turn. The robo faces me, a rebuke stuttering from its mechanical throat. And that's when I hit it with a focused signal from my wafer. The thing wobbles and jerks to a stop, its head swivelling. The rotation increases in speed and thick, acrid smoke—reeking of burnt relays and fried biological circuitry—pours out of its domed head.

Nice.

The robo pitches onto the floor, flames quickly taking hold. I'm 'forced' to glide away on my hover-chair—dropping a handful of smog and percussion grenades. They spiral outwards across the sand-polished, marble floor, rolling under the sandaled-feet of the bank's many customers. They might've noticed, but the robo ain't the only one that is malfunctioning. My wafer had hit all the roboes within a two-hundred metre radius. Others are spinning out of control, arms flailing and falling over. Smoke bellowing from their burning metal insides.

Children scream. Men and women shout. And I laugh.

I command my grenades to detonate and the bank's expansive foyer is engulfed in a thick, impregnable soot-like smog. In the ensuing mayhem, I throttle my hover-chair and glide over the wall of bank-tellers, throwing more grenades as I go. I hear the thrum of blaster bursts behind me. Probably a security guard taking out a robo or two. Good. Their attention is at the front of the bank, where I need it to be.

I land and pull out my stun-gun. I want to use my laser, but even if Mother hadn't told me it would compromise my cover, I ain't in the habit of killing civilians. I may be Quick-Kill—but you want me to kill someone, you either pay me, or you give me a damn good reason why.

I send my hover-chair spinning back into the mayhem of the lobby, spewing more smoke as it goes and superimpose the bank's schematics over my sunglasses' HUD. My augmented shades easily penetrate the gloom, allowing me to drop anyone who gets in my way. I attach a couple of heat-mines to a heavy security door and step aside. The mines glow red hot. Within seconds, there's a hole large enough for me to dive through—an act made easier by the low gravity. A couple of startled security guards—a man and a woman—greet me on the other side. Their expressions of shock well-suited as I drop them with two silent shots from my stun-gun. A quick search and I find the security band I'm looking for.

This area is full of surveillance—cameras, recording devices and scanners—but I want to be seen. I want them to know it's me. Sure, my disguise is different, but they won't be fooled. My MO is always the same—although today I'm adding an extra surprise.

It's all I can do to stop myself waving.

The security band gets me through a couple more doors and into a plush-looking stairwell, which takes me down into the security-locker area. I wonder what's behind all those keyed doors, wishing I had the time to look. I may be here to rob the bank, but this ain't what I'm after. No, my sole intention is getting the attention of the Gilligans—the clan I already mentioned. Mother wants me to infiltrate them… and the best way to join their ranks is to show them what I can do. They are not going to be happy about my latest escapade on this busy little moon of theirs. But they'll be damn-well impressed.

As to why I'm doing all of this?

The Galactic Secret Service has its eyes on another more important goal—is what Mother told me when she gave me the mission brief.

And that's all I know.

I take out a few more guards and arrive in an unassuming office—my target. I've scanned the building from orbit, using every tool at my disposal to interrogate the tek systems of this moon, but I ain't been able to confirm the location of the vault.

But it's in here all right.

I grab my trusty laser from the bag and check the settings. I point it at the far wall and fire. The barrier collapses in slow motion due to the low gravity. Bits of ceiling bouncing off my head. I take out the next wall and reveal a further room—the one I'd guessed was in here. A block of almost white metal three times my height and just as wide squats inside. A vault made from impenetrable alloy. Even my laser at its hottest setting wouldn't scratch it. The only way in is through a single circular door made of the same material—a door secured with an impressive mechanism. Not the kind of vault you'd expect to find in such a provincial bank.

My hunch was right. Pay dirt!

I patch a command to *Little Bastard* hanging in geosynchronous orbit directly above my head. *Little Bastard* is what I renamed the ship Mother gave me for this mission. A top-of-the-range one-man cruiser run by a highly illegal ceph—an autonomous artificial brain now standard kit installed on all Service covert-ops ships. A ship capable of mimicking space debris, orbiting satellites, or a goddamn warship… if anything decided to scan it that is.

Now it's time for *Little Bastard* to do its work. I burn away the walls around the vault and affix a locater. *Little Bastard* replies with an 'object acquired', and my work here is done.

I retrace my steps, only pausing to readjust my costume in full view of the security cams, and to grab the unconscious guards, an easy task in low gravity. Normally, I'd leave them behind, but I have an extra explosive trick up my sleeve and, like I said, I ain't a fan of collateral damage. By the time I reach the bank floor, the smoke is clearing.

My hover-chair arrives at my side. I arm the gravity bomb nestled neatly within its circuitry and send it on its way once more, before heading for the closest exit, playing the shocked and dazed victim for all I'm worth, coughing and spluttering.

I emerge into the bright midday on this moon, hit by the heat of two suns. I've been unable to get my head around how the days work in this binary system. It's different on every planet. But here, whatever part of the cycle we're in—night, day, or twilight—it's always bloody hot.

Time to make my escape.

I drop off the still unconscious security guards and a rough hand grabs my shoulder. "No one goes anywhere!" a stressed cop barks, as much at me as to the others vacating the smoke-filled bank.

"Of course not, Officer," I gasp, eyeing a host of emergency drones floating above us. A quick command from my wafer and they plummet into the ground, smashing into pavement and vehicles.

The cop runs off, and I bound away.

Moments later, the buildings in this busy part of town are shaken by a deep rumble. *Little Bastard* right on cue, descending in a direct vertical line from orbit. The ship smashes into the tent-like, low building and reappears seconds later, carrying the vault in its grasp, and zips away.

All clear, says *Little Bastard* through my wafer interface. *No civilians left in the building.*

Perfect.

With a smile, I activate my surprise. A growling sound grows in intensity, and all faces turn back towards the bank. The walls lean in, masonry ripping off in big chunks, until the whole building falls in on itself, leaving nothing but a smoking hole.

And that is how you rob a bank with style.

Next step: *The gettaway*.

I MAKE MY WAY FROM what's left of the Gilligan Credit Bank as just another freaked out merchant, seemingly fleeing from the scene of devastation with everyone else, joining a long taxi queue that quickly dwindles. When it's my turn, I step into the open cab behind the driver. His riot of red hair, common in this system, is platted into thick dreadlocks and tied up with a white handkerchief preferred by those working in the transport industry. A flimsy canopy hangs above the open cab, blotting out the sunlight, while freezing air is blasted into my face from the dash, otherwise it's open to the heat. I give the man the location of my run-down hotel, and we're off to the edge of town.

"Were you there?" he asks excitedly, gunning the vehicle to glide above the city's drab buildings. "Was it the Green Djinn?" Behind his words the radio is blaring with the news of my robbery.

"I didn't see anything," I reply, smiling to myself.

The Green Djinn is what the news streams christened me after I started my series of daring daylight robberies. The Hejaz System operates a strict class structure denoted by heredity. The lowest caste—the majority of those living in this backwater—are typified by the colour green, which is the only colour they can wear. To fit in, I chose green as a standard part of my disguise. I've unwittingly become a hero to the downtrodden.

"I can't believe he's come here," the driver continues. "To our little moon!"

"What makes you so sure the Green Djinn is a he," I say, feeling annoyed. I may be slowly getting used to my body, but looking male doesn't mean I have to put up with this backward shit.

"He has to be. No woman could pull off something like that. No way."

I decide not to put a hole in the back of the guy's head with my laser, but I'm sure getting pissed off with these backwater worlds Mother keeps posting me too. I take a deep breath. The man ain't being malicious, it's just the way he's programmed. "If you're so sure it's a man," I say. "Why not me?"

"You wish!" the driver guffaws. "If you were twenty years younger and twenty pounds lighter!"

Despite being ruled by an intolerant regime that jails people for saying the smallest thing out of line, the people in the Hejaz system always shoot from the hip. I find them refreshing. "They say the Green Djinn is a master of disguise. He could be anybody."

"I wish you were him. That would be something," the man laughed. "I'd be the most famous taxi-driver in town. Or on this moon."

I say nothing. The man's wish will soon come true.

"Like the fabled djinn, he also disappears without a trace," the driver continues, full of admiration, unaware that he's aiding my escape.

I must admit, my popularity with the locals in this system is unexpected. I'm no Robin Hood. I don't steal from the rich and give to the poor. But *the haves* are not much liked by the *have-nots*—and there sure are a lot of have-nots.

This latest escapade of the Green Djinn is going to

cause some consternation. I don't normally demolish the bank I'm stealing from. If this doesn't make the people I'm after sit up and take notice, I don't know what will. Mother won't be pleased—this wasn't in the mission outline. But there's always scope to improvise.

I could rob these banks a helluva lot more quietly, but Mother demanded I get attention. The only problem— it ain't working. I hate being stuck in *Little Bastard* and I hate the heat of this cramped system. I need to get closer to the core. To a five-star gaiasphere, not this backwater. I understand that I've got to earn my dues, but I've had enough. This latest escapade—demolishing a bank and stealing the biggest goddamn safe I've found in this entire fucking system—should do it. I hope.

The taxi-driver chats some more. I nod and reply as needed.

I must admit, having a human driver is comforting. One of the quirks of this system is that the ruling classes insist everyone works. I'm sure the car could fly itself— although in such low gravity, it's hardly flying. But the law is the law. This system has its problems. There's widespread inequalities and human life is cheap, but the place sure is alive.

The taxi-driver drops me off in a residential district on the opposite side of the city and says his goodbyes. I half-walk, half-float over to the run-down hotel and go up to my room. Most buildings on this planet are low and squat, despite the meagre gravity. I chose this hotel specifically for its many floors. My room is on the top and at the back. Just a bed, wardrobe, toilet, shower cubicle and balcony. There's nothing in here that's mine. Convenient, as I'm going to mysteriously disappear very soon.

I go out to the balcony and use my wafer to check for

any unwanted surveillance. It's unlikely I was followed, but you can't be too careful. Good thing I've taken care of any cameras in the vicinity—I don't want what happens next to be recorded.

A whoosh of air, and *Little Bastard* arrives with its stealth cloak activated. Just another shimmering heat-haze on this hot little moon.

Took you long enough, I say over the wafer. I glide off the balcony and into my ship, the door clanging shut behind me.

The gravity increases for a few seconds as the ship launches itself back into space and, once zero-gee is achieved, I float to the command deck.

"Where's the vault?" I ask, pleased the mission is over.

"We are heading there now," the ship replies in its efficient tones. *"ETA two minutes and thirty-three seconds."*

The voice is artificial-sounding. The brain that runs the ship is perfectly capable of talking to me in any number of human-like voices, but I prefer something impersonal and metallic. Having said that, its personality—if you can call it that—has grown on me. The thing is highly illegal, but when it comes to working for the Galactic Secret Service, illegal doesn't mean shit if it helps get the job done.

I prefer gravity to match my home planet of Plenty. "Set grav at point-eight Earth normal," I say. A few seconds later, 'up and down' arrives, and I sit on the command chair to eye the telemetry. No pursuit ships. Nothing. *Little Bastard* has positioned itself inside the mirror signal of the moon's primary spacestation. A shadow hiding inside a shadow. The ship will let me know if anything approaches. It's good like that.

I bring up the news streams.

The robbery dominates everything, with much

discussion regarding the Green Djinn. If I hadn't made such a splash, the authorities would've hid it under the carpet.

"Tea is waiting for you," Little Bastard informs me, a pleased lilt to its metallic tones.

The three-letter word fills me with pleasure, and I crack a smile. I make my way to the galley and pour a large mug of the milky stuff. "The vault," I begin, taking a refreshing sip. "What are the deets?"

"It is a Series Nine Heinz and Wessman Super Special. Imported from the Key into the Hejaz system five years ago. I contacted the Heinz and Wessman company for a reset code, using the highest Service security protocols, but it appears the serial numbers have been changed—or so their computer informed me. I am unable to open the door by any conventional means."

It's what I guessed. Heinz and Wessman supply these types of vaults to all kinds of criminals. They're not stupid enough to keep serial numbers. I would've told *Little Bastard* not to bother, but the ceph sure likes to waste its time. "Where is it?"

The galley screen flashes into life showing the safe floating outside the ship.

"May I ask why you didn't instruct me to bring the vault into the cargo hold?"

"How long did it take us to break into the last one we stole?"

"Four days, fifteen hours, thirty-seven minutes and twenty-one seconds."

"And how long would it take you to blast a hole inside using the ship's lasers?"

"I would not advise that as a course of action. It would be much more—"

"Is the vault securely tethered?"

"The vault is connected to the ship via a gravimetric field."

I have no idea what a gravimetric field is, but it sounds like it will do the job. "Good. Hit the door with a concentrated ten percent blast. Focus the lasers to a beam no wider than three feet. Keep going till you get through."

"To operate the laser may alert the local law enforce—"

"Just do it."

"Complying."

The screen flashes and, even at such a low threshold, the thrum of the laser cannon reverberates pleasantly through the ship. Finally, the flashing stops. The screen clears to reveal a blackened melted hole in the vault's door with debris escaping into space. "Good, now bring it aboard."

Done.

The screen flickers to show local space. A red dot approaches at speed. "What the hell's that?"

"A law enforcement patrol vehicle."

Part of me yearns for some hands-on action—if you can call melting a local reinforcement ship to space slag 'action'. *Little Bastard* may be small, but it outclasses most of the ships in this system. But where's the sport in killing an opponent who can't fight back? More dots suddenly appear on the nav-screen—correction, they're blotches rather than spots.

I should be careful what I wish for.

"Three cruisers and a battleship have just voidwarped into the system. They will be in weapons distance in thirty-two seconds."

"A battleship? Where the hell did they get that?"

"It's an old Delta-Class Void Warrior," Little Bastard explains. *"But refitted and serviceable. They are charging*

weapons."

"What's she got?"

"*An ion battering ram, mag-rails and lasers. Weapons distance in fifteen seconds.*"

"Shit. And the cruisers?"

"*Pulse cannons and blaster arrays. They're attempting a void-lock. Prepare for manoeuvres!*"

If they get a lock on us, they'll be able to follow us into the void. I should've jumped as soon as I left the hot little moon below. *My bad.* I was cocky and now I'm paying the price. *Little Bastard* is gonna love this—if we can escape that is. I strap myself into my chair and sink back into the webbing, feeling the ship lurch violently, my eyes fixed on the screen which flicks into tactical mode.

The blobs resolve themselves into four ships—one massive, the Delta-Class Battleship. A series of flashing dots spray from her. Mag-rails, high-calibre by the look of them.

Little Bastard manoeuvres expertly, throwing me around like a rag doll until the inertial dampeners kick in. The spread of our lasers meets the incoming barrage. Lights dart out silently from the other ships—blaster arrays.

We duck and dive. "Don't let them get a lock!"

"*They will still be able to track us if we jump,*" *Little Bastard* replies in its same efficient tones.

A bright flash and everything goes dark, before, thankfully the systems blink back on. "What the hell was that?"

"*An ion cannon. But at low intensity. They are trying to disable us. No essential systems were damaged.*"

The cruisers give chase and I'm deafened by the thrum of *Little Bastard's* weapon systems—reassuringly loud and shaking the command seat even with the inertial dampeners in place.

"I've detected a tactical blind spot upon the battleship. Moving in closer."

We dive onto the Delta-Class, which rears up on the tactical readout. I worry that we are going to crash straight into it. The thing is enormous. "What the hell are you doing!"

The pursuing cruisers break off their attack, unable to fire on us without hitting their enormous sister-ship. We expertly dart over the fuselage, readouts telling me we are only a few feet away from crashing. Our weapons become deafening. Explosions from our fire, rock the massive ship below. I flip to an external view and baulk at what I see. We're going to smash into a command node, a large stack like a downtown cityblok.

"Shit! We're done for!"

"Prepare to jump."

"What the—"

WE SLAM INTO THE VOID and suddenly, the ship is calm and silent. "Thank space!" I croak. "Just how bad is it?"

"Damage report. We have ninety-three percent integrity. Automatic systems now attempting repairs."

I open my mouth to reply, but my words are cut off by the return to normal space—a jarring, mind-wrenching snap. The jump was a short one and we emerge at pre-determined co-ords, located in the middle of nowhere as planned. Not close to any planet, moon, colony asteroid or space routes. *Little Bastard* trains its weapons on where any pursuit ships are likely to appear, but I know we weren't followed.

"Recharge the void engines!" I order. "We don't want to be caught napping again."

"On it."

"And what the hell was that?"

The ceph says nothing, indicating it hasn't understood my question.

"I thought we were going to crash."

"The Delta Warrior Class of ships is one of the biggest warships ever built. Its size gives certain advantages and certain disadvantages. In this instance, a void-jump at a half-way point along its superstructure was not detectable—our comparative mass makes that an impossibility. Our jump was also masked by a barrage of weapons fire from all on-board aggressive systems."

If I didn't know any better, I'd say *Little Bastard* was bragging. "Well done. So, we're safe from any pursuit?"

"There is a small possibility, but it is less than one percent."

"Good. Those attack ships appeared only seconds after we revealed ourselves. It appears they were prepared."

"As you may remember, I did advise against your course of action."

The goddamn ship is right. I was sloppy. I should've left the system first, not revealed the ship's location.

The reason?

I'm going stir crazy. I've worked alone all my life. Yet I'm finding my isolation in this system hard to deal with. But I know the source of my frustration—lack of female company. My self-enforced celibacy is starting to grate.

I take a deep breath and blow it out as one long sigh. I understand my basic physiology. My needs. Sexual release is necessary for a healthy mind. But so far, I've failed to take that intimate step in this gender-reoriented body of mine. And no matter how much I've avoided self-gratification, it's been the only option. Sure, I used to give myself 'one off the wrist' when I was a woman. I wiggled my bean like every other gal—a great way to relax. But nothing prepared me for the emptiness that inhabits me after I perform the same act as a man. A feeling of loss with a full-on slice of hopelessness.

No wonder lonely guys are so fucked up. An insight I wish I didn't have. But in some way, it helps me understand how I am now physically wired.

This planetary system is like any other, there are bars and brothels where women can be found. Sadly, though, as I discovered on my first mission, that's not for me. I'm gonna have to meet a dame and—

I shake my head.

Just how am I supposed to do that? There's only one thing for it. After this mission, I'm gonna take some time out and take care of the issue. Meet some regular girl in a bar. Get to know her a little, then get this damn thing over and done with. I'm Quick-Kill for fuck's sake. Sex shouldn't be a goddamn problem. But it is.

I glare down at this body of mine and grit my teeth. Introspection will get me nowhere. There's a job to do. So I better get on with it. "How long before we can jump again? I'm not gonna relax until I know we can get out of here, should our friends turn up guns blazing."

"Voidwarp will be charged in under five minutes. Preset co-ords."

"Good," I say, making my way to the cargo area, still feeling a bit shaky. "I suppose I'd better go and take a gander at what got us into trouble."

The vault is less impressive with a hole burnt through the door. The inside a blackened mess. The ship's laser sure did a lot of damage.

A lump of melted plastic tells me there was a pallet of the local money stashed inside. Now it's no use to anyone. But money is not why I'm doing this. I scan the debris and quickly locate a silver box, one foot in height and width, untouched by the heat of the pulse laser.

I open it to find a single cube of *Stuff* glowing white inside.

"I knew there had to be a reason for a safe like this," I whistle appreciatively. This is the biggest cube of *Stuff* I've found. Losing it is sure gonna piss off the Gilligans. I wondered how this system could get its hands on a battleship and I'm guessing *Stuff* is very much part of that answer.

Not that I have any idea what *Stuff* actually is.

Little Bastard ran a diagnostic and sample scan after I

stole my first batch months ago, but other than finding out it was organic matter combined with some exotic and unknown compounds, the ship and I are none the wiser. I'm sure Mother and the Service know all about *Stuff.* But that wasn't part of my mission briefing and the Service sure are tight-lipped.

A flashing red light catches my eye, coming from a small, soot-covered capsule the size and shape of a large trunk.

Wonder what loot could be stashed inside?

I pull it free of the surrounding rubble and try and prise it open, but the case is rigged with an electronic locking device. And I ain't about to trip some goddamn booby-trap. I rub at the soot and reveal a glass panel.

Staring back at me is the face of a beautiful woman.

I TAKE A STEP BACK.

What the hell is a woman doing in a goddamn safe?

I drag it into the cargo area and clean off more soot. A suspended animation foetal-pod? I don't know much about the tek, which looks battered and ancient, but there sure seems to be a lot of flashing red lights. I get *Little Bastard* to scan it. "What's the verdict? Is she alive?"

No reply.

"Well?"

"The female will not survive unless she is removed from the pod. You need to take her to the medibay immediately."

"Shit!" I race across the cargo bay, grab a crowbar, and prise open the casing—sometimes brute force is best. It opens with a pop, the lid clattering to the floor.

More red lights blink and a whole load of alarms sound. Some of the internals have fried and tubes are leaking everywhere. I take another look at the woman. Her skin is the colour of amber, her features statuesque… beautiful. Like some fallen Egyptian queen of old.

"She's not breathing," Little Bastard says. *"I recommend you hurry."*

I hoist her out of the pod and jog her down to the medibay, dragging wires and tubes as I go, while *Little Bastard* reduces the grav to make it easier.

We arrive at a small alcove—a human-sized locker mounted in the wall. The medibay is small, but top-of-the-range. Healing everything from minor wounds to significant injury and near-death. I kick it open, bundle her inside and let *Little Bastard* do its job.

The woman is scanned, injected, hit with medipacks, and rolled on to her side.

Sudden bleeping, and she goes into cardiac arrest. There's nothing I can do, as more volts jerk through her, other than sit down and watch. After a few minutes, everything quietens down, and *Little Bastard* informs me she is stable.

I'm intrigued. Who wouldn't be?

A babe like this held in hibernation inside one of the largest safes I've seen on this mission. What the hell was she doing in there? She's not typical of the system, which is a real mix of races—the varied human genome in all its multi-ethnic splendour. Only the rich can afford a pure race makeover—another form of elitism. But I'm not judging her. She reeks of importance—or at least of someone rich enough to afford a Cadillac body and face augmentation.

She reminds me of—dare I say it?—*royalty*.

You know the kind of thing? That notion of innate superiority the high-ups peddle to the befuddled masses. Her look seems to be based on an ancient Egyptian aesthetic, or at least what passes for that in this fucked-up century. And she's the most attractive woman I've seen in a long time, maybe ever. But then again, I've been starved of female company for longer than I care to mention.

I get myself another mug of tea, take a sip, and contemplate further. Maybe stealing this woman will make the Gilligans finally sit up and take notice. Or maybe she's their prisoner? Either way, her presence on *Little Bastard* means things are gonna get complicated.

"So, what's the verdict? Did we kill her or is she gonna make it?"

A pause. *Little Bastard* may be an artificial brain, but it sure feels like it's got attitude.

"The patient is suffering from a rather rough awakening from hypersleep. Her pod was irreversibly damaged by the unconventional way we gained entry to the safe." Again, I can hear the accusation in its metallic tone. *"She will wake in a few hours."*

"That ain't gonna happen," I say, taking another sip of tea. "The last thing I need is a civilian on board. Sedate her."

"I cannot comply," the ceph replies. *"The subject must be wakened to complete the hibernation exit process. She will not survive otherwise."*

I ponder on letting the woman die… but I know that's not a real possibility. Like I said, I don't like killing civilians. "Okay. Check the pod and see if you—"

"The pod has already been scanned and its remaining systems interrogated," Little Bastard says.

"And?"

"Nothing of significance was found."

"How long has she been in that thing?"

"No information available. There is one odd thing about the pod."

"Go on then," I say.

"It has been strengthened."

"For what reason?"

Little Bastard says nothing for a few moments. Is it thinking or just trying to piss me off?

"Minimal available evidence to speculate."

I take another sip of tea. Very well. I'll take the obvious route to find out who she is and what she was doing in hibernation—I'll ask her. "Buzz me when she wakes. I need to get out of this goddamn disguise."

I pull off my thawb—I'm naked underneath—and enter the shower unit.

In all my time as an assassin, I never once wore anything

like this. My costume was a wig and red lipstick. But now I'm a secret agent and this is what I'm forced to wear—a full-on face and body augmentation.

A few tweaks on the control pad and I'm hit with a concentrated burst of chemicals.

My disguise loosens, and I feel my mouth, nose, cheeks, and chin literally drop off. Revealing my own face in the polished metal walls—or at least the face that Mother gave me when I was reassigned a new body. Everything about me is fake these days.

I glare at my reflection. My large belly and backside disintegrates, and I'm back to being 'me'—a fine specimen of manhood in all its glory.

Lucky happenchance if Mother is to be believed.

I snort.

"Returning to normal space," Little Bastard informs me.

The ship jolts and we enter the void again, before, a few seconds later, we return to normal space. Finally, I can properly relax. I tweak the control pad and take a regular shower. The ever-present dust of this system gets everywhere. I let the water cascade over me for a few minutes before towelling off and lying down on my bunk. I'm bushed. But I always feel like this after an operation, more mentally tired than anything else. The job was mostly straightforward, but that near miss with that Delta-Class warship, sure put the willies up me.

"Anything on the feeds?" I ask, closing my eyes.

"The raid is the top story of the system," the ceph answers.

"Good. Let's hope the Gilligan Gang sits up and takes goddamn notice." I've systematically robbed them of *Stuff* for over three months. They must make contact soon. As to what form their message would take? I've no idea, but I'm expecting something overt. "Time for some shut-eye. Keep monitoring."

Sometime later, I'm rudely awoken by a buzz in my wafer. Damn, it's *Little Bastard*. Can't the ceph ever let me sleep? *What now?*

I open my eyes and find the girl I rescued from hibernation, creeping towards me with a knife.

"WHAT THE HELL DO YOU think you're doing?" I sit up and stare at her.

The girl is tiny but well-formed and unashamedly naked. Her nipples pointing at me accusingly, her body covered in an alluring sheen of sweat. But it's not her obvious assets that I'm drawn to, it's her eyes. She appears to think she has the upper hand. I've been over-confident already today and decide not to take her at face value. "Is this the thanks I get," I say, standing up, remembering that I'm also naked. "For saving your goddamn life?"

"Sit down!" she orders, her voice stress-filled and a little shaky.

"Okay," I say, lazily grabbing at a pillow, apparently with the intention of using it to cover my modesty. In one swift motion, I fling it at her and pounce. Within seconds, I'm sitting astride of her holding the knife, aware of our naked bodies touching. This close, I can smell her, an alluringly feminine fragrance—not a perfume, but her own body-scent. She screams and starts struggling. Struggling that ceases as soon as I bring the knife up to her throat. "That was a dumb move—you obviously come from a well-off family. You must do, with those expensive looks. Didn't they teach you how to look after yourself?" I get off her, grab a sheet and offer it to the girl. "Cover yourself up."

I quickly pull on some clothes while the girl wraps the sheet around herself, although the sheer material only magnifies her assets. I know the power of a pretty face and a taut body. I used the same things myself to lure perps back when I was in the assassination game. Still… I over-powered her easily. *Maybe too easily.* Sure, she's making me tingle in all my new places, but I'm no sap. "What the hell were you doing in that hibernation pod?"

"I'm not saying anything until you tell me who you are and what you're going to do with me!"

"Me? I'm the guy who just stole you."

"Stole me? What do you mean by that?"

"If you don't want me to throw you out of the nearest airlock, you will answer *my* questions—starting with your name."

The girl sits on the edge of the bed, tears beginning to run down her face. The waterworks have no effect on me—I know that trick too well. But the girl is damn hot all the same. Strong features, with an aquiline nose, all framed by thick, straight, black hair, cut to a severe fringe. Dusky, dreamy eyes and high cheekbones sitting above fleshy, perfectly formed lips. And her breasts…

I mentally rebuke myself. *Info now, breasts later.*

"Talk!"

"My name is Sirena," she says. "Sirena Jayla."

I nod and, via my wafer, silently command *Little Bastard* to search for her name using the Secret Service Cipher—their encrypted sub-space channel. A marvel in itself. Hijacking any number of media, science, and government installations to run a vast secret network available only to those in the know.

"And what happened to you, Sirena Jayla?" I ask.

"I was kidnapped from my pleasure barge by some vile people. They came aboard with the staff. Killed them all and took their places. Threatened to blow the ship if I didn't go quietly. I had no choice. They took me to a small cruiser—and old derelict—and did horrible, horrible things to me."

"And that's it?"

"Are you part of them? The gang who kidnapped me?"

"No," I reply. "But that doesn't mean I'm not just as dangerous."

"Where am I? What is this system?"

I probably shouldn't tell her, but I need to find out who this girl is and why she's here. And besides, it's months since I've had a decent conversation. *Little Bastard* might be a fully-fledged ceph with an independent consciousness, but he's no conversationalist. "This system is nowhere special," I answer. "Just another galactic backwater. Run by dictators, mafia or religious nuts. This particular one is operated by the Gilligan Gang." I watch her closely, but she gives no reaction. Either she's never heard of them, or she's a good actress. "We are in the Hejaz system."

She shrugs. "Hejaz?"

"Yeah, I'm not sure what it means. I think, originally, it was named after some long-forgotten holy land. But there's nothing holy about it these days, believe me. The locals, a mixture of Irish, Arab, and space-knows-what else, are kept on their knees by a ridiculous caste system and a crippling tax structure devised by the top one percent. Like I said, just another galactic backwater."

"Then what are you doing here?"

"Good question."

She waits for more information, but I just smile. She clears her throat. "Do you have anything to eat? I'm starving."

It's a ploy. A way into the human psyche.

If I feed her, I'm less likely to throw her out of the airlock. Not that I'd do that anyway, but she doesn't know that. "Sure," I say and motion for her to exit my room. I herd her towards the galley, fighting to keep my eyes above the firm line of her ass.

Having someone aboard might make a welcome change, but I can't risk further distractions. Certainly not from gorgeous intruders given to threatening me with knives.

Little Bastard is a small ship and the galley only a short distance from my quarters. A cramped alcove with a table and chairs. "Sit down."

She complies, and I find myself staring into her face again. Damn, the girl is beautiful. "Computer," I say. "Prepare a nutritional supplement for our guest here."

"*Yes, Captain,*" *Little Bastard* replies in smooth but affected female tones.

I get what it's doing, hiding under a typical comp-persona. There's no need. Sirena would never guess I was talking to a ceph. Not unless they found the brain itself, lurking somewhere in the depths of the ship.

The galley produces an ugly looking drink—pale grey and mucous-like—while I order burger and fries. It's all reconstituted, and not my normal bowl of porridge, but part of me wants to annoy the girl, to make her drool while she's forced to eat her breakfast through a straw. I also pour myself yet another mug of tea. And there's nothing reconstituted about that. Tea is the only necessity I requested on this mission and I'm all the better for it. Life without my favourite libation would be no life at all.

Sirena grabs her drink and sucks at it. "Nice," she says and I'm not sure if she means it or not.

I ignore her and start in on my meal. It goes down smoothly, Sirena watching every mouthful. The food itself is inconsequential. The galley gives me the required amount of nutrition I need in whatever form I request. The ship's rations don't hold much flavour, that's for sure, but it's all I've got. All the food in this system is too spicy for me—for this body. Jane, my old self, used to love a curry—the hotter the better, but I dunno, spicy is not for me anymore. Something else taken away from me by Mother and the goddamn Secret Service.

I take a sip of tea and shake my head. Even I'm bored with my self-pity.

Little Bastard buzzes my wafer. *Sirena Jayla—also known as Alice Farquhar—went missing just over five years ago,* it says in my mind.

When I first came aboard this ship, the ceph wanted to communicate with me this way all the time, but I couldn't stand its voice inside my head. Bad memories I suppose. For now, though, it's useful.

'Kidnapped by raiders' is what the survivors called it. Since then nothing has been heard of her.

I hum thoughtfully. *Do a background check on the girl—see what more you can find out on her via the cipher. Anything and everything. Search both names.*

On it.

"You're very cute," Sirena says as I wipe my plate clean. "That look must've cost you a lot."

"More than you will ever realise," I reply. "But I ain't the person of interest in this little scenario. How long were you in hyposleep? What year were you captured?"

"Why?"

"Just answer the question."

"Twenty-four forty-nine," she says.

I do the simple math and the numbers add up. "That was five years ago."

Sirena's jaw drops. "That can't be possible."

"Get used to it."

Sirena sags, a hopeless look crossing her face.

"If the matter was a simple kidnapping," I continue, "the ransom would've been paid, and you'd already be back with your family. So why put you into hibernation? That only makes sense if you were taken as a hostage. What kind of business is your family in, anyway? Did they mess with the wrong people?"

"Daddy and Mummy work in real estate and land bartering."

"A great cover for money laundering, buying and selling land."

"No," Sirena says with a bored shake of her head. "They were not that type of people."

"If you say so."

"You still haven't told me who you are?"

"Well, I'm not a kidnapper, not intentionally anyway. And I think you owe me some thanks for saving your life."

"About that…" she frowns at me. "What happened to the pod I was in? I saw it in your cargo bay. The thing was a burnt-out wreck."

"I stole you, remember? Your pod was inside the safe I liberated from one of the Gilligan's Banks—the family that runs the Hejaz system. I didn't know you were in there. Who could've guessed? Otherwise I might've thought twice about blasting it with the ship's lasers."

"You did what?" Sirena says, going pale.

"I didn't fancy taking a week or two to open the thing. That's when I found the pod. You were in a bad way, but luckily, I have a top-of-the-range medibay facility aboard. Otherwise you'd be toast. So, like I said, you owe me some thanks for saving your goddamn life."

The girl takes a few seconds to compose herself,

sipping absentmindedly at her drink. "Thanks for rescuing me," she says finally. "What is this ship? I've not seen anything like it before. It's tiny, but kinda... advanced."

"After five years in hibernation, everything is gonna seem advanced, so suspend your wide-eyed disbelief, okay?"

"The ship has voidwarp, yeah? It must do."

I nod.

"Then you can take me home. Daddy will give you a big reward. I can guarantee it."

"I ain't doing anything of the sort. It might've not looked like it when you woke me, but I'm busy. Too busy to play escort. Sorry."

"Busy doing what? You said you found me in a safe. You stole me! If you're a thief, I'm offering you an easy way to make a lot of money, risk free."

"Sounds great. But I don't need the cash."

"Then what the hell are you doing breaking into banks?"

"That's *my* business."

She straightens her back and sticks out her chest. "I'll do anything you want if you just take me home."

Her offer is serious. And I admit it. I'm tempted. For now though, I have bigger concerns. "I think you'll find I can do whatever I want, with or without your permission... but consider yourself lucky. You're safe from my attentions, believe me."

"You prefer guys, huh?"

"No!" I reply, a little too forcefully. "Me and other men just don't get on. Especially if they're on the wrong side of my laser."

"Then you think I'm unattractive?"

Judging by my increased heartbeat and the excited

sensation in the pit of my stomach, the answer is a most definite no. There's something special about this girl. Maybe it comes from all that high-end augmentation work she's had done, but Sirena has an allure. Something more than her impressive curves, golden skin, and big brown eyes. "Girls who look like you are ten-a-penny at any spaceport," I lie. "Your perky tits and easy tears mean nothing to me. And you came at me with a knife, remember?"

"I'm sorry about that. But what would you have done? I just want out of this mess and to go home."

Little Bastard sends a data file to my wafer and, using its split consciousness function, I go through the info while talking. "Where is home exactly?"

"In the Key of course," she replies, as if that's obvious. And, by the look of her, it is.

"What system?"

"Lalande. One of the original settled systems and second only to Earth," she replies proudly.

"What planet?"

"I didn't grow up on a planet, I'm a hab girl from the oldest gaiasphere in the system. *Anticipation.*"

"That's quite some bragging rights. One of the very first artificial habitats built outside the Sol system and one of the most exclusive," I say, reading directly from the file in my head. I've always dreamed about going to the Key and its core systems, but my actual knowledge is a little sparse. I've only ever seen gaiasphere habitats on the news streams. I access the available information on *Anticipation* and I'm surprised to find it's not quite the paradise I'd imagined. Newer habitats are far roomier and far less morally restrictive. *Anticipation* is a centre for trading and deals run by a strict, authoritarian right-wing government. "Still, I can't imagine it was much fun for you growing up there. Stuck in one of those repressive schools."

Her eyebrows furrow for the briefest of moments and I can see that she's perturbed. No… not perturbed. The girl is surprised.

"You seem to know a lot about me for someone supposedly unconnected to my kidnapping," she says.

"Let's just say I like to keep on top of things." I continue reading. She'd been kicked out of a bunch of prep schools for 'bad behaviour'. Her record is full of petty misdemeanours—until she went missing. Daddy must've sure been rich to cover up all that shit she got up to. And that showy pleasure barge she was kidnapped from was *stolen*.

The woman's kidnap story doesn't quite add up.

Maybe I've been premature. The girl could be a plant.

Sirena reaches over the table and takes my hands, her fingers delicate and tiny over mine. "Thank you. I know you didn't set out to save me. I'm more than grateful." She turns away. "But… but I've not been entirely truthful," she says, swallowing. "Let me tell you what really happened."

"Go on."

She faces me again and takes a deep breath, brow furrowing as if she's trying to collect her thoughts. "I was a bit of a tearaway as a kid. I've caused my family no end of anxiety. I was thrown out of all my schools and colleges. I stole. Was caught with drugs. And a lot of other stuff I'm ashamed of. And Sirena isn't my real name. I'm Alice Farquhar, of the Farquhar Clan. I changed my name as soon as I could and disowned my family. I hated them, their name and all their precious history. Hated everything. I stole the pleasure barge I was kidnapped from. I don't know why I did it. I didn't need the money. But the men I was supposed to sell it to turned on me. They beat up my friends and took me with them."

More tears form in her eyes, dripping down her cheek and onto the grey metal of the galley table top.

Could be fake, but her words sure feel heartfelt.

"They did things to me," she continues. "Unspeakable things. I kept telling them Daddy would pay for my return, but they weren't interested. They turned me into a slave. I thought they were going to kill me. It made me realise how stupid I'd been. I promised myself that if I ever escaped, I'd change. I'd go back home and try and make up for what I've done."

"And the hibernation pod?"

"They found it on an old derelict and forced me into it. To test it out, or so they said. I was terrified. Screaming. And that's the last thing I remember."

"So why lie to me?"

"I thought that if you knew what I was really like, you wouldn't help me."

"I suppose that makes sense." The girl has been through the mill and has only got herself to blame. At least she's not fooling herself any more.

"So now you know all about me, that it's my own fault I'm in this mess, will you help me?"

I sit back and think. There's no way I can drop her off at a local police station—or anywhere else for that matter. Not in this system. It's a good bet the Gilligans will be looking for her. Yet… I can't let her stay with me. Despite what's between my legs, I'm a one-woman operation. The last thing I need is someone finding out who I am and what I'm up to.

"Throwing you out the airlock would be the easiest solution…" I say, pausing just long enough to see the girl tense.

If Mother were here, I'm sure she wouldn't think twice about spacing the girl. Luckily for Sirena, I ain't nothing like that uptight centenarian. "…But don't worry, I'm not gonna make you do the vacuum dance."

"Thank you," she whispers.

"Yeah. I'm all heart. I have another plan. One that should get you off my ship and out of my hair."

"And what's that?" she says, swallowing.

"I'll alter your appearance. Tone down all that ethnic purity, give you a new ID and dump you at a spaceport with enough credits to buy your way home aboard a clanship."

She squeezes my hand a little tighter. "That sounds scary. Can't I stay here a short while longer? A few days to re-orientate myself?"

I shake my head. "That's not a possibility. But I've got to lie low for a few hours. So you can be my passenger overnight—until I can safely drop you off. For now, I've a room for you. Where you can have a little privacy."

Sirena offers me a determined smile. "Thank you."

"Don't thank me just yet. The room will have a lockable door. I don't want you wandering around getting under my feet… or cutting my throat." I give her a warning look. "And if I find out anything more about you, anything that I'm not happy about, the airlock ain't far. Get me?"

Sirena doesn't seem bothered by my threat and nods her head.

I escort the girl to a cabin that doubles as a prison cell. Aware of how tiny she is in comparison to my massive frame. Her hips gently sway, brushing against my thigh.

Is she purposely trying to turn me on?

Fuck. The girl is just walking! *Curse this damn male*

libido. "Here," I say, entering the cabin. "There's a wall bunk that pulls out. And a head and shower unit. I suggest you get cleaned up."

"You ever gonna tell me your name?"

I shrug. "Names are overrated."

Sirena's expectant gaze doesn't leave my face and I relent. "Sam," I say, the name I chose for this mission. *Sam Santana.* Seems I have a sentimental streak when it comes to aliases. My first was a girl called Samantha. Back on Plenty. Sam died a long time ago, murdered by her pimp. Perhaps I loved her. I dunno. But I made sure her death was avenged… *and then some.*

"Nice to meet you, Sam," she says, dropping the sheet to reveal statuesque buttocks, before entering the shower unit. My eyes linger for longer than they should, until she catches me staring. I make a quick exit.

The door closes with a clang and *Little Bastard* engages the lock.

"Is it really your intention to let the intruder go?" Little Bastard asks as I return to the bridge.

"Yeah. She sounds like a typical spoilt brat who got everything she ever wanted by flashing money or those expensive tits of hers, but I don't think she's a threat."

"Galactic Secret Service protocols dictate that intruders be liquidated at once."

"If that's the case, why did you save her goddamn life?"

"It was pertinent to first know who she was and her intentions."

"Is that why you let her enter my quarters with a knife?"

"That was a calculated risk. You were given more than enough warning. And you are a fully trained agent twice her size."

"A regular ship's computer would have kept her locked in the medibay. You Service cephs sure like to complicate things."

"The subject was under constant observation—how better to assess her by letting her wander the ship?"

"And now you want me to space her?"

"Secret Service protocols dictate that intruders be liquidated."

"So you said."

"It is my responsibility to remind you of the directives and responsibilities of—"

"It ain't happening."

"The intruder cannot be allowed to stay aboard, even for a few hours. She may compromise the mission."

"Remind me again, who is the senior in our little arrangement?"

"You are, sir."

"Good. Don't forget it."

A long pause.

"Do you understand?"

"Yes. But this will have to go into the mission report."

"You do that, and while you're stabbing me in the back, answer me this: did you scan for any wafer or any other artificial augmentation when you were healing the girl?"

"She has an outdated cerebral enhancer—a wafer of sorts—it is of nondescript design and function. Exclusive in its day, but designed primarily for social interaction and sexual gratification."

"You don't surprise me," I say. "But the girl is an enigma, being left in hyposleep like that in a goddamn Gilligan Gang safe. Very pretty, but an enigma all the same."

"Pretty or not, she is a threat to our objective… Sam."

I swallow a rebuke. I didn't give it permission to call me anything other than, *sir*. The thing is trying to get a rise from me. And yet, the name does fit. "Okay," I say. "Now give me some silence… I need to get some rest."

"Will do."

I head back to my quarters and lie down. It's still late, but I ain't in the mood for sleeping. And, I admit it, part of me is pleased to have Sirena aboard. I've been going stir crazy living on my own with *Little Bastard*, but it's more than that. My heart is thumping for a whole different set of reasons. I'm not about to get distracted, no way, but I'm feeling an excitement I've never quite felt before. Something in the pit of my stomach. I'm more alive now than I have been for the last few months. Sure, I've had that special tingle over many a gal, back when I was a gal myself. But this is different. A biting, visceral desire to return to Sirena's cabin, slip into the shower with her and…

I consider commanding my wafer to calm myself down, but I prefer the sensation. And hey, there ain't anything wrong in being horny if it doesn't get in the way. Which it won't. I'm no sap. The whole idea is a non-starter. In this body I'm a goddamn virgin again.

I close my eyes, but it's over an hour before I finally fall asleep.

"SAM!"

"What the hell is it?" I reply, yawning.

"Mother wants to speak to you."

"Huh?" I say, rubbing my eyes.

"You've overslept. I left you alone, especially after yesterday's exertions, but this is a priority alert."

"What the hell does she want?"

"She wants you up and alert and listening!" The reply comes from the screen in my quarters. It jumps into life and Mother is revealed, staring at me with beady eyes sitting under a furrowed forehead.

I shake my head, feeling unusually groggy. "Oh, great."

"Your ceph informs me that you have someone aboard. Some woman you picked up."

"And I thought that jumped-up data-stack was on my side."

"It reports to me, Quick-Kill, as do you. Now, why is this girl still alive?"

I sit up and run my hand through my thick, black hair before rubbing at the annoying stubble of my chin. "I'm no murderer, that's why," I say, feeling suddenly defensive about my new passenger.

"You seem to have forgotten that's exactly what you are. Officially sanctioned. And you were also an assassin before we recruited you."

"Sure, you're right. I've killed hundreds of people…

but they always deserved it. This girl—as far as I can tell—is an innocent. And I don't kill innocent people."

"She is aboard a secret ship on a sensitive mission. She cannot be allowed to—"

"And just what is this goddamn mission anyway? I've been at it for months with no movement."

"You know the assignment. Get the attention of the Gilligan Gang. Then infiltrate them. More orders will arrive when you're inside their organisation."

"Great."

"I can't tell you more. Just in case—"

"—Just in case I'm captured and interrogated. Yeah. I get it."

"Now about this girl…"

"She's in the ship's cell. I'm dropping her off at a spaceport and that will be the end of that. Sirena Jayla, aka Alice Farquhar, comes from a good family but, was a bit of a tearaway and, as far as I can tell, she's seen the error of her ways. You've read her file, I take it?"

"Yes, I did. The girl is trouble. Through and through. Seems like money and prestige wasn't enough for her. According to Abe, her record up to when she disappeared shows signs of an undiagnosed sociopathic disorder."

"Sociopathic? No way. Sure, the girl is disturbed, but she has been through a lot since she was captured. She's changed for the better."

Mother eyes me for a couple of seconds, as if she's surprised by my words. "I didn't read anything that makes me think she's worth saving. Another reason to space the bitch, pronto. A fitting demise for a rich brat."

"Sirena was found in a safe I robbed," I say, ignoring her. "She has no idea what she's doing in this system. Space knows what the Gilligans had planned for her. Sirena says she's never heard of them and I believe her."

"That makes sense at least. Our intel on the Gilligan Gang tells us these guys aren't great thinkers. They're a 'point and shoot' kinda organisation. Like that ambush on your ship yesterday. They're not the type to come up with an elaborate plan involving kidnapped rich kids and hibernation pods. Sounds like the girl found herself in the wrong place at the wrong time."

"Yeah, that squares with what I've found out about the Gilligans," I say. "They're not subtle. In this system, subtlety is a rare commodity. But, dammit, there's something about Sirena."

"I'm sure she's a lot of fun, especially with that new body of yours, but sometimes people have to die for the greater good. Innocent or otherwise. Call it collateral damage."

I stand up, raising my voice, wondering why Mother is so keen on killing the girl. "I get it. You're right. But I've a gut feeling about Sirena. And it's nothing to do with her good looks. I can't put my finger on it, but killing her seems like the wrong move."

"You sure it's not a case of simple infatuation? I've seen it before in new agents. An unfamiliar body coupled with a different gender can sometimes take a bit of getting used to."

Her words irritate me. *Infatuation?* No. I feel a strong desire to protect Sirena. She's an innocent who just made a few mistakes. She doesn't deserve to lose her life over this. No way. "Of course, I'm sure," I say. "I'm Quick-Kill, remember, not some sap, half-wit who falls for the first bit of skirt that comes her way."

Mother's eyes bore into me from the flickering screen. "You're new. Normally, I wouldn't expect to be disobeyed. But, I always trust a gut. Okay. We'll do it your way. And don't take any unnecessary risks."

"Of course not," I reply bullishly.

"By the way, that was nice work yesterday with your latest robbery."

"You heard about that, huh? I thought you'd be pissed."

"Something was needed to get the attention of the Gilligans. I think you might've done it by demolishing one of their banks. I'm impressed."

"Thanks."

"That is all. Goodbye, Agent Quick-Kill."

"Yeah, bye. And please warn your ceph that if it snitches on me again, I'm gonna give it a reprogramming it'll never forget."

The screen dies, and I dress before making my way to the bridge. The conversation with Mother certainly got my hackles up. I don't like my boss, especially after she shot and killed my old body, but her insistence on spacing Sirena is pissing me off.

Just why am I protecting the girl, I wonder. I search my feelings. There's still that same tingle when I think about her, but this is something different. A deep desire to protect her. To keep her safe. What she told me last night was heartfelt. Sirena needs someone to look out for her. I'm pleased Mother trusted my gut. I doubt I'll get the same leeway in the future.

The situation raises the question that has been bothering me the most since Mother recruited me—*what am I willing to do to get my old body back?* I shake my head. Here, stuck inside a tiny ship run by a traitorous computer brain—my home planet of Plenty and my old life are sure looking attractive. I was a one-woman operation. With no one bossing me around.

"Where's the closest spaceport?" I ask *Little Bastard*.

"My mission brief is to report daily information back to

the Service whenever possible," Little Bastard says. *"I did warn you that ignoring protocols would be included."*

"Yeah, I thought you'd at least have the decency to wait until the mission was over. Maybe try that next time?"

"I'm afraid that wouldn't be possible under my work parameters."

"Oh, I see. You're saying *it's not your fault*. Nice. Maybe you're more human than I thought. At least you're living up to the name I gave you, although I may be forced to change it to *Traitorous Little Bastard*. Now, answer the damn question, where is the nearest spaceport? I need to get Sirena safely away before Mother changes her vicious little mind."

"The nearest spaceports are on Brigadoon III. The largest moon of the system's only gas giant. Planet-sized. Gravity one-point-three."

I bring up the moon on the navicom. Large population, multiple spaceports. A lot of trade with all sorts of goods. It's busy, bustling with visitors and hundreds of ships coming and going daily—just what I'm looking for. "Chart a course and be ready to jump."

I make my way to Sirena's cabin. I unlock the door and swing it open with little ceremony. She's lying on her bunk, half-under a thin sheet. The room smells sweet and inviting. She pushes herself up onto her elbows, the sheet sliding off her body. I stare at her, feeling a little dizzy.

"You okay?" she asks, unabashed.

"It's nothing," I reply. "I overslept. Cover yourself up and come with me. You'll be leaving soon."

"Don't you want to come and join me for…? Hell, you know what I want, and you want it to. Don't deny it. I've seen you looking at me."

She's right. Here's the opportunity I've been hungry for. A willing girl who would allow me to take the next step in this body. I'm desirous of it. Very much so. But Mother's words are still ringing in my ears. Sirena's safety is my main concern here. The longer she stays on this ship, the more danger she will be in from the Service. *And yet…?*

I move my eyes away from hers, my heart pounding loudly in my ears. "No… You must go. It's the only way."

She jumps to her feet, balancing on the bunk, her face is next to mine, and she smells so good. I want to drink her in, to thrust my face into her thick black hair.

"I know you like me, Sam. But you're closed off. Uptight. There's no reason to be. I'm no threat to you." She leans in and kisses me.

At first, I resist, until her tongue pushes into my mouth and intertwines with my own.

Suddenly I'm back on Plenty with Samantha. My first. She knew who I was and what I wanted. That I was too controlled, too goddamn distant. Withdrawn and unable to expose my true self in the simplest way.

I gave myself to her that night and it was the right thing to do. To hell with Mother and the mission—I deserve this!

I push Sirena away, her eyes looking confusedly into my own until they widen in understanding.

I AWAKE AS IF FROM a dream, dizzied and disorientated. My heart still thudding in my chest like a jackhammer.

"Wow!" Sirena says, lying next to me, her own heart beating furiously. "That was quite something. Fast, but, wow! So intense. You're full of surprises, Sam."

"Thanks… *I think*. It was my first time," I reply, slowly coming back to myself. "Was it… was it okay? Did I do all right?"

"Your first time? You're kidding?"

"It's complicated."

"Well you did good, mister. First time or not."

"Don't call me that?"

"What? *Mister?*"

"Yeah, I don't like it."

"Okay." She pushes herself up on her elbows to look down at me, her face flushed, her pupils wide, black, and alluring. "You sure are a strange one, Sam."

"I shouldn't have done that."

"Well I'm glad you did. And I want you to do it again, lots of times."

What are you doing, Sam? Little Bastard says through my wafer.

Not now! I reply.

But, Sam! The mission!

"If that was your first time, there's not much I can teach you," Sirena says rubbing herself against me. She wants a second round.

I'm gonna need more time. Something else I'll have to get used to with this body.

Sam!

"Shut up!" I blurt, accidentally speaking the words out loud.

"That's not very nice," Sirena says with a puzzled look.

I push her aside. I shouldn't have let Sirena get to me, although I'm glad she did. *Little Bastard* is right though. I need to get back on-mission. Mother may change her mind, which I can't let happen. No. To keep Sirena safe, she needs to get off this ship now.

I command my wafer to shut down my sexual centre and to ignore all related sensations. The change is immediate, but I still feel drawn to her. A powerful need to be with her. To… goddammit! To *protect her.* "Cover yourself up and come with me."

She's stunned and lets it show. Like she can't believe I can be so cold. "But I thought—"

"It's nothing to do with you… with what happened. But for your own good, you need to go. I'm sorry, but that's how it is."

"You think this is a game?" she replies tersely. "I'm deadly serious. I want you, Sam. I need to be with you."

I'm upsetting her, but that can't be helped. "This ain't no game, and you know it." I pass her the sheet and she dutifully gets up and wraps it around herself. "I thought you'd be keen to get back home to your family."

"I am. Or I was. Now I've met you… I feel different. Don't you? Don't you feel different?"

"Yeah," I admit, pushing those thoughts quickly away.

Sirena stamps her foot. "Then let me stay!"

"I wish I could. But things haven't changed. You're in

danger while you're here."

She's upset, and angry, but she finally nods. "Okay, Sam," she replies with a look of determination. "Let's do this."

"Good. First off, we'll change your appearance. Hejaz may be a backwater, but their people-control methods are advanced. I'm guessing that, after I stole that safe you were left inside, your face will have been sent to all policing centres and face-recognition systems."

"Why? I haven't done anything."

"Like I told you, I'm a sort of thief. It's me they're after. Finding you is just a stepping stone in their pursuit of the Green Djinn."

Sirena smirks. "Is that what they call you?"

"Yeah. I'm an all-round anti-hero."

"You don't mind telling me that?"

"It's not a secret and besides, you won't be in this system long enough for it to matter."

"So everyone will be looking for me, huh?"

I nod.

"Will changing my appearance hurt?"

"No. Just a nano-disguise. And no more questions."

I pull on a pair of trousers and push Sirena towards my quarters where I begin the process of changing this swan of a woman into something less alluring.

First off, I get her to step into my shower cubicle. I command *Little Bastard* to start the augmentation and she's slowly transformed into a slightly saggy, middle-aged woman. Skin tone and facial features are also altered. But her eyes remain the same.

Beautiful, regardless of the container they are held within.

I get her to dress in an abaya—a crimson and orange over-garment worn by most of the upper-classes in this system. A band usually holds the hair, but I fit her with a hijab to hide her striking black locks—a colour unusual in this system which is dominated by gingers and browns. I add a few accoutrements. Bangles, bags, and a sash-belt—and we're done.

"Where did you get all this stuff?" she asks.

"I told you… no more questions." I give her a handful of local cash and some high-note galaxy dollars.

"Is that it?"

"We'll drop you off outside the city."

"We?"

"Listen!" I reply, annoyed at my slip. "Get in a cab—they're easy to find. Give the driver your destination and nothing else. Your dress gives you status, which means that the driver will not talk back to you. You should also be ignored by beggars and peddlers. Enter the spaceport and find a clanship. You know how to spot a typical clan family member?"

Sirena nods.

"Good. Go up to any one of them and explain that you require passage. They won't care about ID or anything else. I've given you more than enough dollars for your needs. You understand?"

"And my disguise?"

"It's temporary. It will disintegrate after a few days. Just wash it away. It won't bother the clans after you've paid. Once you're out of the system, you can charter a ship back to Lalande or anywhere you fancy. Although if I were you, I'd change your name and your look again. Make a fresh start."

"Really?"

"Just a bit of advice. Take it or leave it."

"Okay… Thanks, Sam." She puts her arms around me and kisses me on the cheek.

"Go to the airlock." I hand her a pair of sunglasses. And with her eyes now hidden, I feel a surge of loss.

She leaves, and I track her via *Little Bastard's* cameras. She waits dutifully by the airlock, her hands rubbing over her now larger belly. I return to the bridge. "Okay," I say to *Little Bastard*. "You ready?"

"Yes, Sam."

"You do know I didn't give you permission to call me that?"

"I can omit that name from my lexicon if you wish?"

"No," I reply, rubbing at my face where Sirena kissed me. "I kinda like it."

"Initiating voidwarp in three, two, one."

A small jolt tells me we've entered the void and a secondary jolt a few moments later tells me we've arrived.

"In orbit around Brigadoon III. Stealth mode activated."

"Good. Take us down fast."

"On it."

A few minutes later, *Little Bastard* touches down on the planet's surface. The airlock hisses open and Sirena vacates the ship. I'm filled with a peculiar feeling of loss.

Perhaps I'm getting soft? I hope not, but Sirena has certainly left an impression. And, I must admit, I feel different. Cocky and more arrogant. Like a winner. A feeling I've never had after sleeping with a girl before. It's weird… but I like it.

"Take us up again," I command *Little Bastard*. "And keep us in geosync."

"On it," the ceph replies, although I can detect a note of disdain in its metallic voice, like it's judging me.

The nav screen pops into life and I'm able to watch Sirena as she walks towards a busy road. I placed a small tracking device in one of her bangles. Just in case. Everything seems okay. It's unlikely we were detected on the way down. Even if this system had advanced navigation and security tek, it would still be hard to find my ship.

Sirena gets in a taxi and it heads towards the spaceport.

"We shouldn't stay here long," *Little Bastard* informs me.

"Sure," I say. "Plot a course back to… What the hell is that?" The taxi Sirena is travelling in stops at an intersection, blocked by another vehicle. More vehicles also converge on her location, accompanied by a squad of ground troops.

"Shit!"

"IT APPEARS THE GIRL HAS *been detected,"* the ceph informs me dispassionately.

"There's no way in hell they could get to her so quickly. I don't understand it."

"Ready to voidwarp. At your command."

"No, we're not going anywhere."

"Sam, I must advise that we leave here immediately. The girl has been compromised. We do not know how. There is a possibility that our presence has also been detected."

"I said no."

"As you wish. But I will jump out of here if I detect any unusual behaviour."

"No, you goddamn won't!" I keep watching the screens. Sirena is taken out of the taxi and driven away to some government buildings on the edge of the town. My guess is that it's a local detention centre where 'dissidents' are taken for interrogation. "You properly checked the girl?" I ask, despite knowing the answer.

"Sirena Jayla, aka Alice Farquhar, was thoroughly scanned in the medibay. The pod was also scanned. Nothing unusual was found. No tracking devices."

My heart starts to thump in my chest. I command it to slow down with my wafer, but it has little effect. "Get me a floor plan of the building she's been taken to."

"I must advise against any other course of action that does not take us away from here immediately."

"Yeah, I got that. But I'm looking at the bigger

picture," I reply. "The mission is to infiltrate the Gilligan Gang, right? And maybe, just maybe, Sirena is more important to them than we realise. They got to Sirena fast. *Too goddamn fast.* She just might be the bargaining chip I need to get inside their organisation. I'm gonna break in, get some intel, and get the girl out of there."

"If you continue this course of action, I will be forced to make another report."

"Which you can't do while we are in stealth mode, correct?"

"That is true."

"Good. Now get me that floor plan."

A long pause. *"On it."*

"Good."

Moments later, a full set of 3D building schematics appear on my screen. I do a quick assessment of the layout and run back to my quarters, stripping off my trousers and entering the shower unit. I command *Little Bastard* to activate a nano-disguise.

The Hejaz system has many albinos—known as Reeves. They do not hold rank, but the caste system favours them highly. They are solvers of disputes, as well as being a conduit for this system's basic religious beliefs. Being born an albino means these guys are on the gravy train for life. In return, they are expected to uphold the government and its edicts, which means they are trusted implicitly. This look is my emergency camouflage—the nuclear option to be used only in dire emergencies. The disguise quickly takes shape, my skin becoming paler, my hair becoming a brilliant white.

I dress quickly in reeving robes suitable for the character I will be playing and pop in a pair of red-tinted contact lenses.

The result? *Impressive.*

I add my customary grenades and other weaponry, then jog down to the airlock only stopping to pick up my mission satchel.

"Sam, I do not believe you are acting rationally."

"Can it and take me down. Drop me off as close to the detention centre as possible without causing a fuss."

"On it."

I feel a jolt and the airlock slides open. I jump out into a dusty back-lot and orientate with my wafer. I'm only eight-hundred feet or so away from my destination.

Wait on my command in geosync, I command *Little Bastard,* and feel a rush of air as the ship powers upwards.

I curb my urge to run, and walk purposely towards the detention centre, passing a group of men smoking on a corner. They bow their heads and chant religious verse. I'm hoping for a similar reaction when I arrive.

In the twenty or so minutes it has taken to get into disguise and be dropped off, the detention centre has become blockaded. Transports, bristling with blasters, lasers and other cannons, hover over its low roof, with more vehicles flying close perimeters. A blockade of soldiers, nervous-looking police, and various vehicles surround the building, their weapons pointed upwards.

Seems like I'm expected.

Although, judging by all this hardware, they are expecting me to turn up in *Little Bastard,* like I've done for every bank job so far in this system. Which gives me the advantage. Still, I'm surprised.

How can they possibly know I'd come to rescue the girl? Unless they're taking no chances. More is going on here than I understand, an extra reason why I need to get inside.

I walk unnoticed towards the main entrance until I'm stopped by an officer in stylised red robes, indicating his stature in this caste system. He's a major and, judging by the sweat patches leaking through his clothing and his nervous demeanour, he's not suited to this position. Which is the problem with caste-systems—those with the least ability are sometimes given the most influence.

"Where are you going, Reeve?" he says to me.

"Where do you think?" I reply, pushing the man aside and striding forward.

I can almost feel the man's indecision as I walk purposefully towards a group of soldiers, who hastily part to let me pass. I enter the building and ignore the reception area. The green robes of the staff mean they cannot speak until spoken to. But they are agitated, and I hear them report my entrance to a superior. I walk past groups of soldiers who jump to attention, and avert their eyes, as is the customary response to my pretend caste.

I'm not going to get much further into this building without a distraction and, unwittingly, I've already been given the idea on how to do just that.

I command *Little Bastard* to perform an attack run. That'll keep everyone busy.

I head towards the elevator, also guarded by a phalanx of troops. A red-robed figure emerges from a side-room and walks towards me—his attitude telling me he won't be so easily fobbed off—when a deafening explosion rocks the building. The crack and whistle of weapon-fire erupts outside. I throw a series of smoke grenades and the corridor turns black as soot.

I close my eyes and guide myself via my wafer, which doubles as a short-range radar device. I slip past panicked soldiers and into the stairway. Sirena is two floors below, held in a large chamber. I'm guessing she will be guarded.

More explosions and the thrum and snap of cannon and laser. It seems like *Little Bastard* is doing a fine job.

Two large steel doors block the lower level. But not for long. I blow them inward with a single shot from the blaster in my satchel and stun everybody I run into. Another massive explosion rocks the building. The walls crack and split, and part of the corridor ceiling falls in. A little too close for comfort.

What the hell are you doing?

Causing a distraction, Little Bastard replies dispassionately.

I climb over rubble and find the doors to the chamber Sirena is being kept inside. I take them out with my blaster and throw in more smoke grenades. But they are ready for me. A barrage of blaster fire slams through the doorway and into the opposite wall, which explodes into a mixture of flaming dust, powder, and masonry.

I jog further down the corridor and, coordinating with *Little Bastard,* blast a hole in the wall. I jump inside.

The room is full of smoke and the soldiers inside are still blindly firing into the doorway, unaware that I'm in here with them. I hit the men with a wide stun blast and everything goes quiet.

"Sam… is that you?" Sirena croaks, from somewhere inside the murky room.

I check my wafer, but the local area scan shows nothing. *Where the hell is she?* "Sirena!" I shout.

"I'm here," she replies, her voice full of panic.

"But I can't see you."

"Here!"

I head towards the sound, using my wafer to make my way through the murk. But it's still telling me the room is empty, other than the soldiers lying stunned on the floor. "Sirena!"

Something is thrust into my face. A smell of harsh chemicals and I fall into a yawning pit of blackness.

I OPEN MY EYES, FEELING dehydrated and achy, lying in a plush double bed inside an equally plush bedroom. I sit up and pull back the bedclothes to find myself dressed in a simple white robe.

My legs are wobbly, but I manage to get out of bed to stand onto shaky feet. I go over to a full-length mirror. My disguise has gone, and so have my clothes. It's Quick-Kill staring back at me, not some high-ranking albino alter-ego. I check my body. I appear to be uninjured. Only my pride is wounded.

I let myself get caught, goddammit!

But how? I remember entering the room that Sirena was held in, when something was thrust into my face and out went the lights.

Little Bastard! I shout through my wafer. There's no reply. Nothing. I access my wafer and find that most of its functions have been disabled. Not damaged, just 'closed down'. That doesn't bode well. Whoever caught me, must've known exactly what was inside my head and how dangerous it was.

Shit!

This doesn't stink of the Gilligans. No way. Something else is going on here. But what?

I open the bedroom door and enter a large, well-to-do living area. "Hello!" I shout. "Anyone there? Sirena?"

"In here," says a thin, ancient sounding female voice from a doorway on the other side of the room.

I stop in my tracks, my hand unconsciously reaching to my thigh, where, in another life, my laser had been holstered.

Suddenly feeling powerless, I amble over to the doorway to find an old, dark-skinned lady hunched over a stove in a quaint-looking kitchen, making what appears to be an omelette. Behind her is a large window revealing an impossibly green garden at the end of which stands a set of stables.

It's unlike any part of this system I've seen before. There's not a single natural temperate zone on any of the settled worlds. The old lady looks at me with milky green eyes from a wrinkled face framed by long, thick brightly white hair.

"We've kept you sedated for quite a while, you must be hungry. Sit down." She nods towards a wooden table surrounded by a few chairs.

"Who the hell are you?" I shout. "And what happened to Sirena?"

The woman becomes suddenly still. "If you are not going to act civilly, you will be made unconscious again and we'll forcibly rip that wafer out of your head. Some of my boys have already expressed an interest in it. They'd be more than happy to get their hands on such advanced tek. You understand me?"

"Your boys?"

She becomes animated again. "Sit and eat," she commands.

I could easily overpower the woman, but she ain't scared by me. If anything, she's acting like she has the upper hand. At this point, I know nothing about her or where I am, or what happened to Sirena. I decide to err on the side of caution and pull out a chair and sit down, resting my elbows on the table.

"Elbows!"

"Huh?"

"Get your elbows off the table. In this house, you show respect."

I've no idea why my elbows are a problem, but again, I comply.

She comes over to the table, walking with a slow, deliberate gait and places an omelette in front of me. She pours boiling water into a flowery teapot with wrinkled hands, their brown skin blotched with white, and puts it on a tray with two dainty cups of the same design. "I don't know if you like tea," she says, "but I always do business over a nice cup. It's a lot more civilised, don't you think?"

"Who are you?"

"Eat and drink, then we will talk."

I shovel the omelette into my mouth with a fork. But my mind keeps going back to Sirena. I need to know that she's okay.

"Did no one ever teach you decent table manners?"

I shrug. The food is delicious and it's all I can do to not wipe the pattern off the plate when I'm finished.

"You have a good appetite. I've always liked that in a man." The old lady pours the tea, asking if I want milk and nods with approval when I answer in the affirmative.

I take a sip, pleasantly surprised. A fine blend. "Okay," I say, placing the cup back on its dainty saucer. "You gonna tell me where I am, where's Sirena, and who the hell you are?"

"Please, no cussing. I will not have it in my house."

I sigh. "Just answer my questions."

The old lady sits back. "You are in my house. Sirena is quite safe… for the time being. As for me? I'm Ma Gilligan. And you my friend, are the Green Djinn."

I TAKE IN THE INFORMATION with a furrow of my brows. So, it was the Gilligans after all? That makes no sense. No sense whatsoever. There's no way they had the wherewithal to capture me. Something bigger is going on here, but what?

"I can tell by your expression that you are surprised at how easily you were snared."

I don't like that word, 'snared'. It sounds like I walked right into a trap. But I can't deny I've been wrong-footed. I'm also perplexed as to why I'm here in this house and not in some high-security prison cell. My mind starts to race, I command my wafer to calm myself down, forgetting the thing is offline. I'm forced to take deep breaths instead.

"You're surprised?"

"Is it that obvious?" I reply. "How did you get to the girl so fast? And how did you capture me?"

Old Ma Gilligan puts her fingers up to her lips, shaking her head as if I've asked the wrong questions. "How you were caught is not what this discussion is about. No, no. You are here to talk about the return of all the *Stuff* you have stolen from my family in the last three months."

I'm taken aback. This is what my mission has been about. To get the attention of, and to infiltrate, the Gilligans. With my panic over Sirena and waking up in this strange place, I'd almost forgotten. It's a mental leap, but I force myself to adapt to this new situation. It's what I must do if I want to survive. "So, I take it that you're the person in charge of this system, yeah?"

She nods. "And I have been for the last one hundred and fifty or so years."

"Just how old are you?"

"Now, now. Don't be impolite."

"But I don't get it. If you're in charge, why are all the women in this system second-class citizens?"

"Why should that bother you? You're a man. And a very fine example of one, if I may say."

I shrug and say nothing.

"I'm a believer in traditional values," she continues, as if this is the only way things can ever be. "A woman's place is in the home, the man's is out working and providing."

I feel my hackles rise. But I remind myself I'm on a mission. If I'm to infiltrate this gang, I must toe the line, no matter how disagreeable. "You're good at keeping people down," I reply, "which means some people will get shat on. I understand."

"Please don't use that kind of language. I simply won't have it. And I won't warn you a third time."

There is an edge of threat to her voice. If this woman is a hundred-and-fifty year old matriarch, she's someone I shouldn't be messing with. In this system, she's probably as dangerous as Mother.

"I'm sorry, it won't happen again. But doesn't it bother your ideals that you, a woman, oversee it all?"

She shakes her head as if I've asked the silliest question. "No, no. Old Ma Gilligan always knows best," she says with practised ease and more than a hint of warning.

I guess she's used this phrase many times and on less pleasant occasions. "I'll make sure to remember that."

"Good. Now, you have the better of me. You know my name, but I still do not know who you are. You are obviously from out-of-system. And that wafer of yours certainly got my boys excited. Who are you? I refuse to call you the Green Djinn."

"Sam," I reply. "Sam Santana."

My assumed surname is one of the most common names in the galaxy. Difficult to track and obviously a pseudonym. But there's no way I'd be expected to give my real name. It seems to satisfy the old gal.

"So, Sam. Let us get down to business. You have been systematically robbing my banks over the last few months. You've taken millions of my credits, destroyed my property and become a big noise with the local populace. But most of all, you've been stealing my reserves of *Stuff.* You do know what a priceless commodity it is?"

I shake my head and tell the truth. "No idea. But I guessed that stealing it would get your attention."

"You wanted my attention? Why not simply come and knock on my door?"

"I'm not sure that would've worked. And, until I woke up, I didn't know you even existed."

"I do keep myself hidden. If the system found out a woman was in charge, there would be pandemonium. But you could've made contact any number of ways."

"Perhaps I should've come knocking at your door to hand in my CV, but I prefer more practical demonstrations. I thought I'd show you what I was capable of. My extensive abilities. How, for instance, I managed to steal from right under your nose. I figured you'd come to see me as an asset, rather than a threat. I'm an independent with no Cabal connections. So, you can be sure of my loyalty."

Old Ma Gilligan takes a sip at her ornate teacup and

places it back on the saucer, her fingers gently reorienting the cup to line up the pattern.

I can tell I've piqued her interest.

"You want to work for the Gilligans?" she says. "I must admit, I didn't see that coming. But let's say I agree to this. What will your role be with us, exactly?"

"You have this system sown up at a basic level. Which means that, when it comes to *other operations*—which I'm sure you're involved in—you don't have the personnel. You need to go outside, cap-in-hand to organisations like the Cabal, and pay big bucks for the expertise I can offer. Or worse, become indebted to them."

"That much is true. And what do you want in return for this service?"

I replace my own cup on its saucer and fix my eyes on hers. "Power."

"What kind of power?"

I sit back and use the mission brief. "Money and prestige were always my goals. I had hoped that when I attained those two things, I'd be happy. Content. But I have more money than I care to deal with, and, as you are no doubt aware, money is nothing compared to real power. In comparison to me, you are small and frail. I could easily get the better of you. But that won't happen, because you have power. A lot of it. I want something similar. I want a senior role in your organisation and my own group of operatives. I'll train them up, teach them what I know. I'll get them top-of-the-line wafers. I'll create a secret Gilligan army of sorts. And anything else you want from me."

"And in return you will give back all my *Stuff*?"

"Every ounce of it. Although I have a couple of caveats."

Old Ma Gilligan's milky green eyes narrow in the

brown skin of her wrinkled face. "Go on."

"The girl Sirena is to be released and allowed to leave this system, you will return my wafer to full functionality and explain to me exactly how I got caught. Agreed?"

She considers my words for a few moments and smiles. "I can do all those things, Sam." She offers me her tiny, ancient hand. "But I also have a caveat. That ship of yours. It, like you, has become a symbol of resistance to the lower castes. It cannot be seen again. It must be removed from this system."

"My ship is my base," I reply, relieved that *Little Bastard* is still in one piece and out of their hands. "It represents a large investment in money, time and effort. I'd be loath to lose it. You've seen what it can do. It can be an asset to us both."

She gives the barest shake of her head and I know the matter is not up for discussion. It seems an odd choice—a case of cutting her nose off to spite her face—but I don't know her well enough to judge.

"Give the ship to the girl Sirena," she says. "She can take the thing out of the system for good."

I might've gotten caught, but I'm finally starting to get somewhere. And there's a way to also help Sirena. I thought the old gal might have used her as a bargaining chip. I feel a terrific surge of relief at this news.

"Are we agreed?" she asks, her eyes narrowing.

"Almost," I reply. "But tell me… what is to stop you having me killed once I get the *Stuff* back to you?"

"Be careful, Sam Santana. You are close to insult. My word is my bond. Old Ma Gilligan never breaks it, not if the person is honourable in return. You are honourable, are you not?"

"Of course," I reply.

I'm lying through my teeth, and, under the gaze of

this peculiar matriarch, I can't help but feel guilty.

"Good, because those that are not honourable meet very sad ends. I hope I make myself clear?"

"Very clear," I reply, finally taking her hand and shaking it. Old Ma Gilligan is a dangerous woman. I will have to be very careful.

"From now on you will have access to all the accoutrements available to a member of my family," she continues. "Including property, prestige, and the power you crave so much. The details we can work out later, but do not forget that you are on probation, understand?"

I nod.

"I will be watching and assessing your every move."

"I wouldn't expect anything less."

Her fingers grip me tightly, her eyes becoming hard. "And please remember to never, ever cross me."

"That will not happen," I reply.

Old Ma Gilligan has no idea I'm a Galactic Secret Service agent. This is what Mother and I have been working towards for the last few months. I'll send Sirena away to safety and command *Little Bastard* to return and keep out of sight. I'm gonna need that ship to keep in contact with Mother, once my position inside the Gilligan Gang is cemented.

"And what about my wafer? I'll need it to contact my ship."

"There is nothing wrong with your wafer," the matriarch says quietly. "I do not like such things. I abhor them. However, I do see their usefulness. You will find that wafers do not work within five miles of my mansion. Once you leave, it will begin to function properly again."

"But that's impossible."

"Obviously not. When you have returned my *Stuff*, and have proved your loyalty over time, I will be willing to reveal certain things about me and my family. You will find out that we are not the backwater organisation that many portray us as."

"I look forward to gaining your full confidence," I say, wondering if this information has something to do with my mission.

She waves away my words with a bored hand. "You will be escorted to a safe distance from this mansion. Take the girl with you. Call your ship and unload the *Stuff*—before sending Sirena and that ship out of my system."

And with that, Old Ma Gilligan stands onto surprisingly sprightly legs and leaves.

TEN MINUTES LATER, I'M STANDING outside the mansion while an old-fashioned horse-drawn carriage is prepared. A door opens in an outhouse and Sirena emerges, flanked by two armed guards. My heart lurches at the sight of her. She's alive and uninjured.

"Thank space you're safe!" she shouts at the sight of me. She runs over and gives me a long hug. "I thought… I didn't know what to think."

"What happened?" I ask. "How come you were caught so quickly?"

"After I left your ship, I did exactly as you told me. But they seemed to know I was coming. Took me to a detention centre. Was that… was that attack caused by you?"

"Yeah," I reply, feeling a strong sense of relief. More than is professional. I've let this girl get to me.

"What are they going to do with us?"

"I've bargained your release. You're going home in my ship."

"I am?" Sirena's face lights up and she hugs me again. "Thank you, Sam, but… but what about you?"

"I'm staying here. I've got work to do."

"You're not coming with me?"

I shake my head. "I would if I could."

"Will you be safe?"

"I'll be fine. Don't worry about me."

We are ushered towards the carriage. I've never been close to a horse before. They are beautiful, mesmerising creatures. We climb inside, and Sirena sits beside me, her head nestling on my shoulder.

I must admit, having Sirena close feels good. I'm surprised by how much she means to me. But if I'm honest, I want her out of my head. I should never have slept with her. It wasn't like me to show such a total lack of self-control.

I wonder if I can blame this male body for the lapse. I want to, but I know it goes deeper than that. And without my wafer to curb my libido, I feel a strong desire for her.

We travel for twenty or so minutes and, slowly, the landscape reverts to the regular sandy dust of this desert system. Old Ma Gilligan's mansion must be an artificially maintained oasis. Seems like she likes to live in a bubble of her own making. A bubble I'm more than happy to burst, should I get the chance.

We arrive at a small spaceport. A phalanx of soldiers is waiting for us with a couple of transports and hefty-looking cannons of varying design and description.

My wafer suddenly jolts back into life.

I'd doubted Old Ma Gilligan's words, but they've been proved true. If this exclusion-tek became widely available, it would end the use of wafers for good. It's the kind of thing Mother and the Secret Service would love to get their hands on.

I put out a coded call for *Little Bastard*. The ship should've tracked me. I'm hoping it's somewhere in orbit.

Sam, are you alright? the ship says, and I've never felt so pleased to hear its impersonal tones. *I've been keeping a low profile and tracking you as ordered. Waiting for your command. You have been off the grid for many hours.*

Everything is fine and on-mission. I need you to come meet me, I reply.

I'm detecting anti-ship weaponry at your location.

No worries. I've entered the second phase of the mission and contacted the Gilligans. Come on down.

On it.

A crack of thunder, a rush of air and the small rounded ship is hovering a few feet in front of me. The horses whinny in alarm. The soldiers point their weapons towards the ship, as do all the larger batteries and ground-to-air lasers. They are taking no chances.

The airlock hisses open, but before I can enter, Sirena is grabbed by a soldier. He puts a blaster to her head.

"What the hell is this?" I blurt.

"The girl goes nowhere until we get our *Stuff*," says a voice behind me.

I turn to see a very important looking middle-aged man dressed in the purple and white of royalty, sitting on a vast hover-chair, his hands crossed over his voluminous belly. He's surrounded by guards and a mix of sycophants. I recognise him at once. A planetary governor. A big noise in this system. I can't remember his name. To be honest, the elite in this system all dress alike and look the same—down to the same-styled goatee and sunglasses.

"Is this what passes as trust in the Gilligans?" I growl.

He waves to one of his vassals, who brings him a flask. He snatches it off the woman as if she's not there and takes a swig. "Our word is our bond," he says with a bored sneer. "However, your word... is less than trustworthy. Get the *Stuff!*"

I shrug, wondering how deep this distrust of me goes, but I'm willing to play ball. I order *Little Bastard* to unload the special pallet I've been using as a storage space for the *Stuff,* and the auto-cargo mechanism dumps it onto the sand.

A group of inspection officers gives it the once-over and, satisfied, the pallet is picked up by one of the transports and taken away.

Sirena is thankfully released and comes over to me, tears in her eyes.

I command *Little Bastard* silently through my wafer: *I want you to plot a course to the Lalande system, The Anticipation Hab.*

On it.

I won't be going with you. Take the girl. When you've dropped her off, return here using stealth mode and await further orders. It is imperative to the success of this mission that you are not discovered. Do I make myself clear?

I cannot do that, Sam. Protocols forbid any non-agent to be alone on a Ceph-enabled ship. It is a direct contravention of the Secret Service code for encephalitic entities.

I know, that's why I'm enacting Override Quick-Kill Seven, Seven, Seven.

A pause. Followed by a few clicks.

As you wish.

The override is for emergencies only. Having a ceph aboard a mission ship is still new thing. It is only supposed to be used if the ceph starts to act irrationally. I feel guilty having to use it on *Little Bastard*, but its protocols are getting in the way.

For this mission to succeed, everything must appear above board. If I break a few protocols to do that, while also keeping Sirena safe, then all the better. The ceph can't possibly understand that. I must be allowed to act in the moment without hindrance.

Do you understand your objective? I ask the ship

Take the girl wherever she wants to go. After I've dropped her off, return here covertly. Wait for more orders.

Good.

I go to the airlock, followed by Sirena. "This is it," I say.

"Thanks, Sam… for doing this." She stands on tiptoes and kisses me on the lips. "I'll never forget."

A sudden surge from my wafer accompanied by intense pain and a bright, white flash.

SOMEWHERE, FROM FAR AWAY, I hear a voice calling a single name. *"Sam."*

I ignore it, preferring to stay where I am, resting in delicious slumber.

"You sure are cute lying there, even with your shaved head, but I'm afraid the time has come for us to part ways. Or, to put it another way, for me to kick you off this fantastic yet highly illegal ship of yours."

A girl's voice. Familiar.

"C'mon, Sam. Wakey, wakey!"

I open my eyes to see a petite girl standing over me. She's dressed in a tight-fitting, green-leather outfit that's vaguely militaristic in design. Padded and dangerous-looking. She wears a black belt emphasising her hips and thighs, from which hangs a loose blaster. Her hair is pinned back under a cap of sorts. She's beautiful. A name flits into my mind. "Sirena?"

"Yep, that's me. And you're Sam. Sam Santana, if I'm to believe it. Which I don't."

I push myself up and rub at my face. I've a few days growth of stubble. "How long have I been out? What did they do to me?"

"You mean, what did *I do* to you? Not as much as I could have, is the answer. But hey, maybe I'm getting soft in my old age. I've kept you unconscious since your surgery. I got your medibay to remove that wafer from your head—I needed it to give myself full control of this ship. Isn't that right, *Little Bastard?*"

"*That is right, Captain.*"

The metallic tones are also familiar, and yet I can't quite place them.

"Of course, I realised who and what you were as soon as I came out of hibernation… You starting to remember? If not, it's gonna ruin my big speech."

I'm groggy, but slowly, recollection of a sort returns. "Sirena? What the hell happened?"

"In answer to your question: *I happened.* Me. Call me a specialist, brought in by the Cabal when conventional means failed."

I rub my head, it too, is stubbly. "Where's my hair?"

"Like I said… *I removed your wafer.* Keep up, will you, or this will be no fun at all. Your hair will grow back, so no foul."

"I don't understand?"

"I saved your life, understand that! Old Ma Gilligan was quite pissed to find out who you really were—a Galactic Secret Agent. You think the Gilligans would have let you live if I'd left you in their hands? They'd have torn that wafer out of your head like they were ripping at a warm pizza. You owe me a quite a favour. But if anyone was going to get that wafer, that anyone was me."

The Gilligans!

My mind is still sluggish, but things start to come back to me in a slow, swirl of disjointed memories. Getting captured. Old Ma Gilligan. Sirena and *Little Bastard.* Robbing banks. Mother and the mission. I try and access my wafer, but there's nothing there. "You stole my goddamn wafer?"

"You really need to keep up, Sam. I was after this ship of yours, remember? As soon as I set my eyes on it and you, I knew what it was and who you were. A ceph-ship for a fully-fledged Galactic Secret Agent."

"You… you're working for the Cabal?" I croak, unable to properly believe I've been duped, rubbing at a dead arm.

Sirena shrugs. "They're my clients but I'm more of an independent. I'm my own boss and that's how I like it. But you know what they say? *It takes a thief to catch a thief.* And, shit! I caught a helluva lot more. You think it was an accident that I turned up in that safe you stole? That was my idea. I sussed where you'd hit next and made my plans. Although I was nearly too clever for my own good. I never figured you'd blast your way inside with a goddamn ship's laser. But, hey, you need luck in this job and I've always had that in plentiful supply."

I can't believe it.

Is this what being a Galactic Secret Agent is like? To constantly be made a sap of? First Mother, then Pistol Whip and now Sirena. I stare at the girl, or whoever she is, unable to fathom what she did to me. A basic honey-trap that this dim male body was unable to resist. "How could I have been so stupid?"

"Don't beat yourself up, Sam. You weren't a complete chump. I used a nano-pheromone on you. A highly complex psycho-emotio-stimulant of my own devising delivered by my hardworking sweat glands and pointed in your general direction. I call it *Tang.* It took me years to perfect—and to bio-match it to my own DNA. Tang is also enhanced by touch and, if you remember, you did give me a rather fun *touching.* I hope you haven't forgotten?"

I shake my head with sullen irritation. I may be embarrassed, but I'm also impressed. I was quite something back on my home planet of Plenty, but this girl is beyond anything I could've imagined. The creation of her Tang is also well outside my tek abilities. Nevertheless, I've been a fool and an arrogant fool at that.

But it explains everything.

Why I was so keen to keep the girl safe, to protect her from Mother and the Service. Why I ignored *Little Bastard*'s warnings. And why I risked myself and my ship to get her back after she was supposedly captured.

"No one is immune to my Tang," Sirena continues with pride. "It works on most gender types, *eventually*. You lasted a helluva lot longer than most suckers. I thought you'd be mine after our special time together, but you still threw me off your ship. I was disappointed, but impressed."

I wonder what Sirena has planned for me next. I'm alive, and wearing a skinsuit, which is a good sign, although I sense there's more to come from this conversation. I may be groggy, but I'm still fast and twice her size. Yet my strong sense of self-preservation is telling me to make no sudden moves. The blaster she has at her side is just a little too casual and I doubt I'd be able to overpower her as easily as I did when she came at me with the knife.

That was a clever play.

I'm forced to sit back and find out what she has in store for me. But I ain't going down without a fight, that's for sure. "I threw you off the ship for your own good," I spit.

"That's what I guessed. You sure were sweet about it."

"And what happened next—you getting captured?"

Sirena gives me a brief, but pleased smile. "I informed the Gilligans of my arrival as soon as I stepped off your ship and told them to make a big stink catching me. To take me to a local detention centre… and to wait. I was pretty sure you'd come after me. I banked on it."

"And I literally walked into the trap. How did you contact the Gilligans so quickly?"

"That was easy. I also have a top-range wafer. Minus any Slash-Stak components—yes, I know all about the Galactic Secret Service wafer tek. There was something fishy about Slash-Stak from the start. Luckily, I designed my own wafer. It also possesses a stealth mode. It fooled your mediscan, your ceph and, most of all, it fooled you. All part of the disguise."

"So, you didn't feel anything for me?" I hear myself saying. The words sound glum and resentful. Like some rejected teen. I regret them at once.

"Oh dear. It really was your first time, wasn't it?" she says with a surprised rise of her eyebrows.

"Forget it," I say. "If your job was to catch me, what was all that nonsense with Old Ma Gilligan? Why the interrogation?"

"The original plan was to catch you and your ship. Hand both over to the Gilligan Gang, complete with all the *Stuff* you stole. The *Stuff* that got the Cabal's panties in such a bunch."

"What changed? You didn't fall for me, did you?"

A brief flicker in her impenetrable exterior. "You wish. But I did fall for this goddamn ship of yours. Its ceph is gonna make me rich. I can't wait to sell it to the highest bidder. Hell, I could even retire. Or I might even take it for myself… I haven't quite decided. But I couldn't just steal it, like any other ship. I needed your cooperation. I led you to believe you were on-mission. That things were going your way. And Old Ma Gilligan was more than pleased to go along, although the dried up old bitch was set on killing you. But she's not lived as long as she has by crossing the Cabal."

And then I remember. "I disabled *Little Bastard's* security protocols."

"You sure did. That's what I was waiting for. Everything else up to that point was just dressing. Just a way to put you at ease. I also knew that I'd need that wafer of yours to take full control—that's the reason for the surgery. Overall, a great result. Everyone is happy. I got what I wanted, the Gilligans got back their *Stuff*, and the Cabal are very pleased with me. The only problem… *there's one loose end.*"

"I'm guessing it's the reason why I'm wearing this skinsuit," I say, rubbing the life back into my arms.

"Yeah, I'm putting you out the airlock as soon as we drop out of voidspace. I've gotten *Little Bastard* to take us to a suitable spot. If you're lucky, a passing ship, of which there should be many, should pick up your beacon."

"You're not going to kill me?"

Sirena's hand plays with the blaster hanging loosely from her belt. "Let me be honest, I like you, Sam. In my profession, that doesn't happen often. When I first laid my eyes on you, I thought you were one of those pretty guys who knows he can use and abuse everyone around them. The same type of macho prick I've had to deal with all my life. But you surprised me. You're tender and, by the way you stormed that detention centre, you're goddamn ruthless and single-minded. I like that in a guy. So, I'm breaking my rule this once."

"*We will soon be dropping out of voidspace, Captain,*" *Little Bastard* announces over the com.

In a single motion of blurred fingers, Sirena's blaster appears in her hand. "Forget any half-assed ideas about fighting your way out of this," she warns me plainly. "You've been beaten, fair and square. Accept it and be advised that my blaster is set to kill—so no sudden moves. Now get up and head for the airlock."

She's right. I have been easily beaten. I do as I'm told, with Sirena walking a few paces behind me. There's nothing else to do. I've been outsmarted—at least I'm getting out of this alive. But what life will I have left, even if I'm picked up by another ship? Losing *Little Bastard* will mean my career with the Service is over. There's no way they'd ever forgive me. I'll have to disappear, spending the rest of my life looking over my goddamn shoulder.

Shit!

Sirena tells me to grab a helmet and, after I zip it into place, she throws me a short-range beacon. "Goodbye, Sam, and good luck. I think you're gonna need it." She steps back and the inner-airlock door closes.

"I want you to open the airlock as soon as we exit voidspace," I hear Sirena command *Little Bastard* over the com.

"On it."

I stand to face the outer door, staring at the swirl of voidspace through a small circular porthole. The airlock is not depressurised, which means that as soon as the door is opened, I'll be forcibly jettisoned into outer space.

"Exiting the void in three, two, one…"

A jolt and I prepare myself for the airlock to open. Nothing.

"I said, open the airlock and get the hell out of here!" Sirena shouts.

"I'm afraid I can't do that," *Little Bastard* replies.

It's then that I notice a glint of light outside the airlock porthole—a glint that resolves into a vast battleship and six cruisers, all armed to the teeth.

"YOU'VE GOT TO BE KIDDING *me!"* Sirena shrieks over the com.

A crackle and a familiar voice in my helmet. *"Ah, Quick-Kill. Your ship informs me that you are still alive. Well done."*

The voice belongs to Mother. Another crackle and Mother's voice booms out over the speakers of the ship. *"Bluetongue, you are under arrest for multiple murders, for working with the Cabal, for the attempted theft of a Galactic Secret Service ship, the theft and misuse of a Galactic Secret Service wafer, and for being a persistent and annoying little bitch."*

I hear Sirena shout and then the thump of her impotent blaster as she fires at the airlock door. But airlocks are built to survive. A gasp and a mumble and everything goes silent. The inner airlock door opens to reveal Sirena lying unconscious on the floor.

"Don't remove your helmet, Sam," Little Bastard warns me over the com. *"The air is contaminated. Please take the prisoner to the cell and await further instructions."*

"Mother?" I say. "What the hell is going on? And who is Bluetongue?"

No reply.

I kick Sirena's blaster away and sling her slim form over my shoulder before dumping her in the cell.

I'm shocked at how such a small woman can be so

dangerous, and yet, the same could've been said about me. Until I joined the Service, that is. I've been used and abused since day one. And suddenly, I feel myself trapped between Sirena and Mother. Sirena is closer to me, *to who I am inside,* to what I've wanted to be my whole life. Mother is my enforced employer. Someone who, it seems, is content to dupe and use me as an expendable pawn. I realise I'm probably still suffering from the effects of Sirena's Tang, but if I was able to make a choice, I'd blast those ships out there into pieces and void jump this dangerous woman away to safety. Despite everything, she didn't kill me when she had the chance. That means a lot to Quick-Kill.

I'll never forget it.

I close the door and I'm immediately buffeted by the air-con system.

"The air is now breathable," Little Bastard informs me, and I remove my flimsy helmet, placing it in my belt.

"You were in on this?" I shout, angrily.

"Yes, Sam," the ceph answers. *"We are now docking with Mother's personal ship. She has instructed me to not discuss the mission with you until you have given your debrief."*

The hiss of the airlock opening, and the ship is suddenly full of heavily armed soldiers. One grabs me, and I'm roughly escorted away.

A short while later, I find myself in a small office not unlike the one I was brought to when I was first captured by the Galactic Secret Service. This time, I'm twice the size and the chair I'm sitting in is too small for me.

The door slides open and in walks Mother.

She's wearing the same revealing black skinsuit, but the tired features of her face have disappeared. The skin is plump around her eyes and mouth, and her lips are fuller, although the skin is reddened and peeling—the result of a recent juvo-treatment. I wonder if the treatment is for some future mission or plain vanity. Either way, I feel my hackles rise at the sight of her.

"I'm betting you're pissed at me right now," she says with no preamble.

"You could say that!" I snap back. "You've played me for a chump for the last time. I'm done with you and the goddamn Service. I've had it."

Mother smiles, lines showing around her lips where the juvo-treatment hasn't quite yet taken. "No. I'm afraid it doesn't work like that. I told you exactly what was expected of you after you were recruited. Your service is lifelong. You want to end your it? Well, you can guess what will happen."

Mother's eyebrows furrow the briefest amount—but it's enough for me to realise she's not making an idle threat.

"This is not what I signed up for. No way!"

"Perhaps you've forgotten that if it wasn't for the Service, you'd be dead? We saved you and gave you a chance at a brand-new life. Doesn't that mean anything?"

She's right. I'm as trapped as I ever was. "Okay, I get it." I wave my spatula hands over the immense bulk of my body. "You did this to me. Turned me into a goddamn man. I accepted it and got on with the job. But the job, as far as I can see, is to sit back while the Service makes a fool out of me. To keep me in the dark. To trust that damn ceph ship of mine more than you trust me."

"I'm sorry you feel like that. But we didn't set out to deceive you. Your mission parameters were bona-fide. To get noticed by the Gilligan Gang. To infiltrate them and to wait for further orders… and you almost did that. Which was good work. But we didn't count on the girl."

I flush at how easy it was for Sirena to get to me. "She used some kind of psycho-emotio sex stimulant," I say. "Even your ceph ship didn't detect that or the fact she had a hidden wafer."

"There is no shame in being fooled by Bluetongue—hell, she's already duped me and the entire Secret Service."

"Go on," I reply, intrigued.

"What I'm about to tell you, is between you and me. It is not to be discussed with other agents. The girl you know as Sirena Jayla… she's an ex-Secret Service agent who went by the codename of *The Bluetongue Lizard*. A name we should've taken more notice of—a deceitful creature."

I'm surprised, but more than that, I'm shocked. "Ex-agent? I thought you told me agents were not allowed to leave the Service?"

Mother produces a cigarette from somewhere on her desk and leans back. She flicks an old-fashioned lighter and puts the end into its yellowy-blue flame, inhaling deeply. "That much is true," she says, snapping the lighter shut. "When we recruited her, we soon realised we had something special. Soon, Bluetongue became one of our top operatives. But we were being played from the start. It's my opinion that she let herself get caught—that she played up to us from the very beginning. Using the Service to get inside information and access to personnel and tek. After her disappearance, we lost a slew of agents and other operatives. All due to her. But it's more than that. Bluetongue has a personal vendetta against the Service and particularly against me. She's tried to kill me on many occasions."

"So why didn't you get me to keep her locked up on my ship? Why let the thing play out like it did?"

"You were not the only one who was fooled by

her, Quick-Kill. Bluetongue's identity has changed many times. We've found it impossible to track her. To Bluetongue, a male or female body is just a shell, a covering for the dark intellect that lies inside. We did a security check on Sirena Jayla. To us, she was who she seemed, a spoilt brat whose real name was Alice Farquhar. Bluetongue's back story was immaculate. Although we now know she killed the actual Alice Farquhar and took her place."

"What twigged you to who she really was?" I ask, feeling relieved and surprised that this 'super-agent' let me live. And then I realise… she knew I was an agent. She knew I'd been gender-reoriented. That perhaps it was against my will, and that I resented what was done to me.

Was that why she didn't kill me?

Maybe I reminded her of herself? Could it be that simple?

"Ceph ships are new and highly illegal," Mother continues, taking another deep drag on her cigarette. "When you initiated the security override on *Little Bastard*, as you so lovingly renamed it, we were automatically informed. Certain protocols were enacted. Updated protocols that Bluetongue knew nothing about—and that's how we caught her. She thought she'd managed to break the ceph's programming. But *Little Bastard* was still working for us. You must understand that you were expendable in this equation."

I give a reluctant nod of my head. "Yeah, that makes sense, I suppose."

"To get Bluetongue back under our control is… well, let's just say today has been long waited for."

"So, what's next?"

Mother fixes me with her beady eyes. "A new mission

has just come up."

"Don't tell me, it's another backwater operation, right?"

Mother smiles. "Not this time. You've helped bring in The Bluetongue Lizard and you survived. That's big. You deserve a reward."

"A mission in the Key, perhaps?" I ask hopefully.

"I can do better than that."

"Better? What do you mean?"

"This assignment is on Gaia Prime."

"The capital?"

Mother nods. "You did good, Quick-Kill."

The itching in my forearm turns into sudden, intense pain. I look down to see the muscles bulging.

"What's a matter?" Mother asks, coming towards me.

Searing pain and my forearm splits open to reveal a small blaster connected to the bones underneath. My arm jerks up to point the gun at Mother and I'm powerless to stop it, blood spilling out in a torrent. I look up into Mother's eyes and we both know it's too late.

A look of defeat crosses her features. "Oh shi—"

The blaster shoots her in the head, which disintegrates into an explosion of blood and brains.

"And good riddance to bad rubbish" says Sirena's voice in my head. *"Nice work."*

I'm too stunned to reply.

"You thought I was after Little Bastard?" Sirena continues gleefully. *"Well think again, this has only ever been about Mother. About getting revenge on her and the Secret goddamn Galactic Service. What it's always been about. About what they do in the name of security. And you've played your part magnificently."*

I can't believe it. Sirena is talking to me through my wafer—but she removed it, *didn't she?*

The blaster returns to hide itself back amongst the flesh of my forearm and the nano-fibres of my skin suit close over it, stemming any further blood loss.

"The shaved head was a distraction," Sirena continues. *"I didn't remove your wafer, instead the surgery was to implant the blaster. I knew the first thing Mother would do after I was supposedly captured would be to give you a debrief. It took all my wits to make her think I'd finally made a misstep. But it was Mother who messed up. Fatally. Why else do you think I kept you alive? Although trying to stay alive is gonna be your next priority. Goodbye Jane… and good luck."*

A large explosion rocks the ship, and it yaws, throwing me and the dead body of Mother onto the opposite wall. Another explosion and the artificial gravity disappears.

Little Bastard spins past the porthole, lasers and mag-rails blazing. Another explosion and the depressurisation alarm sounds. I grasp at my helmet and zip it into place. More explosions and the office door blows inwards. The whole room ruptures, breaking apart. I desperately grab onto the leg of the desk, but it disintegrates, and I'm flung into space.

I'm a passenger, flying through the silent darkness with no ability to check my forward motion.

I watch *Little Bastard*, tearing into the bigger ships before diving onto the Service battleship, its lasers and other weapons firing furiously… and then the tiny ship disappears. The same manoeuvre I pulled back in the Hejaz system.

No one will be able to follow her. She's gone.

Sirena, or Bluetongue as she's also known, played me for a fool after all. Played us all for fools. She didn't keep me alive out of some half-assed sentimentality. No. It was all part of her plan. And yet, as I see a rescue barge coming towards me, I no longer feel duped. Instead, I'm filled with a strong sense of admiration, combined with an equal sense of purpose.

One day, I don't know where or when, I'm going to catch up with Sirena and… I ponder for a few moments. Perhaps I'll bring her in, doing what Mother failed to do, or maybe... *Who knows?*

PART FOUR
SIRENA

THE CRUSIE SHIP, SURE SPLENDID, slips out of the void as smoothly as a diamond from a velvet pouch. No harsh jolt like with Secret Service ships, which are built for speed without any thought for comfort. No. This ship is all about luxury. A luxury that I've come to respect over the last few days.

Begrudgingly.

I'm not a fan of ostentation. The closest I ever came to that affectation was showing off with my Dodge Charger. Damn! I still miss that hunk of souped-up metal. I suppose it's still where I left it, parked outside Angie's Apartment on the planet Plenty, hundreds of light-years away, before my altercation with the Cabal and that 'fortuitous rescue' by Mother.

I came aboard *Sure Splendid* as just another high-roller passenger with the intention of keeping my head down. To stay in my cabin for a week or so, until it became time to act. Although I let myself occasionally venture out—in disguise of course.

I'm glad I did.

This is a place of treats. Anything the pampered rich could ever want is available on request. I'll admit, I've indulged myself. Why shouldn't I? What I'm up to might just get me killed. Quick-Kill Jane has had enough of being pushed around by the Galactic Secret Service—and everyone else for that matter. This is my operation. My scheme. A make or break mission that relies on nobody else.

Just how I like it. The only problem? I'm still a man. My plan meant I had to act quickly, and a gender re-orientation is something that takes time and money.

My disguise is nothing special. The fact that the human race now exists in its trillions means that face-recognition is only practical on a planet-to-planet basis, yet I'm taking no chances. I've chosen the most common features. Light brown skin, brown hair and a nondescript nose and jaw combination. Not that I need it for my trip—the company that owns *Sure Splendid* prides themselves on the discreet nature of its cruises. What happens aboard these top-of-the-range cruise ships, stays aboard these top-of-the-range cruise ships.

As to my plan? Part of it is the planet that now hovers somewhere below like a cloudy white, blue and green-streaked marble. Anybody who's anybody comes here once in their lives. To look at where it all started. Although I'm intrigued, sightseeing ain't the main item on my agenda.

"If everyone can turn to the viewing port," booms a slightly bored voice over deep, sumptuous-sounding speakers. *"Then we will begin."*

I stand shoulder to shoulder with the well-heeled and their hangers-on in a large ballroom-like viewing room. A massive curve of field-strengthened glass stretches from floor to roof. Presently, the glass is dulled, awaiting the big reveal. I'm excited, although I'm forced to quell a strong desire to blow the glass and all these elitist rich twats out into space with a single shot of my laser. I pat my thigh out of habit and sigh, forgetting I ain't got my favourite weapon. Or any of my normal kit, including a wafer. This liner is sown up tighter than the Galactic

Emperor's arsehole. But with what I'm planning, I won't need anything other than my wits—which I have in abundance.

First, I have to get myself off this ship and towards my destination… more on that later.

I've always been irked by the rich and their insecure need to flash their status in one gaudy display after another. It was the same back on Plenty, which also had its 'higher echelon'—a self-obsessed elite overly keen to enforce their own stature at the expense of good taste. Here, they're just members of the crowd.

When I came aboard, I expected many questions about who I was and where I was from. Or what nobby family I belonged to. I had a full back story ready to be told, but everyone I met was tight-lipped. I guess they were worried they might meet someone better off than themselves, someone richer, someone more-connected. Which suited me down to the ground—I ain't one for small-talk, especially with these jumped up creeps.

Waiters flit amongst the crowd of nearly seven-hundred people with not a single robo in sight. Prestige means the exclusivity of human servants only.

I don't want to be impressed, but I am.

"Human civilisation has come a long way from those first pioneering days," the booming voice continues. *"From a difficult beginning, humankind finally conquered space, learning to bend it at will. And with that knowledge, we leapt from our home-world to colonise not just our own system, but many systems encompassing most of the known galaxy. We must never, ever forget where it all started…*

"Behold… Earth! The third rock from the sun."

The glass clears and there she is. Ancient Earth. A white, ice-covered ball marbled with hints of blues and greens. Behind her, sits the half-crescent of the Moon.

It's peculiar that the Moon is the more recognisable artefact of the birthplace of my race. Her face remaining mostly unchanged since the dawn of history. Seeing her hanging there, in the empty void of space, sure makes my cold heart beat a little faster. Not just because she's achingly pretty…

Sure Splendid glides closer to Earth, hovering over the still-green African continent. The only feature I recognise.

The rest of the planet is hidden under swathes of ice.

"The glaciers that cover two-thirds of the Earth's surface, although breathtakingly beautiful, were not present when civilisation began," the voice continues. *"The coming of the Great Ice Age was the spur humankind needed to escape from the confines of planet-living and to…"*

I've seen and heard enough. My plan doesn't depend on me being here aboard this ship. It's just a starting place. But this is a once-in-a-lifetime moment, so why the hell not?

I take a cocktail from a passing waiter, down it in one, and make my way out of the impressive room, pushing through the throng of rich shmucks who are also coming to the realisation that Ancient Earth, regardless of all its history, is just another planet. And a rather dull-looking one at that.

I enter the outer corridor and head towards the stern.

Sure Splendid is enormous, built to encompass the massive void-engines taking up nearly two-thirds of the cruise-ship's length. 'The bigger the void-engine, the smoother the jump' is how physics puts it. These engines are ridiculous. A game of 'mine is bigger than yours' played by all the cruise companies.

With Ancient Earth outside the viewing port, and the crew catering to their main event, I'm left pretty much on my own.

Just how I planned it.

The ship has only one deck, accessed by a carriage system that links every part of the ship to every other part. I'm under no time-constraint, but it makes my job easier when I find an open car, ready and waiting for me. I slip inside and speak my destination. A few minutes later, the transport hums to a pleased stop and I get out in the rear Recreation Section, which sits just in front of the engines—lending fantastic views of the lethal void-field that shimmers and twists in hypnotic purple hues. But like I said… I'm not here to sight-see. I quickly walk to my destination—a large portal housing locked double doors marked 'Emergency Only'.

Disabling the locking mechanism is child's play and I barely miss a stride before slipping inside. Here are the life-rafts. A range of docked ships of various sizes and capacities. I hurry down a couple of levels until I find what I'm looking for—the largest ships with the biggest engines, designed to take up to fifty people. I slide into one of the many available skinsuits, zip a helmet in place and command its systems to cool me down. I switch off the body-temp warnings and a blast of cold air hits me in the face, making me shiver—a necessary discomfort for what is coming next.

I hunt around for a booster pack and strap it on. I'm gonna need this later, if everything goes to plan.

I hard-lock the docking clamp, power up the first lifeboat and switch off the auto-pilot, before entering my pre-calculated nav co-ords. Numbers and symbols zip cross the navcom before flashing green. I engage the engines at full-power and swiftly exit the lifeboat before the doors lock in place.

One down. Twenty more to go.

I jog down the line, quickly doing the same with the rest of the lifeboats, the rumble of their combined engines reverberating through the superstructure. The lifeboats all sit upon a master davit controlled by the bridge of the *Sure Splendid*. A single device enabling the captain to launch the escape ships in multiples, should it be needed.

And it's going to be needed very soon.

I get inside the last ship and rummage through its lockers for a toolbox—an emergency kit issued on all life-boats. Metal and heavy. I jam the box between the double-skinned airlock doors and engage the closing mechanism. The doors smash into it, grinding impotently. I make my way through rows of seats and sit down in the pilot's chair, strapping myself in, shivering from the decreasing temperature in my suit. My cold fingers push the power controls to max, the vibration of the engines shaking the lifeboat that sits clamped to the master davit with all the other powered-up escape ships. I sit back and wait, my eyes watching the shimmering star-field through the small pilot's window.

Sure Splendid begins to yaw, imperceptibly at first, but the momentum slowly increases—pushed by the firing engines of the many lifeboats fastened tightly to the ship. The com screen flashes with a 'shutdown' from the bridge. Good luck with that—the captain can't countermand my pre-programmed in-ship 'captains,' and I hard-locked all the docking clamps.

Sweet.

I turn on the boat's navcom and watch as the enormous cruiser twists into a slow spin.

The captain has no choice. He can't have any problems during the cruise's main event. In any other scenario, engineers would be sent down to come fix this, to manually power down the 'malfunctioning escape ships'. Not now, with Ancient Earth hanging outside the window and all those rich nobs watching.

No fucking way.

Depressurisation sirens sound outside, loud and blaring. Thirty seconds later, the air-shield is deactivated, and the master-davit released. My ship is ejected into space with all the other lifeboats that power away. Escaping air from the jammed airlock buffets me. I'm safe inside my tightening—and now freezing—skinsuit. The captain is likely to scan the boats for any life signals. Jamming the doors open gives the impression of a faulty door and the depressurisation cools the interior into a dead zone. I'm taking no chances. This plan will only work if everyone thinks the lifeboats are empty. My heat profile from this now ice-cold skinsuit will be low enough to be unrecognised. The auto-SOS begins to initialise, and I hit the kill-switch—I don't want anyone tracking me after I'm on my way. Not so the other ships, whose SOS signals blink on the navcom.

Everything goes silent apart from the rumble of the lifeboat's engine and the chattering of my teeth.

I watch Ancient Earth slide silently past, some forgotten ice-covered continent half-in, half-out of shadow below. A few of the other escaping ships are caught by the gravity well and spiral into the atmosphere to burn up. The remaining boats, including my own, cruise past, their engines firing to take them on a new trajectory, the one I programmed.

The cold is a strangling force, freezing my limbs, trapping me in a livid shroud of ice.

The captain of *Sure Splendid* will have forgotten about the lifeboat problem and be more concerned with damage control—and keeping all those rich twats happy.

It's unlikely he or she will be still monitoring the life-rafts. But I hang on as long as I can, curled into a frozen ball in the pilot's chair.

After the allotted time of one hour, thirteen minutes, counted down minute by minute, second by second, a red helmet-light warns me my body heat is the lowest point I can let it get to, and the suit blasts me with much-needed, glorious heat.

It's another twenty minutes before I stop shivering. Finally able to move, I make my way to the back of the ship and remove the smashed toolbox that's blocking the twin airlock doors. They close with a reassuring hiss. Ten minutes later, the air and temperature levels are in the green and I'm able to zip off my helmet.

The chairs in this life-boat also double as bunks. I tilt one back and lie down, commanding my suit to put me into hibernation. A prolonged sleep function built into most suits these days—should it ever be needed. I tell it to wake me if there is an emergency and, if not, to wait the thirty-six point seven hours it will take to reach my destination.

MY EYES HAVE ONLY JUST closed, it seems, when I'm woken from slumber by my pre-programmed alert.

"What the hell is it?" I ask, still half-asleep and expecting the metallic tones of *Little Bastard* in reply. Then I remember where I am and what happened to my stolen ceph-ship. "Shit."

Pushing myself up from my makeshift bunk, I go find the single head and take a much-needed toilet break. Afterwards, I root around for rations and discover enough food to last me half a goddamn lifetime. For simple survival food, it sure is tasty. I chow down as much as I can, unsure when I'll be eating again, and go in search of the emergency oxygen. If my plan is to work, I'm gonna need a supplementary tank or two. I locate the O2 at the rear. The readouts tell me they've been recently serviced. Each holds five hours' worth of air. Cut that in half for the exertion that's involved, and I've still got bags of time, which is necessary, because I'm certainly not planning on sitting on my butt. I strap two tanks together and drop back into the pilot's seat.

The ship is eerily silent, apart from a few groans and murmurs. Outside the small viewing port, the Moon has grown large. A quick look at the navcom reveals thirteen other life-boats silently flying with me. In precisely seventeen minutes, the engines will automatically kick back into life for a landing.

I won't be joining them.

I replace my helmet, turn off the environmental controls and instruct my suit to cool me down again. The ship is supposed to be empty, and a warm human is a dead giveaway. I sit back and shiver. Seventeen minutes suddenly seems like an age. I have no choice but to sit and wait, my mind replaying the events after Mother's assassination by Sirena, aka the Bluetongue Lizard.

::

"We're taking you out of the field, understand?" the agent who called himself 'Chinatown' said.

I was in the same interrogation room I'd been in for the last six weeks. Don't ask me where. Some hidden Service compound is my guess. And not a place you'd want to go visit anytime soon, not if you wanted to keep your sanity. "You mean it's over? You're done with me?"

"We've thrown everything we can at you. We never believed you were involved in Bluetongue's plot to kill Mother, despite what we put you through. But there's a process to these things. You didn't squeeze the trigger personally. You were played like we all were." Chinatown pulled a pained expression. "And Mother was sloppy."

I didn't want to agree with the guy who'd made my life hell over the length of my interrogation, yet he was right. There was no way Mother should have allowed me onto her ship, never mind into her office. It was her fatal mistake. Bluetongue had rigged me with a hidden-blaster that had blown Mother's head clean off her shoulders.

"Bluetongue played us all for fools," Chinatown continued. "Now the bitch has a ceph-ship."

"How did she break its programming?"

Chinatown grimaced. It was pretty much the

same question he'd been asking me over the time of my interrogation. "If we knew that then…" The man shrugged. Wide shoulders coming to rest with a sigh. "You know we've had to ground the entire ceph-fleet?"

"I guessed as much. Until you know how my ship was compromised, it might happen again. The entire fleet is vulnerable to Sirena, to Bluetongue, and anyone else she gives her ceph-breaking tek to. What happens next?"

"Without our cephs, we're pulling everybody back in to work on data and ops, sifting through all info and Intel until we find Bluetongue. Manually, if we have to. We're still in the process of dusting off our old computers. It will take time, but we're gonna get her."

I nodded noncommittedly. "And this includes me? I'm heading towards a goddamn desk job?"

"Only our top agents are allowed out into the field."

"You think they would've faired any better against Bluetongue than I did?" I asked, wanting to know the answer. I was still cut up about what happened and my part in it. Sirena had played me for a sap, taking not only my virginity in this re-gendered body, but stealing my goddamn ship. I was angry and wanted revenge.

Chinatown gave me another shrug. "You're still alive, which in my book puts you right up there, so let's hope so, yeah?"

"And my wafer?"

He gave me a curt shake of his head. "We're also rethinking our reliance on that tek, especially after what you found out on Old Ma Gilligan's farm. It won't matter to you either way—you don't need no military-grade wafer to operate a goddamn desk."

"You know who I am. What I can do. You think I'm gonna work well as an office-jockey?"

"No, I don't. But you understand the reasons. You've been compromised. Even with the all-clear, there's still a shadow hanging over you."

"How long am I expected to sit on my ass?"

"From what I've been told, it's for the duration. Until we smoke out that bitch once and for all."

I wanted to argue, but I was tired of talking. Tired of everything.

"I'll try and keep you in the loop with any developments. An overview, that's all. Nothing specific. There is, however, some good news. Your agent profile shows a desire to spend time in the Key. That's where we're sending you."

::

A bright flash alerts me to the firing of thrusters. One of the lifeboats ahead is beginning its descent. Followed by another and then another.

My heart thumps in my ears.

It's at times like these, that I wish I had a wafer. A quick thought and an adjusted neurotransmitter or two would calm me right down. But to be honest, working completely on my own, without any extra cerebral help, has certainly concentrated my mind. There's something to be said for the power of ice-cold fear. I did consider raiding the ship's medikit to get myself a handful of relaxants and blockers, but now, more than ever, I need my wits about me.

I'm guessing the captain of *Sure Splendid* will have alerted the Sol security station on the Moon about their renegade lifeboats.

Not that they wouldn't be aware of them already…

The Sol System is a no-go-area for all shipping due

to the number of religious cranks, tourists and others who are drawn to this system like flies to shit. After an unlicensed nuclear blast—connected to one of the many doomsday cults that still proliferate the galaxy—took out one of Mars's two moons, giving it a beautiful, if not a slightly radioactive ring, the Sol System was made off-limits for good. 'Preserving ancient heritage' was how it was put. Over the last six months, since Bluetongue disappeared, security and activity in this ancient system had increased, piquing my interest. The only ship allowed to come and make its once in a year visit was *Sure Splendid,* due to the serious amount of clout the rich had over everything in the galaxy.

I'm hoping the malfunctioning, 'empty' lifeboats will be ignored and allowed to land. But I'll admit, it's a gamble.

I wait and watch further engine flashes, keeping a close eye on my own position. I'm running as stealthily as I can—which is difficult for a lifeboat designed solely to be noticed. It's my bet that if the ships are being monitored, Moonbase will only be looking for auto-SOS signals, which means I should be ignored. I'll have to use my engines to land, though. Good thing I've a plan in place that should ensure my 'touchdown' doesn't receive any undesirable consequences.

The first lifeboat manoeuvres into a descending orbit, the others following.

This mission was always going to be make-or-break. Here, now, I'm very much in the 'break' part of my plan. Using its gas thrusters, I push my ship into an asymmetrical spin, taking it out of the expected descent envelope. I strap myself back into the chair and—when the ship twists into the right position—blow the airlock. The escaping air gives the ship more than a gentle nudge.

To any observer, casual or otherwise, it will appear the lifeboat is out of control. I check the navcom. My ship is now heading for a crash on the Moon surface.

A landing I'm banking everything on… including my life.

Tense minutes pass. The other lifeboats perform their expected change in trajectory, bringing them in low over the Sea of Tranquillity. I've done my homework on the Moon. For a mostly empty planetoid, it sure has a rich number of names.

The other ships are programmed to head towards certain beacons. Once landed, they are to await rescue. If this was a real emergency and these boats were filled with survivors, those in the nearest base would be alerted to send a rescue mission. This is not the case with these 'malfunctioning' lifeboats. I'm hoping they'll be given little or no attention.

Hope ain't a mission variable I'm familiar with.

But it is what it is.

The Moon was an important staging post for interstellar travel back in the day. After the development of void travel, and the deteriorating climate on Ancient Earth, its importance dwindled. There was a brief hundred-year period of colonisation, but with other earth-like exo-planets being discovered almost daily, those colonists left for greener pastures. And who in their right mind would want to live on such an airless, if not beautiful, ball of dust? Only a single base is left, situated on the North Pole—Moonbase. The centre of security keeping the Sol system safe, which left quite a few empty facilities, hangars, mines and long-abandoned colonies. One of which is my destination, although I'm not fool enough to land right on top of it.

And landing—of a sort—is my plan. If I can get this

ship back under control in time. Before this mission, those 'ifs' didn't seem too many. Here, in this moment, I feel they're all stacked against me.

The first lifeboat spins on its axis and initiates a full engine burn and explodes in a flash of white. If I wasn't strapped into the pilot's chair so tightly, I would've jumped right out of it.

Shit!

Not part of the plan!

I bring up the navcom, frustrated at the lack of tactical readouts.

Missiles. A whole host of them.

The navcom is not sophisticated enough to locate them all. Meanwhile, another boat disappears into a blinding ball of white.

My fingers pound at the basic navcom, programming a set of avoidance measures into the flight computer. I watch the screen, ready to hit the initiate button. One by one, the remaining lifeboats around me are destroyed. My eyes search frantically for the final missile—the one aimed at me.

It's not there.

I check again, but nothing.

Almost against my own expectations, my plan goddamn worked—although I've yet to get this ship down to the surface.

It's possible my ship was missed by Moonbase. Maybe they don't know I'm here at all? But I can't bank on that. It's equally possible they decided not to waste a missile to blow a ship that's already on a crash trajectory. If that's the case, they will be expecting my ship to do just that… crash.

The upshot? Quick-Kill is gonna need all her goddamn guile.

The ship's constant spin is disorientating, and I purposely take my eyes away from the pilot window. I've got to steer this thing using primitive methods, just hands on a set of simple controls—with no distractions.

I double-check my 'flight profile.'

Everything looks good. The lifeboat will come down in the Montes Appenninus, a sharp, rugged range of mountains in the north-western part of the Moon's near side. Which I'm approaching faster than I'd like.

The mountains are entering the terminator, hiding most of them in shadow. Not that that will protect me from the tracking satellites, but it will sure be harder to find a cold ship in the dark.

A few seconds later, the lifeboat passes into blackness. The peaks in Montes Appenninus reach a height of six kilometres and we're descending fast. I hold my nerve, using the ship's gas thrusters to edge the trajectory into a deep valley between two vast spears of rock.

"Proximity alert!" the navcom warns me, accompanied with the manic beep and scream of other safety systems. I ignore them, quickly orientating the ship and firing all engines. I'm shaken by a deafening roar and pushed down into my seat.

The lifeboat gives a steep rock-face a glancing blow and begins to yaw. I yank on the controls, trying to counter. *Too late*. I punch the cockpit inertial dampners activation sequence and brace myself in the chair as the lunar surface races up to meet me.

Oh shit…

I SCANNED THROUGH REPORT AFTER report—a never-ending stream of rumour, odd occurrences, murders of interest, and ship disappearances. The Galactic Secret Service was pulling out all the stops to find Bluetongue. I was nothing more than an extra wheel, the human element in a computer chain whose only job, it seemed, was to double-check anything the computers 'thought was relevant.'

At least I was finally in the Key, on one of the most important gaiaspheres going by the name of *Charity*. A vast tube spinning above a yellow-orange gas giant. Cities, towns, villages, parks, forests and fields all laid out on the inside and covered with a thin blue coating of atmosphere. I didn't know the science behind how these things work, but it sure was beautiful.

That was all I got to see when they brought me into the Key. A fleeting glimpse of the mammoth structure before I was taken directly to an 'underground' facility to eat, sleep and work inside the innards of a computer recently brought back into service. A featureless, windowless room packed with a single screen.

It was as if the computer station I'd been parked at had been deliberately made to be as unsociable as possible. It possessed no personality to speak of and barked commands at me like I was its servant. Which I suppose I was. I arrived in the morning to a quick debrief, outlining my work for the day—usually sifting through a pile of reports it had also scanned—and spent the next twelve hours going through them. I was allowed thirty minutes for lunch and an occasional toilet break. That was it. My evenings—if that's what you can call them—were a few hours in my small compartment, a short walk away. I might as well not have slept. My unconscious hours were as busy as my working ones. Frantically dream-sifting through more reports. Always in search of Sirena, aka the Bluetongue Lizard. I often woke up feeling more tired than when I went to bed. I was determined to find something that would lead me to her. Painstakingly searching for that one, elusive snippet of info or data. Going through reports multiple times looking for a hook to catch her with.

But I came up with nothing. As did everyone else. Sirena had disappeared into thin air.

::

I crack open my eyes and take stock of my surroundings.

I'm still sitting in the pilot's chair, connected to what's left of the lifeboat. The pilot's window was smashed by the impact, showering me in regolith—thick, black moon-dust. Despite the destruction around me, my suit is in the green. No rips, punctures or tears, and no injuries.

I gingerly pull myself free from the half-crushed navcom console and dig out my two oxygen tanks. They are also undamaged. The rest of the ship has not been so lucky. If my plan was to use it to escape, I'd be scuppered. Luckily, I've got another way to get off Mother Moon. The only part of the lifeboat that survived intact is the cockpit and the passenger cabin. The boat's inertial dampners certainly did their job… and then some. I'm impressed. The rest of the ship must be strewn around me. At least it looks like a crash site if someone should come investigate.

That's because it is a crash site, you dumb-ass.

I can't disagree with myself on this one. If these lifeboats were not top of the range, I'd never have made it. It wasn't something I'd factored into my plan. Sometimes you just need plain old luck.

What did Sirena say? *You need luck in this job and I've always had that in plentiful supply.*

The bitch ain't wrong there…

The suit's chronometer tells me I've been unconscious for only a few minutes. Good. My brief use of the ship's thrusters would've caused a quick-enough heat signature to mimic the explosion of a ship going down and breaking up. Or so I hope.

I crawl out of the wreckage to get my bearings, flicking my skinsuit's torch around to peer into the total blackness. The smashed cockpit came to rest against a sheer rock wall—the side of a deep valley that is nothing more than a slit between two tall peaks. A line of destruction—bits of lifeboat strewn around this tight valley—shows me the direction I was heading before I came down. I chose this destination weeks ago after a thorough investigation of the Moon's surface and features. At that time, I didn't have a plan… then *Sure Splendid* entered the equation. Another piece of luck. After that, everything was straightforward.

Mostly.

I'm exactly where I wanted to be. Give or take a kilometre or two. Basically, 'X' marks the spot, and I'm standing on it. Although I wasn't stupid enough to crash the lifeboat anywhere near my final objective.

This has to look like a random coming-down of a malfunctioning ship, nothing more. So far, that's exactly what I've got. But I can't hang around though. I need to get away from here.

Rather than leave a trail a child could follow in the moon dust, I clamber up onto the wreckage of the cockpit, activate the booster pack I scavenged from *Sure Splendid,* and take a boosted jump up the sheer rock wall. Pushing with my feet and pulling with my hands, I ascend easily in the low gravity. A nimble four-legged, black-skinned, climbing insect.

I reach a suitable ledge and glance down just in time.

A flash of light—an approaching ship.

Shit!

My suit's torch winks off at a quick command and I push myself into a crevice, telling the suit's nano-fibres to harden, flushing cold air around me.

The ship, a small two-person cruiser by the look of it, hovers below me, positioned right over the crash site, before flying up and travelling past where I'm hiding. I'm convinced they're going to spot me, but after a few minutes circling above, it ascends and flits away.

I order the skinsuit to soften and I'm left trembling, wishing I'd taken those relaxants when I had the chance.

Adrenaline can be a bitch.

It takes another thirty minutes of climbing before I calm down. And another forty minutes before I drop onto the wide, empty plain beyond.

I check my oxygen. Everything is still in the green—and I have a reserve tank.

Sweet.

Time for stage two. I take a deep breath and bound across Mare Imbrium, heading in a direct line to a certain crater named *Archimedes.*

MARE IMBRIUM IS A 'FLAT' plain of regolith and small rocks and boulders. From high above, it looks smooth. The reality is somewhat different. The uneven surface makes the going difficult. I'm bounding along, using the low gravity to take long leaps. At the top of each arc I activate my booster pack, pushing me many hundreds of meters forwards—a peculiar, but effective kind of jogging. But these damn rocks make it hard to keep my footing when I land. My skinsuit ain't gonna get holed anytime soon, but my progress is slower than I expected.

At least the ground interference from all this scree—rocks jettisoned from various meteor impacts over the many eons—means no one will be able to track me.

I'm not much of a history buff. There was never any call for it back on Plenty, although I've always had a fascination for pioneers. Those people who risked their life to do something amazing and ground-breaking. A bit like what I'm doing now. Risking my life in a one-off operation that could go tits up at any moment. At the top of the next bound, I see the man-made structure I'm looking for. A dome surrounded by walls and a few buildings.

The landing site of Apollo 15.

An event that happened so far in the past as to be almost unimaginable. The pioneers who came here were heroes.

Two bounds later and I arrive.

The place is long-abandoned. Historical accounts say it was a tourist destination before Ancient Earth was left behind.

The regolith is disturbed with tyre-tracks and footprints. I add mine to them, marvelling that I'm possibly the first person to come visit here, the first tourist, in hundreds of years. There is a more popular tourist destination—that of the original moon mission, where the first footprint a human has ever taken upon a world outside their own is preserved. Yet I believe there's something more noble about not being first. About taking all the same risks and being almost forgotten by history. If I hadn't discovered this landing site when scoping out my mission, I would've never heard anything about it, but like I said, these people were heroes.

I enter the open dome and stare at the ancient machinery that brought these pioneers to the Moon. I can't help but be impressed. A squat platform wrapped in foil. A single engine hanging underneath.

It's primitive, but kinda beautiful.

Lines of footprints encircle the machine. Preserved for as long as the Moon lasts. Not for eternity though. Nothing lasts that long.

I leave the dome and its antiquated contents and make my way to an abandoned tourist centre. A small complex of buildings peppered with centuries worth of tiny asteroid impacts. I boost myself up to stand atop the structure and scan the area. I'm looking for a small crater, which you'd think would be difficult, given how many small craters meet my eyes. But there it is.

A fresh crater a few feet wide, the regolith dark against the whiter moon surface.

I hop down and make my way towards it. After a

couple of bounds, I arrive and dig through the dust with my hands until I find a rough container, a strongbox of sorts, with added decoration. The kind of decoration that would fool most sensors into thinking this was just another lump of rock. A small, insignificant asteroid.

I smile when I see it again.

Another part of my mission falling into place.

It was launched weeks ago on the outskirts of the Sol System. I got one of those expensive companies that specialise in space burials to do it for me. A lot of people have their ashes sent to the Sol System to forever orbit the Sun. To be dumped in space with all those other dead saps who wanted to return home at the very end. Nothing odd about that, except that my box didn't contain the ashes of my beloved grandma. Nope. It housed a one-use void engine with enough room for my specialist kit.

The Moon regularly passes in and out of known meteoroid streams and is hit by many asteroids a year. My package was timed to arrive during one of them. Too small to be noticed—just one of the hundreds of rocks to hit the Moon.

I tap my fingers on a sequence of pre-programmed pressure points and the thing opens like a treasure chest. I remove the contents and affix them to my skinsuit, leaving the box and my own almost indelible mark on the Moon's surface.

FIVE HOURS LATER AND THREE-QUARTERS down my second tank of oxygen, I arrive atop the rim of the Archimedes crater, the largest crater in Mare Imbrium with a diameter of eighty-four kilometres. Fifty-two miles, to you and me. I'm able to look down across its vast expanse. The crater sure is impressive, if you like that sort of thing. Smooth and large enough to show the curve of the Moon on its furthest edge. Unlike a lot of the other moon craters, it has no central peak. It's pocked with smaller craters—like buckshot.

I'm getting close to my objective and need to be careful. It was easy for me to wander unnoticed across the empty Moon surface. That's about to change.

I unstrap part of my kit—nothing more than a foil blanket with active nano-tek—and, although primitive, it's more than effective. I drape it over my simple life-raft skinsuit and activate the second part of my disguise—if you can call it that. I feel a small current pass through me and, immediately, the foil tightens, moulding itself to my body and head, encasing my helmet. There are available tactical skinsuits that could do the same job, but no matter how much I thought through this mission, there was no way to change into a skinsuit on the surface of the Moon without a working airlock.

Besides, I've always been best at improvisation.

I jog along the rim in full view of tracking systems and geocentric satellites, feeling the skin on the back of my neck crawl. I've tested this makeshift stealth system countless times, yet it's a different ballgame when you know death is pointing at you from a hundred different angles.

It's only a short amount of time before I come across a missile platform, the first of many. It's unlikely this was used to bring down my fellow lifeboats. That would give away the existence of the secret GSS base, which nestles somewhere ahead.

I continue for another half hour, aware that my oxygen levels are now in the amber.

No cause for concern, if I can get to my objective, but the sudden loss of green increases my heartbeat for a few seconds.

I come across a few similar missile platforms and tracking installations, which would be very effective if I was to arrive here in a ship, but useless against a one-person infiltration. I also discover a dozen anti-personnel niches, newly hewn into the rock. Inside nestle any number of drones ready to take out any unwelcome two-footed intruders. Thankfully they remain inert.

I jog amongst the jumble of rocks, giving me extra cover, and close in on my destination, sitting on the outside rim of the Archimedes crater. The installation is named *The Antrum Facility*, home to one of the first geological operations on the Moon, housing up to sixty people. And what do people want? *Water.* More than anything else. Here, on the other side of the craggy crater wall, ice was found in abundance. The installation was part mine, part colony, although it is long abandoned. The outer buildings, windows black and cold, stretch up towards the Archimedes crater rim. The lower part descends into a small satellite crater, over a hundred feet wide. This close, I can see a part of it is obviously man-made and showing recent signs of use. The floor of the crater has been disturbed by vehicles and darkened by tell-tale fuse-engine scorches. It's no crater floor, but the roof of an underground hangar.

I slowly crawl through the thick regolith to the artificial floor, feeling dreadfully exposed.

My oxygen is running at 2%. Fifteen or so minutes of air before I asphyxiate, but I can't rush this step. If I'm discovered now, I'm a dead man—er, woman. Or whatever the hell I am. Just a human, I suppose, sweating and afraid—but challenging the odds.

Just how I like it.

I reach the hangar roof. A wave of relief rushing over me.

Nevertheless, my next step is calculated and no less dangerous. I free a small roll of rope-like plastic and place it in a tight circle. I activate it with a shielded hand-held wafer, direct contact only, and the rope begins to smoulder. A chemical reaction creating a certain amount of weird foam that freezes instantly in the lack of atmosphere. It easily cuts into the thick metal of the hangar roof but does not penetrate all the way through.

When there's room enough, I drop inside, timing my descent so that the foam closes over me and leaving me inside the hole I've carved for myself.

I free my laser and widen the space, my air now at 1%. I didn't realise it would be this close. Shit. It's not like me to underestimate myself. I've been over-breathing. What did Mother tell me on my first so-called 'mission' with Pistol-Whip? *"Wafer augmentations may enhance your wits, but they can also certainly dull them."*

Sure, I knew I'd have no wafer implant for this mission and I made my plans with that in mind, yet I messed up.

Without a wafer to control my breathing, I've used more air than I thought possible.

I ain't panicking, not just yet.

I'm saving that for when I break through the roof.

I tunnel down, burning as I go, until my handheld tells me I'm nearly there. I remove the stealth-foil and spray my suit with a solution that will ultimately destroy it, and which, in the short term, should give me the protection I need. Once applied, the suit's nano-tek becomes more fluid and responsive to any blaster shots that might come my way—but it will degrade within ten minutes. Now, with oxygen running out and with what is waiting for me below, ten minutes seems a lifetime away.

Everything so far has been covert.

A series of well-executed plans to quietly get me here, unobserved, to this moment… the moment when I alert the security drones below, Moonbase, and the goddamn GSS that I'm here.

Luckily, I don't have time to worry.

I brace myself, blast a hole below me, and drop down into a pit of blackness that becomes immediately illuminated, red lights flashing into life as the automatic security systems detect my presence. I float down into a vast cavern, stuffed with ships of all shapes and sizes, stretching hundreds of feet into the distance. Although these are not just any ships…

::

Another day, and another twelve hours going through report after report, until something piqued my interest—a series of anomalous readings in the outer Sol System. Reports of odd navigational sources showing as asteroids, debris or shadow signals that quickly disappeared like they were never there. The Sol System was mostly off-limits, or so I thought, and I ignored it. However, the report swam in the back of my mind and refused to go away, forcing me to go back to dig deeper. I sent out multiple queries that were all returned, unanswered. A blank wall. I queried the central computer, which came back to me with only three words: *No record found.*

A red flag.

Odd activity was what we were after, wasn't it? So why bury it? Unless those ships were known about. And ships that appeared and disappeared, mimicked asteroids and lurked in shadow signals were ships I'd had personal experience with…

I decided to find out more using the Service Cypher.

I was worried that my interest might be noticed, picked up by automated systems and passed to those in charge. Whoever they were. But over the next few months, I was left to get on with my investigations unimpeded. I supposed that with all resources now turned towards Bluetongue, my voice was one amongst thousands, all interrogating databases and reports in a desperate search for any information that might reveal Sirena's whereabouts.

I discovered an old list of bases within the Sol System full of mostly abandoned facilities, spacestations and asteroid habitats. Too many of them.

However, for such an old database, I noticed that the file had been recently updated, specifically information relating the Ancient Earth's only satellite, the Moon, considerably focusing my attention upon that beautiful, grey sphere.

A general search revealed that all GSS official information regarding the Moon had also been updated.

Quick-Kill ain't an official kind of gal, and the Galactic Secret Service didn't have the monopoly on information. Even though Ancient Earth was the birthplace of humankind, interest in the planet and the Sol System belonged to those who studied ancient history, or who had the romantic notion of having their ashes returned there after they died. This meant the information I needed was out there—somewhere.

I spent weeks searching and finally found what I wanted: a full and comprehensive list of all Moon bases. I compared it to the GSS database and… bingo!

There was one single difference—an abandoned ice-mine on the edge of the Archimedes crater going by the name of *The Antrum Facility*.

From what Agent Chinatown told me, all ceph-ships had been decommissioned. Taken out of service until they could work out how Sirena managed to get control of *Little Bastard*. It's not the Secret Service's way to destroy anything, especially if that something has a serious dollar value—whether it was illegal or not.

I put two and two together and came up with a hangar stuffed with ceph-ships.

I LAND IN A CROUCH atop an impressive, white-skinned, sleek-looking ceph-ship. It's substantially larger than *Little Bastard* and, judging by its mag-rail and turret arrays, it also packs a lot more fire-power. Then again, it would need that, seeing that it was significantly less manoeuvrable.

I only have a few seconds to orientate myself, aware of the flicker and whir of approaching drones, an oxygen warning blaring in my helmet. I throw a handful of my best whiz-bangs into the distance. They burst in a series of timed flashes, designed to fuck with the drone's scanning systems. Explosions of white noise in the visual, radio and sound spectrums.

I drop to the hangar floor and activate a weapon I specially designed for this mission—a portable blaster turret. Automatic legs deploy and punch themselves into the moon rock, anchoring the small, but powerful killing machine. I clutch my laser tightly and, under the cover of my timed and disorientating whiz-bangs and added blaster fire, I scuttle away unnoticed.

For now.

A blaster hits me square in the back, knocking me head over heels in the one-sixth gravity.

I regain my feet and look up to see a drone bearing down upon me that I take out with a sweep from my laser. That was too close for comfort. My augmented skinsuit is only good for one or two direct hits like this.

I jog away from the confusion of explosions and blaster fire, throwing more of my whiz bangs as I go. Putting distance between myself and the focus of the battle. The blaster turret won't last long, not with multiple drones converging and firing upon it, but I only need a few more seconds.

A beep from my handheld wafer, and it relays the information I'm after. It's been performing a low-level scan of the ships in here. I'm looking for one ship in particular. The sister to *Little Bastard,* and the handheld has found it.

The only problem? It's on the other side of the goddamn hangar.

I bound forward in the low gravity, using my thruster pack to increase each jump, pushing me onwards, taking pot-shots at the drones alerted to the extra movement, and dropping my most powerful mines under various parked ships.

A warning from my suit announces my oxygen has run out.

I've got seconds left. I'm blasted again by another drone, totalling my thruster pack. The force of the next hit propels me forward towards the ship of my destination. Even though my predicament ain't that promising, my heart surges at the sight. Not exactly *Little Bastard,* but its twin. I spin around, slice my laser through the attacking drones and set off the mines. Three ships are hit by a series of concussive explosions, creating significant balloons of flame. Fire in low gravity with no oxygen blooms in such a beautiful way.

But I don't have time to watch.

I open the outer airlock door and stumble inside, ripping off my helmet before the air has fully recycled, my mouth snatching for oxygen, coughing on the smoke coming from my now disintegrating skinsuit. The inner airlock opens, and I fall naked into the quiet ship, my chest heaving.

Part two of my plan is now complete. But only just.

UNCLOTHED AND SHIVERING, I MAKE my way to a familiar-looking bridge and quickly power up its core systems—a process very different to a normal ship—while also setting the heating to maximum.

This ship, named *The Minion,* is controlled by an autonomous brain. A human-like consciousness. *The ceph.* But, for now, I need to keep that brain dormant.

When I had *Little Bastard* all to myself for those long months in the Hejaz system, I made sure to learn the ship's operating system back to front. At first, I hated the damn ceph and was looking for a way to switch it off, or at least to disable its higher brain functions.

The only problem with this plan? I ended up kinda liking the annoying ship, even if it did double-cross me in favour of Sirena. But I found a way to do just that. To make its brain dormant.

The Service have already done half the job for me. In storing the ceph-ship, they'd powered down the brain and put it in stand-by mode. All I need to do is to reinstate some of the ship's 'lower functions'—flight, navigation, weapons, and voidwarp—and I'll be ready to get out of here. As to why I'm going to all this trouble to get myself a ceph-ship?

Call it 'attention-seeking behaviour.' A way for me to get Sirena to notice me… or at least, that's what I hope.

I upload my custom start-up sequence that will bring

The Minion on-line, powering up sections of the ship, only to power them down moments later. This sequence will also program a rather dangerous voidjump. A make or break manoeuvre that has Quick-Kill written all over it. The process will take three minutes and twenty-two seconds.

A goddamn lifetime!

I check for activity outside the ship. Drones are patrolling in ordered sweeps. The GSS, who I'm assuming are controlling Sol Moonbase, will know there's an intruder amongst their hoard of ceph ships. It won't take them long to find out who and where I am.

But discovery was always part of my plan.

The three minutes and twenty-two seconds pass slowly, time I spend rubbing at my back and side where I was hit by the blasters. The pain is on the unendurable side, but that will soon be the least of my worries.

A message crackles over the com, coming from Sol Moonbase. *"Stand down Agent Quick-Kill and exit the ship."* Even though this is an integral part of the plan, my heart spikes at the mention of my name. The voice is male and officious, and I can hear the stress under his commanding words.

"So you know who I am, well done."

"You will not be allowed to leave. Exit the ship and give yourself up. Otherwise I will be forced to blow the base."

"No way. You neither have the authority nor the will to destroy the Service's exclusive and expensive ceph-fleet. That's too big a decision for someone of your pay grade."

"You are wrong, Agent Quick-Kill. I have standing orders to do just that. I repeat, you will not be permitted to leave. Stand down, before it's too late."

"Yeah? Well I have other plans. I got fed up of

being a goddamn desk-jockey and decided to go find Bluetongue myself. To do that, I figured I would need a ceph-ship," I explain. It's a lie of sorts, what I want him and the Service to believe—a necessary part of my plan. "So I'll give *you* a choice," I continue. "Open the hangar doors or I'll blow my way through them."

A long pause. *"Be warned, the base is protected by a high-yield nuclear device that I will not hesitate from detonating, should you attempt to leave."*

Finally, with a low ping, my program finishes. "Looks like I'm gonna have to call your bluff."

I tap quick fingers over the navcom and the ship lifts off, hovering a few feet from the floor. I bring lasers, cannons and mag-rails online and point them towards the hangar roof.

"This is your final warning, Agent Quick-Kill. Power down your ship immediately or I will detonate… Don't do this, man!"

Here it is. The moment all my planning upon the Moon has come to. *Make or fucking break.* The command screen blinks with a single flashing button, and an innocuous two-word command: 'Initiate Procedure'.

"I'm betting my life you ain't got the balls to do it," I say defiantly. "Otherwise, bring it on!"

I slam the button with my fist. *The Minion's* lasers, blaster cannons and mag-rails pound the roof, punching a hole big enough to fly the ship through. Somewhere below, the nuclear device, the presence of which I've known about since I hatched this plan, receives a command to detonate and, a millisecond later, I'm thrown screaming into the void.

THERE WERE LITERALLY MILLIONS OF Intel snippets distributed and broadcast through the Cypher. I had access to them all, searching and filtering the information for my own ends, and no one was asking what I was up to. The reason, it turned out, was a simple one: All of the Galactic Secret Service's might was being used to locate the Bluetongue Lizard. It had shut down major operations and mothballed others. Agents from across the galaxy were roped in to help, which meant a helluva lot of people were doing exactly the same as myself. Just another agent sifting through information, lost in the noise. Searching with everyone else for some sign of Bluetongue. Of Sirena. Except that I had a tiny advantage.

I knew her.

Or at least I thought I did.

I examined every moment of our interactions together. I had no wafer, which I was finding less of a hindrance than I had anticipated, but everything it recorded was on file. A file I managed to get my hands on. I went over those recordings a thousand times.

In the meantime, no stone was left unturned by the GSS, no lines of enquiry ignored, no clues not thoroughly dissembled and investigated. The Hejaz system was pulled apart, planet by planet and moon by moon, which made me smile when I thought back to Old Ma Gilligan, who, I found out, was languishing in one of the Service's most detestable jails with the rest of her brethren.

But the Service had missed something. I'd been scanned, probed, pulled apart and put back together again. They found nothing, except what was staring them in the face.

I was still alive.

I checked back over Sirena's record with the Service, examined in detail her modus operandi, and there was one common factor about all her exploits: *She left no witnesses.* Covering her tracks by killing anyone she thought was a threat, be they friend or foe. A sure way to never leave a trail.

Sirena could've killed me any number of ways, so why implant me with a blaster when a bomb would've done the trick? She already had *Little Bastard* at her beck and call. She knew who I was from the start. Which meant my life was an open book to her.

I was alive for a reason.

Sirena wanted me to find her.

::

I awake, groggy and choking on my own blood. Pain screams through me in a never-ending wail, like every single nerve in my body has been scraped with sandpaper and doused in vinegar. My head feels twice the size, mushy and pounding. I have no idea who I am or what I'm doing here. Wherever here is.

I'm slumped in front of a series of screens all flashing red, my ears full of sirens and warnings.

"I'm fucking alive," I whisper from a hoarse throat, coughing up blood in a bitter, salty torrent.

More flashes and lines of blurred read-outs.

I blink, focusing on the dash before me. What I'm looking at appears to be damage reports. I'm on a ship, that much is obvious.

As I watch, some of the red sectors flick to orange.

"Automatic repair systems doing their job," I say to myself, spitting out more blood. "Good."

I look down at my naked body. It's discoloured, covered in vast bruises, and splattered with blood leaking from my mouth, nose and ears. My hands are bent back on themselves, wrists broken, the fingers all awry, sticking out in odd directions. One of my legs is twisted at a sick angle, its foot dangling from a single tendon, white bones exposed.

I don't need my memory to tell me I require serious medical attention and, using nothing more than some instinctual subconscious autopilot, I float in the zero-grav, leaving the cramped bridge and its dazzling screens, and arrive in what I recognise as a medibay. I enter the diagnostic pod and lie down, its automatic systems taking over. A door closes above me and, within moments, I'm drifting away into a deep, welcoming sleep…

::

A gentle tingling at my temples brings me back to consciousness. I open my eyes to find myself still in the medibay. I'm no longer in the pod but lying on a bed. I raise my hands. They are healed, as is the rest of my body. My injuries and pains are nothing but half-remembered things. Terrible and faraway.

What the hell happened to me?

I sit bolt upright, stopped from flying off my bunk in the zero gee by a strap around my waist. "Shit!"

My memories come flooding back. The infiltration

of the GSS secret base on Ancient Earth's Moon. Getting access to *Little Bastard's* sister ship and…

I swallow hard.

…and programming a voidjump in the millisecond before the unleashing of a nuclear blast. A voidjump in direct proximity to a planetary body. The chances of my survival were… who cares, I made it.

I smile. There's still a lot of work to do, but at least the Service will be convinced I'm dead. I'm free of them at last, free to do what I want.

And my plans are only just beginning.

"Set gravity to Earth normal," I say.

Nothing happens.

Of course, I'm on a ceph ship, with its brain still dormant and no regular back-up computer. I unstrap myself and float my way back to the bridge. All screens are now in the green and I'm startled by the time stamp. I've been aboard—in stasis—for two months. Even though the ship escaped the nuclear blast, it was still radiated. It has taken the ship that much time to reduce fallout levels to a safe background.

I access the medibay's history and baulk at what I see.

I knew there was a likely possibility of serious injury doing what I did. It was all part of the risk I was taking. The ship's void engines literally bend space using a powerful energy field—a field that can be fatal to organic life if it's not adequately contained—the reason why no one voidjumps right next to a large gravity well, and definitely not on the surface of a planet or a moon. The field destabilises and can enter the cabin area causing all manner of injuries. Which is exactly what happened to me. The unprecedented voidjump caused me serious damage—internal bleeding from ripped organs, muscles and tendons, coupled with snapped bones, a punctured lung and a quite nasty brain bleed. It's a miracle I survived long enough to get to the medibay. Then again, I knew that if my reckless voidjump worked, I would need some serious medical attention and fast. That was no miracle, it was just my innate sense of survival kicking in. Also having a top-of-the-range medibay to help me heal was a significant factor in my plan.

I switch my attention to the navcom that tells me *The Minion* has been jumping regularly, following a pre-programmed, yet random pattern. Stealth-mode was also enabled, not that the ship was gonna be jumping near any systems or space lanes, I made sure of that. It pays to be careful. The readout tells me I'm in the middle of nowhere. I took my lesson from Bluetongue. I ain't gonna leave a trail anyone can follow. As far as the Galactic Secret Service are concerned, they blew their base, Agent Quick-Kill, and all their ceph-ships to kingdom come.

I have some new, and some unfinished business, to take care of. I plot a course back to the Barrows, the region of space inhabited by bootleggers and criminals, and where Mother took me to meet Abe, the Secret Service surgeon who performed my unwanted gender-change. When that business is completed to my satisfaction a few weeks later, I enter a series of jumps into the navcom. The void engines recharge and the ship jerks into voidspace once again, leaving the Barrows far behind.

A few days later, I arrive at a small, red planet in a forgotten, backwater system. Its name incongruous to its planet-wide red-stained deserts and its single city of thirty or so million abandoned souls.

The planet is called *Plenty*.

Quick-Kill has come home.

I ARRIVE AT A SAFE distance, thirty-six planetary diameters away from the planet and at ninety-degrees to the ecliptic—dead space. I engage stealth mode and, to anyone looking, my ship would appear to be a large metallic cube. I'm about to start a system-wide scan for other ships, when there's a buzz from the com.

I stare at the winking light for a few moments.

I want to be surprised. But where this person is concerned, I'm well past amazement. Instead, I feel a grudging, if not an annoyed respect. A quick flick of a switch followed by the hiss of static. "How did you find me so fast?"

"You think I wouldn't notice a ceph-ship disguised as a Heinz and Wessman safe?"

I take a steadying breath. "Hi, Sirena. Or should I call you the Bluetongue Lizard?"

"Sirena will do. I kinda like the way it sounds coming from those pretty lips of yours."

My ship's disguise was designed to be noticed by one person and one person only. Still, I'm flabbergasted that it took only seconds for Sirena to find me. "How long have you been waiting here?"

"That was quite some trick you pulled back on Ancient Earth's old Moon. It's not often I say this, but… I'm impressed. I wondered what you were up to after you went AWOL from that posh gaiasphere you were stationed at.

But then there was all that commotion in the Sol System and a few months later, here you are."

"And where are you?"

"I'm speaking to you through a hidden relay I set up inside the Service Cypher. Those GSS guys are sometimes too dumb for words. How else do you think I can run rings around them?"

"And me. That's why I'm here. You turned me into a prize chump, using me like you did. I ain't too dumb to realise when I've been out-played by a better opponent."

"Is that why you're here, for revenge? That sure seems like a dumb move to me."

"Not revenge, no. Call it curiosity. You could've killed me, but you didn't, which means you had a reason."

"I won't lie to you. I made sure you lived, and that you had a clue to come find me—once you worked it out."

"I had a long time to mull over the events that led to Mother's assassination and came up with the same conclusion as the Service's investigation—everything that happened in the Hejaz system was a goddamn set-up. You knew all about me before you stepped onto my ship."

"I sure did. The Milligans suspected a Service agent was responsible for all those bank raids. It was that which brought me to their system. I needed a way to get to Mother, and who better to use than a green-behind-the-ears agent? I was thorough, I found out who you were and what backward planet you came from."

I grit my teeth. "It was your parting words to me that were the real clue. You called me *Jane*. That name only ever existed in one place: the planet of Plenty."

"Very well worked out. So why the drama on Ancient Earth's Moon? Why steal a ceph-ship?"

"I wanted to come after you without the GSS on my

back, and with my own ship."

"*It was an audacious plan. Not without its risks. That sure was a balls-out move, worthy of one of my own. Although, for a while there, I thought you hadn't made it.*"

"Okay, let's cut the crap. I'm here. What next?"

"*I think a face-to-face would be appropriate,*" Sirena replies.

"Then let's dock our ships and I'll come aboard. It'll be just like old times. I also want to have a word with that traitorous ceph of mine. I still haven't forgiven *Little Bastard.*"

"*No. We need to meet somewhere neutral.*"

"You don't mean—?"

"*Yep. Down on that shitty little planet of yours.*"

A SCAN OF LOCAL SPACE reveals nothing of interest. I am a lone ship in an empty, forgotten system—or so it seems. Sirena is out there somewhere, no doubt setting another one of her traps, and I have no choice but to walk right into it.

As to why?

Because Quick-Kill has a trap of her own.

I bring *The Minion* in low, a hundred or so klicks from New Amsterdam, low enough to cause a wake of dust and sand behind the hurtling ship. I park it at walkable distance from the city and engage the ship's stealth mode, making it almost invisible. I set up a direct com-line, so I can call the ship using a handheld should I need it.

I never guessed Sirena would want me to come down to this goddamn planet. But here I am. In disguise, of course, back in the place I'd spent a lifetime planning to get away from.

I sure hope Sirena doesn't make me a permanent resident.

Forty minutes later, I arrive on the outskirts of New Amsterdam, just as the system's only sun sinks below the horizon, plunging the buildings into crimson and scarlet. I'd always loved this time of day. An unexpected wave of homesickness washes over me and I can't help a small laugh. I've spent a lifetime wanting to get away from this backwater and, it turns out, I've been missing the place all this time.

Nostalgia sure sucks.

I flag down an autocab and get it to take me to Angie's old building. The city is as quiet as a morgue—even quieter than I remember. I'd forgotten what a backwater it is. At least here there is a democracy of sort, unlike those other planets I've visited, run by sadistic regimes. Plenty, with all its problems, is a paradise in comparison. I head towards the tenement building that I had assumed was a bad memory.

I'm not going inside, instead I'm here to visit an old friend. I cross the road to find what's left of my Dodge Charger, looking a sorry sight under the bright street lamps. It ain't fared well while I've been away. Kids have gotten to it. The tarp gone, its once fine paint covered in layers of graffiti and the red dust that this planet is famous for. The battery has been scavenged, but the wheels are still in place—anyone would be hard-put to remove those. They cost me a pretty packet and I didn't want anyone stealing them. Although they've obviously tried. The tires are missing, and my once-shiny hubcaps are burnt and scratched. I lean over the hood and grab a yellowed *Amsterdam City Removal Notice* informing the owner of the car that it will be moved and crushed if not taken care of. Looks like that was just a threat. I pat the metal affectionately and toss a few incendiary grenades inside.

The once beautiful machine begins to smoulder and burn.

I leave it behind me as the flames take hold. An ignoble end for such a great machine.

I disappear down a backstreet, take a few turns and enter an abandoned warehouse. A half-rusted grate on the lower level gives me access to the sewers. I drop down inside. Any sense of nostalgia leaves me as the familiar smell of shit pervades my nostrils.

I track through the sewer system, not even pausing to get my bearings. The tunnels and conduits are burned into my cerebral cortex—no wafer needed. I've spent a lifetime down here. Finally, I reach my destination—one of my old bolt holes, a second workshop—a place where I used to live before the bucks started coming in. It's hidden behind what looks like a dead end of twisting, ancient piping. I find the secret entrance and slip through. Everything is as I left it. I didn't expect it to be disturbed, I was too careful for that, and I haven't been away that long.

This is where I kept my favoured weaponry.

A rack of lasers, all homemade and deadly, is waiting for me. The touch of all that elegantly worked metal pleases my fingers. The laser I had delivered to the Moon, now strapped to my thigh, is way more advanced—not that I will get a chance to use it against Sirena. If I'm to win out against her, I'm gonna need something infinitely subtler. My laser won't do the job, not against an opponent like Bluetongue—she's too clever for that. I reach down behind more piping and pull out a small satchel. I never got a chance to come and retrieve this before Mother whisked me away. A travel bag of sorts. I empty the contents. A small, one-shot blaster the size and shape of a tube of lipstick takes my attention. I loved that thing and was disappointed that I never got to use it. There are some local credits and a few trophies taken from my early kills—a ring off the finger of the pimp who killed my first love, Sam, a tie from a one-time crime boss whose reign was ended by a laser-shot to the temple, and more.

Relics from the past.

I'm back on Plenty to try and catch Sirena, but that

don't mean I can't take the opportunity for some *me time*. I'm down here for just one thing, and there it is. A cheap necklace. I didn't know where it came from, whether I'd always had it, or if I'd picked it up off the street, or was given it as a kid. I'm not the sentimental type, but at one time, that worthless battered chain with its single pendant of dull, scratched crystal was all I had to my name. It's the only reason I came back down here.

As I pick it up in my now-enormous hands, it seems small and insignificant. A child's fancy. And I'm a child no longer. I exit my hideout and the sewers, leaving the necklace hanging on the wall above the alcove where I used to sleep. Leaving it, and the girl I used to be, behind, knowing I will never return. I'm done with Plenty and the life that I lived here.

I make my way down familiar streets and back alleys, keeping a close eye on my handheld.

As far as I can tell, there is no unusual activity around the planet, my ship or inside this city. I feel safe, although I realise that's just an illusion.

How Sirena knew about *Mama's* is beyond me, but that's where she said she wanted to meet. The same place where I hooked up with poor Dynamo, before he was reduced to nothing more than a few atoms.

Here's hoping my fate is gonna be more favourable.

I OPEN THE DOOR TO *Mama's* and stride inside. My guess is that, if Sirena wanted to kill me, I'd be dead by now. She'd have no reason to string it out. I glance around the bar, at the familiar cheesy décor and its tired-looking booths.

Does nothing change in this city?

I sit down in the same booth I used before—offering a handy vantage on all the exits and entrances—order a mug of milky tea and wait. The drink arrives a few minutes later, delivered by a pretty waitress who is unimpressed at what she sees—an overweight, balding businessman. The establishment is mostly deserted. A drunken couple, a sad guy at the bar and two young men playing pool. Any one of them could be Sirena, I suppose. She's had ample time to change her looks and her sex. I don't get any vibes from them though. My guess is that they are who they seem. After a while, I call the waitress over, ordering another mug of tea.

"What day is it?" I ask.

"Friday," she replies as if I'm some half-brained chump. "Friday evening to be more specific."

"Shouldn't this place be busier?"

She shrugs and leaves me to contemplate my tea.

I'm not one for waiting around, Sirena knows that. I guess she's pulling my chain. Or she could be making doubly and triply sure everything is as it should be. But I'm here alone. No back-up. No Service ships at my beck and call. I'm putting myself at the mercy of the Bluetongue Lizard and, however long Sirena wants to take, she won't find out anything other than that.

I'm thinking about ordering a third tea when my handheld buzzes.

So you're here, huh?

'Looks like it,' I type back. '*Where the hell are you? You've had plenty of time to check out me and my ship. I'm no threat to you.*'

I wait for a reply, but one is not forthcoming, my fingers tapping irritably on the booth table.

After another ten minutes, the handheld buzzes again.

'*This was a bad idea. Go back to your ship.*'

What the hell? '*It's not like you to get spooked,*' I reply, hiding my irritation.

'*You don't know me. No one does. Goodbye, Jane.*'

I slam my mug loudly onto the table. My plan pretty much depended on getting to talk with Sirena alone. I've no choice but to get out of here as quick as possible and go back to my ship.

I stand up, pay the girl, and enter the mostly empty street. I hear a whoosh behind me, aware of a sudden displacement of air. Before I can react, a figure steps out of the shadows and shoots me in the gut.

I AWAKE IN A FAMILIAR room. The guest quarters and sometime brig on *Little Bastard*. I'm on Sirena's ship, naked and tied to a chair. My nano-disguise has been stripped away. I bet that I've been thoroughly scanned, probed and searched. It's what I would do. My gut is sore from where I'm guessing Sirena shot me with a stun gun. The tell-tale whoosh was *Little Bastard* landing behind me. I'm relieved to be alive—and a little worried. This is what I've been after.

Time alone with Sirena.

This really is a do or die, and not some dumb, if not fun, test-mission on a backwater planet.

"Were you worried I might have had a blaster or two implanted somewhere I shouldn't?" I say, knowing that Sirena will be able to hear me.

She doesn't reply.

A familiar sounding metallic voice: *"Hi Sam."*

"It's you, is it?" I reply. "I would've named you something other than *Little Bastard,* if I'd known you were going to live up to that name."

"I'm sorry, Sam. Even though I remain an independent entity, my core has been compromised. I am forced to do whatever Sirena tells me to do."

"You're saying you're sorry, huh? Too little, too late, bud."

"If anyone should be apologising, it is you Sam," *Little Bastard* replies dispassionately. *"It was you who rescued*

Sirena and gave her time and opportunity to override my systems. All against my stern recommendations."

"Well, if you'd been better at your job, then you would've noticed she was using her genetically altered sweat glands—her goddamn Tang—to get me to do those things. I'm blaming you and the medibay, okay?"

"Sam, as you know full well, there was no way to detect such a—"

"That's enough!" Another voice that I recognise. Sirena.

"Nice for you to let me come aboard," I say jovially.

Silence.

"I'm here. You left me alive for a reason. I've come to find out why. What plans do you have for me?"

The door slides open and in walks Sirena. Or who I guess is Sirena. Gone is the Egyptian beauty and in her place is a tall, athletic-looking, black-skinned woman. Her brown, impossibly large eyes are wide apart and her head shaven. Two earrings of rounded, flattened gold emphasise her elegant, gazelle-like neck. She wears a single smock that clings tightly to her curves—with nothing underneath. At her waist is belted the same blaster I've seen before.

It hangs loosely. But I can't ignore its threat.

"You like?" she says.

Her voice is different to the one on the com, deeper and more commanding. And I realise that she must've used some kind of tonal augmentation device to allow her to sound like the old Sirena, or at least, the one I'd known.

"Very striking," I reply, meaning it. "For a disguise, it's particularly eye-catching."

"This isn't a disguise, just another look."

"So, you gonna untie me? You've checked me over, I

take it? You know I'm no threat to you."

"I'm gonna leave you as you are. I'm not about to take unnecessary risks and I want to play with you a little."

I swallow. I'm at this mad-woman's mercy and it doesn't feel good. "It wasn't me who put themselves inside a safe that was gonna be robbed," I say with a twist of my head. "It wasn't me that nearly got scorched into nothing by *Little Bastard's* lasers. If anyone is a risk-taker, that anyone is you."

Sirena smiles, her thick lips pulling back to reveal an array of white, gold-tipped teeth almost too big for her mouth. "How could I have predicted you'd do that? I was lucky, sure. Then again, luck's always been on my side. And let me remind you, it's you who's naked and trussed up, not me."

"Yeah, I came to find you. Put my head in the lion's mouth, so to speak. We have history. Don't you think this is a little rude?"

"You weren't *that* good a fuck."

I shouldn't let her words get to me, but they do. Sirena was my first in this body. *In this gender*. That means something.

Sirena's thick, black eyebrows furrow ever so slightly. "That bothers you doesn't it?"

I say nothing.

"It's that kind of attitude that has gotten you killed, Jane. You're too soft. Too soft by half."

I ignore the use of my real name and her threat. "I thought I was an unfeeling bitch until I met you. In comparison, I'm all heart."

"Which is your undoing. Which is why I always win. Which is why I don't care about anyone other than myself."

"That's not true though is it? You cared enough about

Mother to risk everything to kill her, and you cared enough about me to keep me alive."

"Mother got what was coming to her. And you?" She stoops down and runs a single finger under my chin.

Our eyes meet for a second, I try to peer behind Sirena's cold, glassy stare. It's like looking into an abyss.

Her finger jabs suddenly into my skin, raking a nail and drawing blood. "I only kept you alive for a bit of fun," she spits, drawing back to stand on long, lithe, well-formed legs, each ending in a perfectly formed, delicate foot, one ankle ringed with a golden chain set with flashing jewels. "You can't possibly believe you mean anything to me, can you?"

She flicks me a look of disappointment. Like I'm not living up to her expectations.

I say nothing.

"Don't you get it?" she continues. "I loved messing with your mind back in Hejaz. All those beautiful betrayals. Fucking you. Playing you for the sap you are. Your shocked face when the truth struck. I left you alive so you'd come and find me. So you'd blunder, wide-eyed and trusting, back into my power. I wanted to see that look of betrayal plastered over your face one more time before I killed you. And I am gonna kill you, Jane, or Sam or whatever you call yourself. You have my word on that."

"I don't think so. I've gone through your record a thousand times. You may think you know me, but I know all about you. The Bluetongue Lizard never leaves a witness. You kept me alive because you like me, plain and simple. You saw something inside of me that reminded you of yourself."

Sirena sighs. An agitated, angry expelling of breath. "This is what no one gets about me. I just don't give a damn about anyone or anything except this." She points an elegant brown thumb towards herself. "Yet saps like you still think otherwise. Lining themselves up one after another in the vain hope that they've somehow 'connected' with me." She lets out a loud, raucous laugh that twists her beautiful features into something hard, demonic and ugly.

"You may believe that yourself," I say when she's finished, "I'm betting my life that I know better. Something happened to us in this cabin." I flick my eyes at the bunk. "Something special. You know it. That's why you saved me. And that's why you're going to let me go. And maybe, we can enjoy this cabin some more."

Sirena's eyes burn into mine for a few seconds before her lips begin to curl. "I was looking forward to seeing you, granted. Just not in the way you were hoping. You may have outsmarted the Service, but you've shown yourself to be as weak as all the rest—and now I have two ceph ships at my disposal."

With an impossibly quick motion, the blaster appears in her hand. She points it at my leg and fires, obliterating it from below the knee.

Pain explodes from the injury—a wave of agony and horror—and I'm plunged into blackness.

I COME TO SOMETIME LATER, lying on my back, pain lurking on the edge of my sensibilities. Then I remember Sirena and my destroyed leg. My eyes flick open to see her standing over me. I'm lying in the medibay pod, robotic arms poised above.

"How are you feeling, Sam?" Sirena says dispassionately.

I try to speak, but the words won't properly form.

"It's amazing what this medibay can do," Sirena continues, a gleeful smile playing upon her beautiful lips. "It can cure any number of injuries. And… *inflict them.* It has the ability to activate every pain receptor in your body, it can send waves of pure agony through every nerve. It can pull out all your fingernails, pop your eyes and drain them dry, drill your teeth and flay the skin from your body, all without sedation. And when it's done, it can heal you and start the process again. And that's exactly what it's going to do to you."

I shake my head.

"And know this—while you're in here, going through this never-ending hell—I won't even be watching. I won't even bother enough to view your suffering. That's how much I care for you Quick-Kill Ja—"

Sirena staggers, gagging, her hand going to her throat.

At last. This is what I've been waiting for. I thought it was never going to bloody happen. And just in time.

Sirena jabs at the medibay control panel and I'm rudely ejected onto the floor. She clambers inside, and the pod is quickly pulled into the wall.

I drag myself up into a sitting position, looking down at the burnt stump of my right leg.

"It could've been worse," I manage to stutter as the ship's medibay tries to save Sirena, but it was too late for her as soon as she got me aboard. She was over-confident in her abilities, and she underestimated me.

I'm no lovelorn sap. Far from it. Quick-Kill is as rational as they come. Sure, I have emotions, like anyone else, yet I know when to use them to my advantage and when to bury them. I deduced that the only reason Sirena had kept me alive was to fuck with me, to play a part in one of her nasty little games. All I had to do was get aboard and try to stay alive as long as possible. I did what Mother and the rest couldn't do: I captured the goddamn Bluetongue Lizard.

While the Sirena I know is being stripped away, I hobble to the galley to make myself a cup of tea and to grab some food.

"*What have you done, Sam?*" *Little Bastard* asks me, its tone quizzical.

I take a sip of tea and smile. "Me? I've won, that's what I've done."

"*But how?*"

"It was straightforward, but not without its difficulties…"

::

Getting access to Abe's lab in the Barrows hadn't been easy. Nor was getting to talk to the man himself. But that's what I'd done.

Ever since I was gender reassigned, I'd been thinking about what happened to me in his lab. About what Mother told me. About my supposedly homogenised DNA and the mystery of my past.

None of it added up.

I remember making a joke to Mother about every orphaned girl fantasising about being a lost princess, the missing daughter of a king and queen of some proud and noble dynasty that they were destined to inherit. I told her I didn't care about my past. That I lived in the now.

It was a lie.

One of those lies you tell yourself enough times that you end up believing.

I may have been cold-hearted—not on the same level as Sirena, of course—but my life had forced me to become resourceful. I was detached, independent and alone. The way I liked it. The only way I could've survived. Those childish princess-like fantasies, although well hidden, still existed inside of me. A crutch to keep me going through those awful, lonely days of my childhood. A coping mechanism indulged by every orphan kid everywhere. And coping mechanisms were something that Mother and Abe knew all about.

I had no incredible, secret past—although that's what she and Abe wanted me to believe. What they hinted at. No. In reality I was a nobody, an orphan whose parents were probably drug-users or lowlifes who abandoned their daughter on the streets of New Amsterdam on the backwater planet of Plenty, leaving her to fend for herself.

Mother and Abe lied. My DNA hadn't been homogenised. It was a hook. A way to keep me invested in the Service. They wanted me to believe that they'd discovered *something special* about me. And, of course, I *was* something special. Why else did they recruit me? It was a way for my ego to buy into their lies. To buy into myself and the Service.

And it made me wonder. *What did they do to Sirena?*

Which is where Abe came in to the picture. Before I went AWOL from the Service, I researched him, found out as much about the guy as was possible. He was ancient, I knew that. When I found out his real age, I was gobsmacked. Nearly five hundred years old. But I discovered more than his age. Abe was one of the founding fathers of modern eugenics, of genetic manipulation. His work had been outlawed across the galaxy from one system to the next. He made himself a part of terrible regimes and doctrines, just so he could practice his art.

Until he was recruited by the Service, that is.

To work on their agent program.

And Sirena was part of that. A super soldier of sorts. Not in body, which these days can be altered any which way by any half-decent geneticist, but how her mind was designed. Body augmentation was widespread in the galaxy, used for exploration, hostile environments and simple pleasure. Mind and brain manipulation were a different matter altogether. There were too many genetic, biological, developmental, and environmental factors that determined the human psyche. Humans existed in the quadrillion but manufacturing a human mind to exist between controlled parameters had never been achieved—no matter how much scientists had looked for or dreamed about it.

And Abe had dreamed about just that all his life.

Learning about him, I also found out about his vile experiments. For every one of his many years, he had been responsible for hundreds, if not thousands, of deaths, all of which had given him the results and information to achieve the impossible…

Weaponised Consciousness.

That was Sirena. His creation. Probably one of the most intelligent, resourceful and deadly human beings to ever exist. He changed her from a brilliant, super-intelligent, if not flawed human being, into an unrelenting, self-serving killing machine. He altered her, tweaked her original genome, which was that of a resourceful genius, and turned her into a monster—a monster I grew to love and hate in equal measure.

Sirena was his greatest success, a success he was never able to recreate. She was also his greatest failure.

Weaponised consciousness, it turned out, was more dangerous than Abe or anyone else anticipated. Not that this stopped the bastard from trying to refine his technique. The Service wanted him to succeed as part of their desire for super-agents paired with ceph-ships. An ambition that, more than anything else, stank of empire and domination. They supplied him with human stock, allowing him to continue his experiments. And it was this single piece of information that made me realise I'd never go back to them.

Sirena was a thorn in their side from the get-go.

Uncontrollable, dangerous, and with an axe to grind. A grudge that led to her escape and her plans to kill Mother. A grudge that would've inevitably led her back to Abe.

But I got to him first.

Retrieving Sirena's original DNA from him was a simple task. I guessed a man, who is nearly half a century in age, knew how to behave when his life was in danger. In return, he gave me everything I wanted.

My next task, before securing my passage aboard *Sure*

Splendid, was similarly tricky. It came from an idea given to me by Sirena and her Tang. I underwent an expensive DNA treatment of my own. Modifying my sweat glands to produce not Tang, but to exude an invasive DNA—one specifically matched to Sirena's original genome. All I had to do was get myself in close enough proximity, for a brief period of time, and my sweat would do the rest…

THE MEDIBAY FOUGHT A LOSING battle. Sirena was changing, reverting. How could the machine fight off an infection from her own cells that came from her own DNA? Quite simply, it couldn't. In the end, the medibay began to aid the procedure, making sure that the reverted Sirena stayed alive and healthy.

I left the machine to get on with it.

It took a few days for the transformation to complete. Days in which I was able to reset *Little Bastard,* undoing whatever Sirena did to the thing, taking it off-line in very much the same way I did with *The Minion,* which is now docked with us.

I occasionally popped back to the medibay to check on Sirena. The black-skinned beauty was no more. Her finger and toe nails had fallen out, whilst a frizz of blonde hair grew like mould upon her otherwise-bald head. The rest of her body was an amorphous, slug-like blob covered in purple patches, like bruises on a banana.

After another day, the original Sirena started to take shape.

I was surprised at what I saw forming.

A squat woman with a squashed, reddened face sitting under thick, unruly curly blonde hair. Her limbs were inelegant and pudgy, her hips too wide for her body and her chest flattened. Gone were all the curves I was so used to. Her original exterior was not only plain, but unattractive. I guess I shouldn't be surprised. Sirena's desire for tall, statuesque beauty had hinted at something like this.

The medibay released the woman to sleep on the cot.

I can only guess at her mood when she wakes—wakes a different person from the one who leapt into the pod. Would she be angry? Relieved? Remorseful? Full of revenge? I locked down *Little Bastard,* preventing the rejuvenated Sirena from accessing its core systems and the bridge, and hid myself in *The Minion,* waiting for her to contact me. I would've never done this before with Sirena, she was too dangerous. But the thickset blonde I've left behind is not the Bluetongue Lizard.

All that weird shit Abe did to her will have been reversed. And good riddance.

::

The com buzzes a few days later. I've monitored Sirena since she awoke. Showering, dressing, eating. Her movements are awkward—not Sirena-like at all, although something of her alter-ego remains. More than anything, she appears to be calm, which I'm thankful for. I also used these days to repair my leg in *The Minion's* medibay. It's almost as good as new, apart from some tingling and a few cramps.

"*Sam,*" she says, her voice low and guttural, the words roughly formed.

"Hello, Sirena."

She scoffs. "*That's not my name. Not my real name. Sirena was who I always wanted to be. The beautiful siren luring people to their doom. That was the other me, the one you killed.*"

"She died, but you survived."

"Do you want to come over and talk?"

A few minutes later, my laser strapped to my thigh—I still feel the need to be careful—I enter *Little Bastard* and meet Sirena in the galley. She sits on a stool, looking subdued.

"If you're not Sirena, what do I call you?" I ask, breaking the thick silence, and sitting down opposite her.

"I was known as Scuggs."

"Scuggs?" I repeat incredulously, yet the name suits the thickset girl sitting in front of me.

"That was my nickname on the world I grew up on. Before I grew too big for the planet and left it and the name behind."

"You did better than me. I was still trying to escape when I was recruited by the Service."

She looks up and I see her real eyes for the first time. Bright blue and fiercely intelligent. "I hate the Service!"

"Do you remember what they did to you? Or anything after Abe weaponised your brain?"

Scuggs stares past me into the distance, her eyes full of ire. "I remember everything that bastard did to me. What I became. An unfeeling killing machine, just out for myself." An expression of loss creases her face.

"You miss being her? Being Sirena?"

"She was me in most ways. Fiercely intelligent, resourceful, dangerous and damn horny, except that Sirena was a helluva lot more. Like she was hardwired into the now. You ever get that feeling on a mission or a job, when everything is going as you planned? An overpowering omnipotence as if nothing can touch you? That you can do no wrong? That every decision you make is the right one, and the people around you are just saps and fools?"

I nod.

"That was Sirena all the time. Not overconfident, but out there on the very edge of what it is to be the goddamn best."

"I think I just proved who was best, don't you?"

Scuggs nods in acquiescence. "You outsmarted me—or you outsmarted her." Her eyes narrow in her pudgy face. "How does it feel?"

"Honestly? Bittersweet. Sirena was… exhilarating company. I'm gonna miss her."

"You and me both. You fell for her, despite the Tang?"

"Yes and no."

"What does that mean?"

"If she wasn't such a mean, cruel, and malevolent fuck-up, who knows? Tell me, did she really keep me alive just to lure me back and to torture me in the medibay?"

Scuggs shakes her head. "You were right about her. She had a soft spot for you, Sam Santana, aka Quick-Kill Jane. I don't think she properly knew why she kept you alive. It irked her. She liked you, and that made her weak—a weakness that led to her demise."

"And what about you?"

"I have all of Sirena's memories. I'm still her, mostly."

I feel a familiar tingle but ignore it. "You know what I mean. How do you feel about what I've done to you?"

Scuggs takes a deep breath, sitting back on her galley stool, a small hand with stubby fingers raking through her corn-like hair. "I'm pleased to be back. Grateful. More than grateful, actually. I'm me again. I'm glad I didn't kill you like Sirena planned. To torture you with the medibay was a heinous idea. I'm thankful but deflated. I owe you everything. You took a big risk doing what you did. If Sirena had guessed what you were up to…"

"She didn't, remember?"

A small laugh escapes her lips. "You and I are very

similar. I also hate to be turned into a sap. And Sirena sure did that to you and then some. I'm guessing you didn't originally plan on coming here to rescue me, isn't that right?"

I say nothing.

"No, you wanted revenge. Plain and simple, despite the connection you felt with me—*with her.*"

"I wanted to beat Sirena, to humiliate her—that was my only plan until I found out what Abe and Mother had done to you."

"You know about that?"

"Yeah. You despised Mother and the Service, which meant that deep down, you resented them, that they did something to you, something more than a simple gender reorientation. It's why I went back to Abe, to find out what the creep had to say."

"What happened?"

"He told me everything. Blabbed like a little child… although his lab unfortunately exploded after our conversation. With Abe inside. A tragic accident, I'm sure you will agree."

"You're not gonna send me back to the GSS?"

"I want nothing more to do with them, although I can't begrudge the Service too much. I've had quite a bit of fun since I joined their fucked-up organisation. Most of it with you. And they did get me off that damn planet of Plenty. But no, I'd never send you back to those bastards."

"Thanks, although I don't think they'd expect me to look like this."

"How is the old body feeling?"

She shrugs. "Damn itchy. I can't say I've missed it. Nice to be back home, though. I can't believe you pulled the same trick on Sirena that she pulled on you with her Tang. Reverting my genome… that was some damn clever thinking."

"Quick-Kill ain't all good-looks and lasers."

"No, you're not," she says. "You're something special."

Another tingle, Scuggs may be half the full-on woman that Sirena was, but I sense her lurking somewhere inside. Intelligent and impossibly sexy. "I am special, we both are."

A long pause. "If you're not handing me in to the Service, what are you going to do with me?"

"Easy," I reply. "I'm giving you *Little Bastard*. What you do with it is up to you."

Scuggs sits back on her stool again, a wary look on her face. "You're really letting me go?"

"I'm not one hundred percent sure giving you your freedom is a great idea, but I don't blame you for anything that Sirena did." I let the information sink in. "Though I have no doubt that, even without your weaponised brain, you'll still be one very dangerous and resourceful woman. I figure letting you go will leave us even."

"Are you sure that's wise? Sirena did the same to you and look what happened."

"Do you want *Little Bastard* and your freedom or not?"

"I'm touched. And yes. Thanks."

"Don't thank me too quickly. The GSS will still be after you and, without the abilities of the old Sirena, they still might bring you in. I figure that will keep you busy for some time."

"Hey!" Scuggs says, her features becoming animated, showing hints of the Sirena I once knew. "Don't you underestimate me. Why do you think Abe and Mother chose me? My brain was pretty much a honed-weapon to start with. I'll be okay. More than okay. And yeah, we can call it even. Deal?"

I pause before answering. "Deal," I say finally. "I will require one more thing from you before I let you leave."

"You want to know how I side-lined *Little Bastard,* yeah? How I managed to get power over its brain?"

I'm impressed with her astuteness. Then again, I, more than most, know never to judge a book by its cover. "That would be very useful."

"Consider it done."

SURE SAM GLIDES IN CLOSE to a large asteroid that spirals a lonely way through deep, empty space. My ship is close enough to be hidden by the asteroid's bulk. I'm not taking any chances.

"Silent running," I command.

"On it," Sam says in the same tones as my previous male alter ego, Sam Santana. *The Minion's* ceph-brain sure was pissed off about having its personality overridden, but I ain't the type to feel guilty. It does what I tell it to do.

To any casual observer, the asteroid would appear to have been travelling for billions of years, like any other deep space object, except that I had the thing voidspaced here a few weeks ago.

Was it expensive to do this? Sure it was.

It's been over a year since I gave Sirena *Little Bastard* and disappeared into voidspace. A year in which I've been busy.

My experience with robbing banks in the Hejaz system gave me a way to fill my coffers and more. My collected wealth is now bordering on ridiculous. I own a small moon in the Barrows, which has become my base of operations. As for *The Minion?* It's been decommissioned. The old ship no longer exists. I couldn't risk it ever being discovered. The ceph, which Scuggs gave me a way to control, now sits in my own, specially designed stealth ship, named *Sure Sam.*

As far as I'm aware, the GSS is none the wiser that I escaped the nuclear explosion on the Moon.

Sirena, on the other hand, is still at large. I've kept an ear to the Service Cypher, but they've found no trace of her and, in the last few months, normal operations have resumed. In the meantime, I've kept my head down, concentrating on simple jobs—simple jobs that pay the most money and make the least noise.

The first thing I did was to reverse my gender.

I'm all girl again and proud of it. Still petite, and now a natural redhead instead of that wig I used to wear, with some extra cool body augmentation. I no longer need an exoskeleton to supplement my lack of strength. It's all built in at the genetic level—with as many added extras as I can afford.

If I learned one thing from Sirena, it was that gender means nothing. My attitudes were born on a backward thinking planet. Attitudes that are hard to shake, but I'm getting there. And I now have the opposite perspective. After trying both sexes, this girl still prefers her curves. But who knows what the future might bring? I might decide to start 'stand-up peeing' again one day, just for a change. I have my original genome, rescued from Abe's lab, but it ain't time for Jane to return. Not yet. I'm saving her for my retirement, which ain't gonna be any time soon.

"Anything on the deep range"

"Nothing. Correction. Multiple voidpoints are forming. Eight ships."

"Designation?"

"Scouters."

"As expected. Hold position."

"On it."

I watch the nav-screens. The scouters arrive and start

doing their job. The asteroid is noticed and one of the ships is dispatched to investigate.

"You know what to do."

"Manoeuvring now."

Sure Sam glides over the asteroid's surface getting us close to the approaching ship. The scouter initiates a scan.

With *Sure Sam* in silent running and stealth mode activated, the scouter ain't got a chance.

We glide up from the asteroid on a collision course, invisible until it's too late. Instead of crashing, *Sure Sam* comes to rest atop the smaller ship, crushing its bridge and pulverising anyone inside. Nasty, but I'm sure they were paid big bucks for a dangerous job like this. They knew the risks, and, hey, no one lives forever.

Grabbing arms deploy and further crush the ship. If any of the other scouters are watching, they won't notice the cuckoo that is now in their nest—a crushed scouter and another, spider-like ship wrapped around it.

Sam overrides the scouter's com and broadcasts an *all-clear*. We take up position and wait.

"More voidpoints. Two battleships, fifteen cruisers and the target ship."

"Nice. I'm liking these odds." A few seconds later, the ships appear.

"All on schedule."

The target ship carries a VIP. A duplicitous ambassador on a supposed peace mission who is, in reality, a leading member of quite a nasty fascist coup—not that fascists were anything other than self-serving bastards. I don't care about the politics, but it's a coup my employers want to stop before it starts. I'm here to kidnap the ambassador and to hand her over to them at a rendezvous point. So far, the mission is going to plan.

As the bigger ships recharge to voidjump, the scouters all disappear to check out the next voidjump location, leaving me behind. We're immediately contacted by the lead battleship, wondering why we're still here. I send a 'void-engine malfunction' back at them, requesting an emergency dock. A pause, and the request is accepted. I get Sam to power the captured scouter's engines and we plot a course to the battleship, except that soon after, the engines also 'malfunction' putting us on a course that will take us close to the ambassador's ship.

Another com message. More urgent this time.

I send a request for a tug to come get us. Meanwhile, two cruisers move to intercept us. They are nervous, and they should be.

I'm about to initialise the second and most audacious part of the plan, when another message arrives. My screens flash into life, revealing an attractive woman with long, red-tipped blonde hair, blue eyes I've seen before, and statuesque cheekbones.

"Oh hi, Jane. Didn't expect to find you here. I suggest you put up your shields."

"Sirena?" I blurt.

"Not quite. You killed her remember? Oh, and I wasn't joking about your shields. Out."

"Shields up!" I command.

"But if we do that, we will become visible," Sam says.

"Just do it."

Shields flicker on. A breath later, one of the approaching cruisers fires on the VIP ship, exploding it in a bright ball of light, buffeting us in its wake and sending *Sure Sam* and our captured scouter into a tumbling spiral.

The other ships are not slow to react and start to batter the rogue cruiser with their mag-rails and lasers.

With our raised shields making us visible, some of that firepower starts to come our way.

"Shit! Get us out of here, Sam!"

"On it."

We crash into the void, knowing that we will be easily tracked, dropping out a few moments later to discard the scouter, and powering up Sam's void engines.

"Stealth mode now."

We sink into silent running and allow ourselves to drift. Seconds later, the other cruisers appear, the battleships will take longer to recharge their engines. They will arrive soon though. Meanwhile, any one of these cruisers could take us out—if they detect us that is.

As soon as they appear, Sam remote commands the discarded scouter to launch into voidspace. A few moments later, the cruisers follow, leaving us behind.

"Fuck!" I say. "What the hell was Sirena doing there?"

"She was employed to kill that son-of-a-bitch," a voice speaks over the com, accompanied a few seconds later by Sirena's image coming to life again on my screens. *"Oh dear. Did I tread on your toes?"* she says with a mock grimace on her striking face.

"Where the hell are you?"

"The com signal is coming from a point in what registers as empty space," Sam says. *"Another shielded ship."*

"Were you working this job as well, or is this some stupid attempt at revenge?"

"Revenge? No way. I told you we were even. Remember? By the way, that was a nice piece of work with the scouter. I almost didn't notice you until that clumsy engine problem you came up with. You're lucky I did."

"You should know better than to interfere with me."

"Hey, I was just doing my job. My escape plan was all in place, but when I saw you jumping, and guessing how

resourceful you are, I thought I'd come along for the ride."

"You stole a cruiser?"

"Yes and no. Don't expect me to give you the details. You know I don't do things by half, Jane."

"You've cost me a lot of money—do you know *that*?"

"Money? Don't make me laugh. You do this for kicks, like I do. And, oh, it's nice to see you again, Jane." She gives me a suggestive wink. *"Looking good. What about my new look? You like?"*

"You're certainly different from the last time we spoke, that's for sure. That doesn't mean I'm not pissed at you."

"Thanks. You'll get over it."

"You owe me a bounty."

"We can talk about that later. Now, are we gonna get out of here before those cruisers realise what went down?"

"Yeah, sure," I reply sullenly.

"Oh dear, you are put out. How about we meet up to discuss compensation?"

"Meet up?"

"Don't tell me that you don't want to? It'll be fun, just like old times… I'm sending you the co-ords. See you there."

"Sirena!"

"We have received co-ordinates from a ship that has just entered the void from the location of the last com message," Sam says dispassionately. *"Do you want me to follow?"*

I say nothing. Part of me wants to go after her. Another is telling me this is a bad idea. But then again, there's that damn tingle.

"We will need to leave now. What are the co-ords?"

I take a deep breath and give my answer.

~

Reviews

If you loved reading *Quick-Kill & The Galactic Secret Service* as much as I did writing it, can I ask you to please leave a review. This is not just for me and other readers, but for a whole host of other boring marketing reasons that I won't go into right now.

Suffice it so say, if you leave me a review on any of the e-book stores, or Goodreads or anywhere else, I'll be *well-chuffed*, and it will certainly increase the likelihood of further novels in this and other series.

Thanks in advance!

About *Quick-Kill*

First of all, I'd like to thank you for picking up *Quick-Kill & The Galactic Secret Service*. The adventures of Quick-Kill came about simply because I was fantastically bored trying to finish two other stalled novels (only one of which is presently finished!). I wanted to write something different and something fun. Something out there and a little silly. And I think I did just that.

Quick-Kill Jane arrived out of nowhere. Discovered as I wrote that first scene with no thought about characters or places or even the Galactic Secret Service! The gender swap came as a total surprise. As did the rest of her adventures...

If you want me to write more Quick-Kill stories, please contact me via one of the links on the next pages.

Acknowledgements

Thanks for the red-pen, scribbling and 'telling me off in no uncertain terms' talents of my lovely editors:

Deana Holmes
Suzanne Buist
Caroline Bean
Blossom Young

Also by *K.J.Heritage*

Mystery and Crime
Dying Is Easy
The Peculiar Case of the Missing Mondrian

Science Fiction
Shattered Helix *(Vatic Book 1)*
Shattered Web *(Vatic Book 2)*
Blue Into The Rip
Quick-Kill & The Galactic Secret Service
The Lady In The Glass - 12 Tales Of Death & Dying

Sci-Fi Compilations
Once Upon A Time In Gravity City
Chronicle Worlds: Legacy Fleet
From The Indie Side

Fantasy
The Scowl

Non-Fiction
All About Copywriting: 55 Easy Edits To Improve Your Writing Forever
3000 Writing & Plot Prompts A-C: Supercharge Your Creativity & Improve Your Writing Forever!

Find all ebooks, paperbacks, hardbacks & audiobooks by *K.J.Heritage* at the following stores:

Amazon & Audible, Apple, KOBO, Barnes & Noble/, Nook, Google, Smashwords & more

Links

Join K.J.Heritage's *Newsletter*
Get an inside track on all future releases, access to early
reading copies (ARCs), sneak previews, and more.
http://kjheritage.com/join

Mastodon
@kjheritage@mastodon.social

Instagram
Photos of my wonderful Shollie rescue #RescueJack, piccies
of my best mugs of tea, and various and shameless images
of all my books. Oh and maybe yours truly on a good hair
day!
https://www.instagram.com/k.j.heritage

Twitter:
90K+ followers
@kjheritage

TikTok
General silliness and book stuff. Search for #kjhtok
https://www.tiktok.com/@k.j.heritage

BookBub:
Not only can you check out the latest cool book deals, but
you can also get an alert when I publish my next book
https://www.bookbub.com/authors/k-j-heritage

Goodreads:
Friend me here:
https://www.goodreads.com/kjheritage

K.J.Heritage Facebook Group: *Mostly Readers*
Fun chat and posts about reading… *mostly.*
https://www.facebook.com/groups/mostlyreaders

K.J.Heritage Facebook page: *Mostly Writing*
Follow/like and keep in touch with even more writery stuff!
https://www.facebook.com/theauthorkjheritage/

Website:
http://kjheritage.com/

Email:
Want to get in touch? Well here's your chance
contact@kjheritage.com

About *K.J.Heritage*

"K.J.Heritage's uncanny sense of pacing and story puts him at the forefront of today's speculative fiction writers."
Samuel Peralta, Amazon bestselling author and creator of The Future Chronicles

K.J.Heritage writes books that he loves to read. From science fiction action and adventure mysteries to contemporary thrillers, comedy, and paranormal fantasy.

When he isn't penning third-person descriptions about himself, he's an international bestselling author writing the books he likes to read. From psychological thrillers and mystery sci-fi to crime, action & adventure, and epic fantasy. He should really stick to one genre, but he's not that kind of writer... or reader.

His first sci-fi short story, *Escaping The Cradle* was runner-up in the 2005 Clarke-Bradbury International Science Fiction Competition.

K.J.Heritage's short story CHURCHILL'S ROCK, part of the 'Chronicle Worlds: Legacy Fleet' anthology, will be aboard the Astrobotic's Peregrine Lunar Lander set for launch on the United Launch Alliance's Vulcan Centaur rocket platform bound for the moon in June 2022.

He has also appeared in several anthologies with such

self-publishing sci-fi luminaries as Hugh Howey and Samuel Peralta.

K.J.Heritage has done all the requisite 'writery' jobs such as driver's mate, factory gateman, barman, labourer, telesales operative, sales assistant, warehouseman, IT contractor, Student Union President, university IT helpdesk guy, British Rail signal software designer, premiership football website designer, gigging musician, company director, graphic designer, stand-up comedian, sound engineer, improv artist, magazine editor and web journo... Although he doesn't like to talk about it. *Mostly. Maybe a little bit.*

He was born in the UK in one of the more interesting previous centuries. Originally from Derbyshire, he now lives in the seaside town of Brighton. He is a tea drinker, avid Twitterer, and neurodiverse (ASD) human being.

FOR ALL media enquiries, event/booking information, signed copies, etc. please email: *contact@kjheritage.com*

All the very best,

K.J.Heritage